APOLLONIUS OF RHODES

ARGONAUTICA

APOLLONIUS OF RHODES

ARGONAUTICA

Translated by
STANLEY LOMBARDO AND CYNTHIA C. POLSLEY

Introduction by
TARA WELCH

HACKETT PUBLISHING COMPANY
INDIANAPOLIS

Copyright © 2025 by Hackett Publishing Company, Inc.

All rights reserved
Printed in the United States of America

28 27 26 25   1 2 3 4 5 6 7

For further information, please address
   Hackett Publishing Company, Inc.
   P.O. Box 44937
   Indianapolis, Indiana 46244-0937

   www.hackettpublishing.com

Cover design by Brian Rak
Interior design by E. L. Wilson
Composition by Aptara, Inc.

Cataloging-in-Publication data can be accessed via the Library of Congress Online Catalog.
Library of Congress Control Number: 2025933199

ISBN-13: 978-1-64792-230-6 (pbk.)
ISBN-13: 978-1-64792-238-2 (PDF ebook)
ISBN-13: 978-1- 64792-239-9 (epub3)

The paper used in this publication meets the minimum requirements of American National Standard for Information Sciences—Permanence of Paper for Printed Library Materials, ANSI Z39.48–1984.

∞

CONTENTS

Glory Projected: An Introduction to Apollonius's *Argonautica*	vii
Translators' Preface	xlv
Suggestions for Further Reading	xlvii
Maps	xlix

Argonautica

Book One	3
Book Two	45
Book Three	84
Book Four	127

Glossary	181
Appendix: Excerpts from Euripides's *Medea*	205

Glory Projected

An Introduction to Apollonius's *Argonautica*

There once was a priceless and numinous artifact, a shimmering Golden Fleece hanging in an oak tree in far-off Colchis and guarded by a dragon. The Fleece was the hide of a magical flying ram, the glimmering offspring of Poseidon by the Thracian princess Theophane. That ram would later be sent to Boeotia by the cloud goddess Nephele to rescue her children, Phrixus and his twin sister Helle, from the murderous machinations of their unhinged stepmother, Ino. Just in the nick of time, the golden ram rescued the twins from slaughter and carried them on its back eastward across the sea. Helle fell off and drowned along the way, giving her name to the slender gap between Europe and Asia (the Hellespont). Phrixus arrived at Colchis on the far side of the Black Sea, where he married the local princess Chalciope and sacrificed the ram to Zeus.

It is this artifact that motivates the plot of the *Argonautica* (as its first readers referred to it), an epic poem by Apollonius of Rhodes written around 250 BCE. Apollonius was born in Alexandria in Egypt, a large and diverse city at the mouth of the Nile River. Likely a pupil of the great poet Callimachus, Apollonius became head of the Alexandrian Library—one of the great cultural institutions founded and fostered by the Ptolemaic dynasty, rulers of Hellenistic Egypt after the death of Alexander the Great. Apollonius's subject specialty there seems to have been foundation stories and local histories. His epithet "of Rhodes" suggests some association with the island—perhaps, as later biographies suggest, a poor initial reception of the *Argonautica* drove him to retire there and revise the text into the version we have today.

The *Argonautica* is a masterpiece of Hellenistic literature with all the hallmarks of the contemporary literary taste: erudition, refinement, generic experimentation, and lexical skill. Like so much work emerging from the Library, it is deeply rooted in the Homeric tradition yet reflective of contemporary concerns.

Glory Projected: An Introduction to Apollonius's Argonautica

The Quest

The opening of the epic announces the acquisition of the Fleece as the goal of the heroic expedition of the ship Argo and its crew of Argonauts:

> Beginning with you, Apollo, I will recall the glory
> of the ancient heroes who, commanded by Pelias,
> rowed the Argo down through the Pontus
> and the Clashing Rocks in their quest
> for the Golden Fleece. (1.1–5)

The four books that follow trace the Argo's outbound voyage from Iolcus in Thessaly to Colchis (Books 1–2), the Argonauts' stay at Colchis and acquisition of the Fleece with the help of Chalciope's sister Medea (Book 3), and the return to Greece with Fleece and Medea in tow (Book 4). The voyage of the Argo is visible very early in the Greek literary record. It is implicit as the model for many of Odysseus's adventures, particularly Odysseus's visit with Circe; Circe, after all, is sister to King Aeetes of Colchis and, therefore, Medea's aunt. In fact, Circe mentions the Argo to Odysseus, warning him not to go the way of the Clashing Rocks since only the Argo has survived that passage (*Odyssey* 12.71–74, Lombardo transl.). The *Iliad* refers to the tale as well; in *Iliad* 7, Jason's son by Hypsipyle provides the wine for the Greek funeral celebrations (7.481–83, Lombardo transl.). Hesiod is also aware of the myth; *Theogony* includes Medea's genealogy, and the *Catalog of Women* includes Jason's. The fragments of Mimnermus, who wrote in the mid-seventh century, touch on Jason's quest to gain the Fleece. But how did such disparate allusions to the Argo myth become a staple of the written epic tradition? A Jason epic that predates these sources, shared orally but never textually codified, seems a likely culprit. Such epic material must also have fed those versions of the story that appeared in the Classical era: Pindar's *Pythian* 4, Herodotus's *Histories*, a handful of lost plays by Aeschylus, and above all Euripides's *Medea*.

The archaeological record also supports widespread and very early popularity of the myth of the Argo's voyage. Iolcus, Jason's hometown in Thessaly, was prominent until the Mycenaean age but not thereafter, suggesting an early mythogenesis for Jason's origins there. The west coast of Italy is rich in archaeological and topographical evidence for the Argo's presence, such as the worship of Castor and Polydeuces (two of the Argonauts) at Rome, and the folk-etymology of the town Caieta from "Aietes."

Glory Projected: An Introduction to Apollonius's Argonautica

Readers have long recognized the voyage of the Argo as a myth of Greek exploration and colonization, an aspect that underlies the *Odyssey* and perhaps also the far-flung labors of Heracles. The varied locations and interactions these myths treat teach a Greek audience about peoples on the edges of their world and work through the implications of cultural contact. Unlike Odysseus and Heracles, the Argonauts come from all over Greece, and no two sources present the same roster. Any city-state could imagine itself in the Argo's enterprise. The Argo's outbound journey is remarkably consistent across narrative sources for the myth, but the return journey varies widely. This suggests that the Greeks had not yet crossed the Black Sea when the myth took shape: they didn't know how the Argo might return home. In addition to the exploratory aspects, the fact that the expedition sought to recover a golden artifact speaks to one of the impulses of exploration and colonization: to gain access to natural resources available in other lands. The fact that the Golden Fleece was brought to the East by the Greek Phrixus serves to justify Jason's actions as one of recovery rather than exploitation. From the eighth century onward, Greek colonies arose around the coast of the Black Sea, first on the south shore, then the east, then the north and the Sea of Azov.

Written many centuries after this initial exploration, when the contours of the region were much better known, Apollonius's text similarly navigates expansionism and cross-cultural interaction. In Book 2, for example, the Argonauts put in at sites along the Black Sea's southern coast, a region rich in trade ties to Ptolemaic Alexandria. The loving attention Apollonius gives to local geography and history in this book strengthens those ties by writing them back into the mythic past. The Argonauts' long wandering through Libya in Book 4 puts Greeks in northern Africa long before Ptolemy settled his capital there. The epic even closes with a reference to Ptolemaic expansion. While wandering in Libya, the Argonaut Euphemus receives a clod of earth from Triton, which he later throws into the Aegean. Apollonius tells us that this clod would become the island Thera—mother city to Libyan Cyrene, which the Ptolemies subjugated, and itself home to a religious festival honoring the Ptolemies.

Yet, however much history lies behind or is grafted onto the Argo's journey, the tale of the quest for the Fleece also offers its audience the crowd-pleasing satisfaction of discovering familiar mythic tropes set in new contexts. The Argonauts traverse the known and unknown worlds. They meet friends and enemies, monsters and gods alike. They visit death, pass through a sort of underworld, and are guided by a hero. It is to this hero that we now turn.

Glory Projected: An Introduction to Apollonius's Argonautica

The Hero

Jason is the well-known hero who retrieves the Fleece from Colchis and brings it back to Greece. He fits securely in the roster of Greek mythic heroes, journeying like Odysseus, rescuing artifacts like Heracles, and courting a maiden like Theseus. However, Apollonius makes it difficult for his readers to assess him by that yardstick. For starters, he doesn't even come into focus until well into the first book. The opening lines of the poem speak of "the glory of the ancient heroes" (1.1–2). Jason is not named until line 10, and even then, not as a hero but as the shoeless man predestined to murder King Pelias. Pelias quickly assigns Jason the task he hopes will spell doom for Jason, and then the poet spends two hundred lines describing everyone else—all the heroes and adventurers who came together "to serve Aeson's son Jason" (1.216). This is Lombardo and Polsley's rendering for the strange Greek word *summēstores*, or "fellow-counselors." While this word is seldom attested in Greek, the uncompounded form *mēstor*— "counselor"—frequently appears in Homer, referring to Patroclus, Diomedes, Neleus, Priam, and Zeus himself. Apollonius's Argonauts notably act as advisors *together*, and *together for Jason*. This is a group effort.

Another hundred lines on, after a lament by his mother, the spotlight finally turns to Jason. The Argonauts are ready to sail, and Jason seizes his moment to take the lead:

> "All of the gear a vessel needs is here in good order,
> ready for us to embark. There is no need to delay
> on that account. We're only waiting for a tailwind.
> We all want to return to Hellas after our voyage,
> and we are united in reaching the land of Aeetes.
> So putting selfishness aside, choose the best man here
> as our leader, the best to settle our internal disputes
> and to deal with all our foreign alliances." (1.321–28)

It's a skillful speech, crafted to build confidence in the Argonauts' journey and unity of purpose. Jason emphasizes their solidarity with first-person plural nouns and verb forms—"us," "we," "our"—and another striking word, *xunos*, "common," which he underscores in successive lines (in "we all want" and "we are united"). With goodwill, Jason asks them to choose "the best man here as our leader." Lombardo and Polsley's translation captures a wonderful feature in the Greek: the separation of "the best man" from "leader" across the break of a line, in Greek, *ton ariston . . . orchamon*. *Ton ariston* on its own often marks out the hero, as in Homer's "the best of the Achaeans." Imagine Jason's surprise, if not dismay—and the reader's—when the Argonauts clamor in unison, "Heracles!"

> At this, the young heroes all turned their eyes
> toward Heracles, the great hero, sitting in their midst,
> and with one shout, they approved him as their leader. (1.329–31)

Jason did succeed in uniting them, granted. Heracles quells this would-be election by acclamation without even having to get up; he says no, and all the Argonauts assent.

This is the first of many crises of authority in the poem. At fairly regular intervals, Apollonius draws attention to the fact that Jason's leadership is not a closed case. A few examples will suffice to demonstrate the theme. Even before they set sail, the braggart Idas loudly and publicly all but calls Jason a coward for brooding over a troubling prophecy (1.445–47). This causes a ruckus, and another Argonaut, Idmon, has to dress Idas down publicly. A brawl would have erupted "if their companions, and Jason himself, hadn't restrained them," and Orpheus distracted them with a song (1.476, 477–502). As before, Apollonius uses line divisions to make Jason's action a bit of an afterthought; the phrase "and Jason himself" appears in Greek a line after "their companions" (1.493–94 in Greek). Later in Book 1, Jason seems content to linger with Hypsipyle at Lemnos. It is Heracles who prompts their departure, talking to the other heroes apart from Jason:

> "Let's each of us get back to business and leave Jason behind
> in Hypsipyle's bed until he's populated Lemnos
> with his offspring and attained great glory." (1.859–61)

Apollonius describes Heracles's speech as reproachful and angry—he "lit into" and "upbraided" the Argonauts for allowing the delay (1.851, 862). The Argonauts immediately respond to the great man and rig the ships. Yet again, when the Argonauts fall into despair and recrimination at the loss of Heracles at Mysia, Telamon, prompted in part by Jason's aloofness, accuses him of scheming to be rid of the greater hero (1.1279–91). In Book 2, after a boxing match and battle with the belligerent Bebrycians, the crew yet again grumble to each other about a gap in leadership: "Imagine what they [the Bebrycians] would have done, the cowards, if a god had somehow brought Heracles here. If he were here I think, and no doubt about it, there would have been no boxing bout at all . . ." (2.135–38). At the tail end of the expedition, Heracles's specter appears again; the Argonauts just miss him in the land of the Hesperides, where the lion-clad hero has usefully uncovered a freshwater spring in the desert. "Even from afar, Heracles has saved his comrades" (4.1482–83), the Argonauts say.

In many of these moments, Apollonius and his characters employ counterfactual statements that imagine what the quest—and the epic—would look like with different heroic configurations:

> Theseus, though, foremost of all of Erechtheus's sons. . . .
> [wasn't there but] would surely have lightened
> the labor of all the rest of the heroes. (1.95, 99–100)

> . . . and the strife would have continued
> if their companions, and Jason himself, hadn't restrained them
> with cries of indignation. (1.475–77)

> . . . they would have lingered there longer,
> had not Heracles assembled his crewmates
> apart from the women and lit into them . . .
> "Let's each of us get back to business and leave Jason behind . . ."
>   (1.849–51, 59)

> . . . they would have turned back
> then and there to the land of the Mysians, driving
> through the deep sea and unrelenting storm-winds.
> But the two sons of Thracian Boreas restrained Telamon . . . (1.1293–96)

> "Imagine what they would have done, the cowards,
> if a god had somehow brought Heracles here.
> If he were here I think, and no doubt about it,
> there would have been no boxing bout at all." (2.135–38)

> "How uncanny! Even from afar, Heracles has saved
> his comrades, wracked with thirst. If only we could somehow
> find him walking along as we pass through the mainland!" (4.1482–84)

Glory Projected: An Introduction to Apollonius's Argonautica

Such "what if" and "would have" moments evoke unreal or unrealized narratives—alternative epics, if you will. And note that such paths not taken, whether expressed counterfactually ("would surely have lightened the labor of all the rest of the heroes") or merely propositionally ("Let's move on without Jason" or "Let's prioritize the recovery of Heracles over the Fleece") are imagined by both narrator and characters. Some of these might reflect Apollonius's awareness of alternative traditions; in some versions, for example, Theseus actually was an Argonaut. Within the text itself, however, the recurring alternatives promote a sense of self-consciousness that the *Argonautica* is a text comprised of thousands of authorial choices rather than a myth to be taken at face value.

The repeated invocation of alternatives to Jason—even, perhaps, better alternatives—invites Apollonius's readers to focus on his shortcomings as a hero. Chief among these is his recurring helplessness, often coupled with despair. This is the case even at the outset. After Idmon prophesies that they will attain the Fleece and return home despite painful challenges, the Argonauts relax while Jason sits apart, downcast:

> But Jason, at loose ends, was brooding over events,
> and seemed to be preoccupied and somewhat depressed. (1.442–43)

He falls into despondency several times in pursuit of the Fleece. When they lose Heracles near the end of in Book 1, Jason spirals into despair:

> And Jason, bewildered by this predicament,
> never said a word, neither this nor that,
> but just sat there depressed, eating his heart out. (1.1281–83)

In Book 3, Jason maintains composure throughout his first meeting with the haughty King Aeetes, even moderating more rash companions. But after Aeetes issues the dire conditions of relinquishing the Fleece, namely, yoking the fire-breathing bulls and slaying the Earthborn men, Jason quails, pauses, and agrees:

> Hearing this, Jason stared at the ground and sat stock-still,
> speechless, utterly helpless in this dire situation.
> For a long time he thought things over, but couldn't find
> the courage to take on this insurmountable task. (3.414–17)

xiii

Glory Projected: An Introduction to Apollonius's Argonautica

As he later tells his companions, he had no other ideas (4.495–96), which also prompts their despair. The Greek word that recurs in these instances is some form of *amēchania*—a sense of helplessness, being without recourse. The word captures more a mental state than the externality of a situation. Inner turmoil does not disqualify a hero of mythology; Odysseus, Agamemnon, Achilles, and Hector feel it at times. What sets Jason apart is the frequency with which Apollonius characterizes him this way and how often others have to pull him out of it. But one additional instance of the word complicates the picture of Jason's helplessness: after passing safely through the Clashing Rocks in Book 2, Jason professes his despair explicitly:

> "Tiphys, why do you soothe me this way, in my grief?
> I made a mistake, acted like a fool.
> I was helpless, caught up in my abject delusion.
> When Pelias issued his command, I ought to have straightaway
> refused this mission, right there on the spot,
> even if it meant I was doomed to death, torn limb by limb.
> As it is, I'm beset by unbearable angst, bewildering terror,
> dreading the thought of sailing through the icy-cold sea-waves
> and dreading the moment when we'll set foot on the mainland.
> I'm hemmed in on all sides by implacable foes.
> At the close of each day, I pass the endless nights in anguish
> ever since, for my sake, we first gathered together,
> always mulling over every detail." (2.620–32)

> Thus Jason, testing the heroes. They responded by shouting
> words of good cheer. This warmed his heart, and he went on:

> "Friends, my heart swells with courage at your valor." (2.639–41)

This episode recalls *Iliad* 2 when Agamemnon tests his troops by pretending to despair and proposing they return to Greece in shame. But where Agamemnon's experiment is a near-disaster for him because it gives his troops the opportunity to show their desire to quit the war (there was a universal mad dash for the ships, says Homer), Jason's experiment succeeds. His men are behind him, and a brief exchange of mutual encouragement follows. Of one purpose again, they get back to sailing. Jason's helplessness, rather than being an indelible heroic

Glory Projected: An Introduction to Apollonius's Argonautica

blemish, brings opportunities into the text for the Argonauts to work together to find solutions. In this respect, *Argonautica* is not a Homeric epic, and Jason is not a Homeric hero. Where Achilles, Agamemnon, and Odysseus strive for personal glory at the expense of others, Jason's heroism relies on shared responsibility and cooperation. Many astute readers have seen this aspect of Jason's heroism as well-suited to the Hellenistic context of his poem's composition, an era when diplomacy rather than personal martial prowess typified the stratagems of the successful dynast. When Jason asks his men to choose their leader, he defines what he means by that term: "The best to settle our internal disputes and to deal with all our foreign alliances" (1.327–28). He can be seen doing both in the course of the epic. Recall that Telamon criticizes Jason for abandoning Heracles. When the hero regains his senses and apologizes, Jason is quick to forgive and restores harmony within the group:

> And Jason, choosing his words carefully, answered:
>
> "My friend, you denounced me vilely, and that's a fact,
> openly declaring that I wronged an admirable man.
> No matter. Know full well that I won't cultivate anger,
> although it is true that earlier I was vexed.
> After all, it wasn't over flocks of sheep or goods
> that you became so inflamed with rage,
> but a man who is your trusted friend. I hope
> that if a like situation were ever to befall me,
> you'd fight another man on my behalf, too."
>
> He spoke, and as of old, they sat down together. (1.1331–41)

In meeting new peoples, Jason's first approach is to seek peaceful relationships. He welcomes additional heroes onto the quest (Heracles's friends, Phrixus's sons, King Lycus's son) and secures the goodwill and aid of locals in various ports (Lemnians, Doliones, and Mariandyni). He even tries to negotiate with King Aeetes for the Fleece, offering the Argonauts' services in subduing Aeetes's enemies. Soft words are his instrument of choice, and Jason uses them on everyone, ranging from his mother to his helmsman to Medea. Various expressions in Greek convey his tone ("gentle," "fawning," "prudent," "pleasing," "well-chosen"), but his technique in every case is the same, as he suggests to the Argonauts in a moment of candor: "What strength can hardly grasp, a word's light touch can grip. A fitting phrase can smooth the way to fill a wanting need" (3.181–82).

Nowhere does he exploit his verbal skill more than in his exchanges with Medea. Apollonius sets the tone when they first meet at the shrine to Hecate in Book 3. Hera has already arranged for Medea to be smitten by Love's arrow. Here, in a scene reminiscent of Odysseus among the Phaeacians, Hera spruces up Jason for the meeting:

> Never before had there been such a hero,
> not even of those descended directly from Zeus,
> as on that day Hera made Jason, both in his looks
> and in how he spoke. (3.924–27)

Mopsus reminds Jason to use shrewd words to persuade Medea (3.950), and Jason is very careful in his first speech to Medea. He garners sympathy for his plight, flatters her a bit, and—unlike Odysseus, who hints to Nausicaa about a happy marriage—promises only moderate deliverables in return for her help, which she has promised anyhow:

> "And in return,
> you'll win my thanks forever after for your help, which is
> only right, and is proper for those who dwell
> in another part of the world. I'll secure you a name
> and glorious reputation, and the other heroes will
> likewise celebrate you after returning to Hellas,
> as will the heroes' wives and mothers, who now,
> I suppose, sit wailing on the shore." (3.996–1003)

Jason offers gratitude, a name, and a reputation both from him and from his companions. He emphasizes the distance that exists—and presumably will exist—between them. He expressly does not mention marriage, only later conceding that he would wed her (3.1141–43) *if* she ever comes to Greece. That becomes a necessity after Aeetes surmises Medea's betrayal, but even then, he says he will marry her when they arrive at his home (4.98–99). He seems to be hedging his bets. Even as Medea hesitates boarding his ship, Jason "[calms] her down with some cheerful words" (4.108) so they could proceed to retrieve the Fleece.

Glory Projected: An Introduction to Apollonius's Argonautica

However effective Jason's communication skills are at building an alliance, securing the aid of strangers, and ultimately achieving the goal of his quest, his verbal manipulation of Medea becomes increasingly troublesome for any reader who would defend his heroic status. He is prone to half-truths. In their first conversation, Jason recounts to Medea the story of Ariadne and Theseus as if it were a fairy tale: the Cretan princess helped the wandering hero overcome the mandated challenge and then sailed off with him into the sunset and was honored by the gods (3.1005–13). Jason omits the next chapter in which Theseus abandoned Ariadne on the island of Naxos, though we find out in Book 4 that he surely knew of that denouement (4.423–35). We will speak more about the Ariadne parallel below. For now, it suffices to submit it as evidence that Jason knowingly misleads Medea from the start.

More insidiously, Jason talks Medea into complicity with Apsyrtus's murder. After she learns of the Minyans' covenant to keep or give her up according to the ruling of a third party, she accuses Jason of oath-breaking. He uses soothing, fawning words ("trying to calm her down," 4.409) to convince her the covenant is part of a ruse (*dolon*, 4.404) to lure Apsyrtus to his death. She works up the details, but the idea is his. Whether the Minyans' covenant was originally conceived as a trick or whether this is Jason's quick reinterpretation of it under necessity, we cannot know. We can only see Jason use his power of persuasion to deflect Medea's legitimate criticism of him and cast at least some responsibility for their predicament on her ("because of you," 4.397).

After the murder of Apsyrtus, Jason fades from view as a hero, leader, and even lover. The witch Circe speaks only to her kinswoman Medea and reduces Jason to an indefinite pronoun, "whoever this man of mystery is" (4.754). He remains unseen indeed, with lackluster appearances that can be cataloged in this brief paragraph here. Like Circe, Thetis ignores Jason and advises Peleus about their passage through Scylla and Charybdis. Orpheus's singing distracts the Argonauts as they pass the Sirens. At the Phaeacian court, Medea parleys with the king and queen and pleads with the Argonauts. As Jason and Medea consummate their marriage promise, all Apollonius says of Jason is that it wasn't how the hero had planned it (4.1175–76). Wandering the sands of Libya, Jason turns over to Peleus the interpretation of the local nymphs' message. Jason appears as an afterthought at Mopsus's death in the desert: "His comrades, including Jason, gathered around" (4.1549). The Argonauts initiate the sacrifice to Triton (4.1613). Medea single-handedly defeats Talos (4.1680–718). Apollonius finishes up the epic with a successful prayer to Apollo for immediate help and an interpretation of a dream.

The Sidekick(s)

Achilles has Patroclus; Theseus has Pylades; and Gilgamesh has Enkidu. Even Agamemnon and Menelaus function as a sort of pair, as do Hector and Paris. The sidekick advises the hero, complements his strengths, tempers his excesses, and spurs him to glory. The sidekick also provides an interlocutor in conversation with whom the hero can reveal his motivations and troubles. Jason has fifty sidekicks, many of whom are big-personality figures who take the spotlight at times. We have already seen how Heracles almost steals the spotlight both while he is part of the expedition and even afterward, as the Argonauts keep making him the topic of conversation. Others among his companions are great as well—Telamon, Peleus, Meleager, and Castor and Polydeuces (the Dioscuri). They are a well-rounded bunch, including seers and augurs (Mopsus, Idmon), helmsmen (Tiphys), swift messengers (Euphemus, Zetes, and Calais), spotters (Lynceus), and shapeshifters (Periclymenus). There is even someone whose function seems to be "the grouchy one"; all Idas does is grumble about all the departures of this mission from what he considers proper heroic form (e.g., Jason sulking, relying on a woman, using magic potions).

Heracles aside, one sidekick stands out for the frequency of his contribution and for its novelty. Orpheus the musician is named first in Apollonius's catalog of the Argonauts. Orpheus appears on the Argo among the myth's earliest sources, but his presence confused some of Apollonius's ancient readers, called scholiasts, because he was weak (schol. on 1.23–25). Apollonius gives Orpheus a prominent role to match his primacy in the catalog. Practically, his chanting helps the rowers keep time (1.524–25, 552–53). He frequently initiates and performs ritual activities on behalf of the crew, such as when he prompts them to stop at Samothrace to be initiated into local mystery rites (1.908–11), prays to the Hesperides on behalf of the crew (4.1431–43), and takes the lead in supplicating Apollo with the dedication of a tripod to aid them during their wandering in Libya (4.1569–73).

Such instances allow Apollonius to include local religious lore in the story, tapping into his own Alexandrian intellectual interests. They also give him, as author, a surrogate presence in the text. Consider, for example, an episode in Book 2 in which Orpheus initiates rites to Apollo after the god's epiphany:

Finally Orpheus, addressing them all, said:

> "Come, let's call this island the Sacred Island
> of Apollo of the Dawn, since he has manifested himself
> to our eyes at the break of day, and we will sacrifice
> what offerings we can, building an altar on the shore.
> If he later grants us a safe return to the Haemonian land,
> then we will lay the thighs of horned goats on his altar.
> As it is now, I urge you to appease him by offering
> the savory steam of sacrifices and libations.
> **But be gracious, our king, gracious in your appearing!**"*
>
> Orpheus said this, and they quickly constructed
> an altar out of stones. (2.682–93)

After the sacrifice, Orpheus's singing continues with a hymn that Apollonius presents, in indirect sequence. Halfway through, the narration itself shifts into direct speech:

> ... Orpheus, son of Oeagrus, chanted as he played
> his Bistonian lyre how once below Parnassus's peak,
> Apollo shot with his bow the monster Delphyne
> when he was still young and beardless, still reveling
> in his long, fine hair. **Be gracious, O Lord.**
> May your locks be forever unshorn, ever unravaged,
> as is only right. And no one but Leto
> may ever stroke them with her dear hands. (2.702–9)

It is as if Apollonius, like Orpheus, is also hymning Apollo. Apollonius often interrupts the narrative in his own voice (a feature discussed below), but this instance situates him within the epic's events rather than omnisciently outside of it. This overt elision of author and character prompts readers to scrutinize other Orphic moments in the text. When Idas and Idmon quarrel in the first book, Orpheus distracts the whole band with cosmology: a song on how strife among the cosmic elements led to their partition, how the earth and its inhabitants grew, and how the earliest generations of gods ruled the young world. The song engages

---

* Emphasis here and below mine.

Glory Projected: An Introduction to Apollonius's Argonautica

early Greek thought on the origin of the universe (found in Hesiod, Empedocles, and even Homer—again, showing Apollonius's access to the resources of the Alexandrian Library) and offers poetry as a path from strife toward resolution:

> He ended there, stilling his lyre and immortal voice.
> But even after he had finished they sat in silence,
> leaning forward, listening for more,
> so enchanted were they by the music's spell. (1.496–99)

In an epic that sends Greek heroes all over the known world to learn, ally, exchange, and establish relationships, and in which the Argonauts' distant past leaves visible traces for Apollonius's readers, the reconciling function of Orpheus's song gains meaning.

Or consider the episode of the Sirens in Book 4. Apollonius makes pointed changes from his Homeric model, in which Odysseus famously plugs the ears of his crew and binds himself to the mast so that he alone can hear the Sirens' song safely. And he does: the Sirens beckon Odysseus with a promise to sing about the Trojan War and to share knowledge of his future. In Apollonius's text, no ears are plugged, and Jason gains no special knowledge. Rather, Orpheus sings a rival song as the Argonauts row past:

> . . . where the **clear-toned** Sirens,
> daughters of Achelous, used to beguile sailors
> with their **sweet songs** and then destroy them. (4.900–902)

> . . . they deprived many sailors from their sweet return home,
> wearing them away with wearying desire,
> and now suddenly sent forth from their lips to the heroes
> their **delicate voices**. The crew would have cast the hawsers
> out onto the shore, had not Thracian Orpheus,
> plucking the strings of his Bistonian lyre,
> sounded the notes of a **rippling melody**,
> making all their ears ring with the **rhythm**
> as he swept the strings **tumultuously**,
> and the lyre **drowned** out the voice of the Sirens.
> So the west wind and the resounding waves
> rushing from behind bore the ship onward,
> as the Sirens kept voicing their ceaseless song. (4.909–21)

Glory Projected: An Introduction to Apollonius's Argonautica

The Sirens sing in clear tones, sweet songs, and delicate voices. Orpheus, in contrast, sings accompanied by lyre, with rippling melody, rhythm, and tumultuous and loud accompaniment. Orpheus's song wins out and, but for one Argonaut who heeded the Sirens' song, the Argonauts avoid this danger. The final descriptor of the Sirens' song, "ceaseless," emphasizes Orpheus's skill since his song succeeds. Orpheus (Apollonius) can evidently sing songs of purposeful distraction. What, then, do we make of the fact that he sings the marriage hymn at Jason and Medea's premature wedding at the land of the Phaeacians and the celebratory song the next morning?

The Love Interest

Jason's saga takes a sharp turn in Book 3 when he meets Medea. Not only is Medea the catalyst for Jason's achievement of the Fleece, but in the latter half of the epic, she overshadows him as a character both in the consistency of her presence in the text and in its intensity. Few characters in the mythic tradition have exerted as much influence as Medea, the Colchian princess who aids Jason in securing the Fleece and then elopes with him to Greece. Like the Argo, Medea is present very early in the textual and archaeological record (Hesiod *Theogony* 992–1001; rites at the temple of Hera Akraia at Perachora). Earlier versions of her story vary in terms of whether she is a goddess, priestess, or layperson; how many marriages she makes and to whom; and how many children she has and what their fate is. In the mid-fifth century, though, Euripides, in his tragedy *Medea*, exploded and then reconstituted her tradition around one aspect: the notion that, scorned by Jason, Medea killed his new bride and her own children and then fled to Athens. *Argonautica* narrates an earlier phase of Medea's story than the events Euripides dramatizes at Corinth, but Apollonius deftly renders his heroine as one who could grow into that tragic figure.

The invocation to Book 3 launches Medea's presence in the story:

> Come now, Erato, stand at my side, and tell me
> how Jason brought the Fleece back to Iolcus
> aided by Medea's love for him, for you share
> Aphrodite's power, and charm lovesick
> unwedded girls, and your very name means Love.
>
> So the heroes waited in ambush . . . (3.1–6)

Glory Projected: An Introduction to Apollonius's Argonautica

In Book 1, Apollonius calls upon Apollo for divine poetic inspiration. For Book 2, he needs no new infusion of vision. But here he seeks out a specialist: Erato, of course, is the muse of love poetry. Standing by his side, Erato will not share the love story *per se* but rather how Jason got the Fleece back home with the help of Medea's love. The delay of Medea's name (and the prepositional phrase in which it is embedded, "by Medea's love") until after the mention of Jason's quest, and its grammatical subordination to that quest, prime the reader to see Medea as Jason's tool even before we meet her. While "you . . . charm lovesick unwedded girls" is Erato's general domain, it is an apt description of Medea. Finally, in a passing phrase meant simply to give Jason's whereabouts, Apollonius mentions that the Argonauts wait hidden in ambush. To the repeat reader, aware of how grievously Jason uses this girl, this phrase is painfully multivalent. Even the first-time reader soon learns that Medea's love causes her great physical and emotional distress from the outset.

And indeed, when we first meet Medea herself walking unsuspecting in the palace, she cries out at the sight of unknown men so close by (3.244). Soon thereafter, Eros—himself hidden in ambush—hits her with a fresh arrow, and the damage is done. So far, Medea has been a victim of the goddess's plotting, but Apollonius reorients the reader to the nuance of her character with a perspective-shifting simile worthy of the Homeric tradition. The simile describes Medea just after she is shot with Love's arrow:

> *As a poor woman piling dry twigs around a burning brand—*
> *a woman who makes her living spinning wool*
> *so that she might have a fire to keep her warm*
> *when she awakens early—and the flame flares up*
> *wondrously from the small brand and consumes*
> *the whole pile of twigs:*
>   so too Love the Destroyer
> enveloped her heart and burned secretly there.
> Her soft cheek's complexion fluctuated between
> pallid and red in her spirit's confusion. (3.279–87)

The lead-in to the simile implies that Medea is the poor woman feeding the fire, but by the simile's ending, we realize she is akin to the thing burned. Her flush and pallor, here marking her confused spirit in the moment, also foreshadow the juxtaposition of lovestruck innocent and canny sorceress that we will see for the remainder of the epic.

Glory Projected: An Introduction to Apollonius's Argonautica

Apollonius grants generous space within the text to reveal the inner workings of Medea's mind and heart—much more so than to Jason, himself by far the most diffident of all the heroes. Medea's dream, which she experiences after Aeetes's harsh terms are articulated but before she is approached to help, is a masterwork of psychological subtlety:

> A sound sleep had relieved Medea of her love pangs
> as she lay in her bed, but all of a sudden,
> she was assaulted by the sort of anxious,
> deceitful dreams that trouble those in grief.
> She thought that the stranger had agreed to the contest
> not to win the ram's Fleece, had not come to Aeetes's city
> for that reason at all, but to lead her away
> to his own home as his wedded wife. And she dreamed
> that she herself had contended with the oxen
> and completed the task with superlative ease,
> but that her own parents refused to fulfill their promise,
> contending it was not the maiden they had challenged
> to yoke the oxen but the stranger himself;
> and from that there arose further arguments
> between her father and the contingent of strangers,
> with both sides laying the final decision on her,
> and that she suddenly rejected her parents and chose
> the stranger, causing them immeasurable grief,
> and that they cried out in anger, and with that cry,
> sleep released its hold on her. (3.617–36)

Her dream reveals uncertainty about Jason's motivations (lines 621–24), confidence in her own ability to fulfill the terms of the contest (625–26), anxiety about whether her contribution disqualifies Jason's success (or his heroism?; lines 627–29 and cf. lines 456–57, "Whether he shall meet his death as the most magnificent of all heroes or as the worst of them, let him go!"), and finally fear that those aspects really indicate an absolute choice on her part to favor one side or the other (632). Only Penelope's dream in *Odyssey* 19 comes close in terms of its psychological rumination on responsibility and future action; there are even some verbal parallels between the two dreams. Each dream also permits its author to explore narratological issues such as interior or layered focalization.

But unlike Penelope's dream, which is a message from the gods and includes its own interpretation, Medea's dream stems from her inner turmoil. Her waking behavior shows the same turmoil as she continues to resist desire's pull in thought (3.641–45), movement (3.652–61), and speech (3.687–91). Even after promising Chalciope to help Jason, she wavers and suffers to the extent that she contemplates suicide (3.755–814). In one of the most poignant moments in the whole epic, she recalls life's simple pleasures, such as her joyous playmates, and regains the will to live (3.815–21).

For a brief while, Medea enjoys these simple pleasures, and an episode ensues that is her happiest in the epic. Medea sets out to meet Jason and offer her tangible help. Their meeting and its lead-up of a dream followed by a conversation with a family member draw inspiration from Nausicaa's meeting with Odysseus and accentuate the idea of a Medea who is (or starts out) good and innocent. Like Nausicaa, Medea goes on this field trip outside the palace in a horse-drawn cart (*apēnē* in both texts), accompanied by her companions (*amphipolos* in both texts). Like Nausicaa, she drives the cart with her companions jogging alongside. Both girls meet heroes who have been made more handsome for the occasion, heroes who speak winning words (soothing words for Jason, soft and winning speech for Odysseus). Both girls are impressed by the hero before them, offer detailed instructions for the hero's next steps, and fear the reproachful eyes of their own community members. But while Nausicaa is circumspect with Odysseus about her romantic interest in him, and Odysseus neglects to mention that he is already married, Medea and Jason are more forward, at one point even making eyes at each other:

> And now **they both**
> cast down **their** eyes in embarrassment, but soon
> were throwing glances **at each other**, smiling
> with love-light beneath **their** radiant brows. (3.1028–31)

Apollonius emphasizes their mutuality with repetition of the plural pronouns in boldface type above, in Greek rendered by the compact phrase *amphō allote* (3.1022 in Greek), with the dual pronoun *amphō* joining the lovers tightly and the adverb *allote* locking them in repetition.

But Medea's Nausicaa-like optimism is short-lived for all the reasons she had perceived in her dream—fear, guilt, shame. Other departures from the Nausicaa intertext tip the reader off/darken the horizon for Medea/paint a more nuanced picture. Both girls are likened by simile to Artemis with her entourage:

Glory Projected: An Introduction to Apollonius's Argonautica

> *Artemis sometimes roams the mountains—*
> *Immense Taygetus, or Erymanthus—*
> *Showering arrows upon boars or fleet antelope,*
> *And with her play the daughters of Zeus*
> *Who range the wild woods—and Leto is glad*
> *That her daughter towers above them all*
> *With her shining brow, though they are beautiful all—* (*Odyssey* 6.101–7, Lombardo transl.)

> *After bathing in the warm water*
> *of Parthenius or in the Amnisus River, Leto's daughter stands*
> *in her golden chariot, rolling over the hills*
> *with her fleet-footed deer for a rendezvous*
> *with a steaming hot hecatomb. She comes attended*
> *by nymphs, some from the Amnisus, others from glens*
> *and the high mountain springs, and around her*
> *the cowering beasts whine and fawn as the goddess*
> *speeds along.* (*Argonautica* 3.879–87)

Nausicaa's likeness to the virgin goddess honors her status as an unwed maiden and emphasizes her mother's pride in her physical eminence over her nymph companions. Medea's likeness has a different tone: Artemis is headed for a sacrifice, and her superiority is over the animals that cower and whine before her. Nausicaa inspires joy, Medea fear. The heroes' similes in this episode also distinguish the episodes. Odysseus emerges from the sea like a hungry lion, sure of itself and ready to attack. But just before the simile, Odysseus covers his nakedness with a leafy branch, clearly attempting to frighten the girls less, and just after the simile, he debates how best to approach them and chooses a cautious and respectful way (*Odyssey* 6.126–47, Lombardo transl.). In contrast, Jason bursts into the scene dazzling and dangerous as the Dog Star:

> *. . . like Sirius rising*
> *up out of the ocean, bright and beautiful*
> *to behold, but bringing indescribable harm*
> *to the flocks . . .* (3.963–66)

Jason's immediate effect is Medea's physical lovesickness—pit in the stomach, inability to speak or move, and the like. "Indescribable harm" is not a bad description of his long-term effect on her and many others in their future together (her brother, his father, the children, his new bride). The Sirius simile also brings in both warrior Achilles and husband Hector from the *Iliad*, casting shadows of vengeful violence and marital tragedy into Medea's first conversation with Jason. Medea herself articulates a warning at the conclusion of this first conversation. Whereas Nausicaa had only said to Odysseus, "Farewell, stranger, and remember me in your own native land. I saved your life" (*Odyssey* 8.498–99, Lombardo transl.), Medea says to Jason:

> "Simply do this: when you do reach Iolcus,
> remember me, and I, even despite my parents,
> will remember you, too. And may a rumor reach my ears
> from afar or a bird come as messenger to report
> when you've forgotten me, or may swift gusts sweep me off
> and carry me over the sea from here to Iolcus myself,
> so that I can reproach you face to face as I remind
> you that you escaped due to my goodwill. May I then
> appear as an unexpected guest at your palace's hearth!" (3.1123–31)

Despite the fact that Medea's love was plotted by the gods and activated by Love's arrow, and despite the fact that she has tried to resist it and suffers deeply because of it, with these words, there is no mistaking that Medea is not—or would not remain—innocent, naïve, or helpless. As she departs with Jason (in possession of the Fleece, thanks again to her help) and they voyage away from Colchis, Apollonius comments more on her actions than on her inner thoughts, as emphasized in the opening to Book 4:

> Speak now, divine Muse, and in your own voice recount
> the laborious schemes the Colchian maiden now wove.
> My own soul quavers with speechless bemusement
> as I try to decide whether she left the Colchians
> out of sheer panic or love-stricken grief. (4.1–5)

Medea's inscrutability prompts a moment of keen and private (speechless) poetic self-reflection. Whatever Medea is, she prompts Apollonius—and us—to reckon with her. He asks for help again when he must tell of Medea's most horrific deed in this text—her part in the murder of her brother Apsyrtus.

Glory Projected: An Introduction to Apollonius's Argonautica

> Ah, pitiless Love, humankind's greatest curse,
> you are the source of deadly strife, lamentation
> and groans, and you are grief's stormy birth-mother.
> Arise, Divinity, and take up arms against
> the sons of our foes as you did when you filled
> Medea's heart with ill-fated madness. Tell us how,
> by what evil doom, she murdered Apsyrtus
> when he came to meet her, for we must sing that next. (4.446–53)

His poetic aporia covers plot; "by what evil doom" is Lombardo and Polsley's rendition of the dative of means in the Greek. More profoundly, it covers interpretation. "How" reflects the Greek *pōs*, a Greek adverb that expresses manner ("with what attitude"), usually with a sense of disbelief, shock, or dismay. The rest of this poetic interjection, while it fits the immediate situation with Apsyrtus (he is indeed the son of Medea and Jason's foe), also fits the circumstances of the Medea we already know from Euripides's tragedy. In that play, after Medea accuses Jason of ingratitude for the crimes she committed in his name (including betraying her family), Jason famously claims it was Love who compelled Medea to save him.

The killing of Apsyrtus is sparked when Medea perceives she is about to be abandoned. As she confronts Jason, she delivers a harangue that is surely modeled on a similar harangue in Euripides's play (*Medea* 465–519). She speaks:

> "Son of Aeson, what conspiracy are you all plotting?
> Have your triumphs gone to your head, erasing your
> memory? Do you have any regard for what you said when
> you were trapped by necessity? Where went your oaths to Zeus,
> suppliants' god, where went your honey-sweet promises?
> Because of them, against all decency and fixed
> on shameless purpose, I forsook my country, the glories
> of my home, my parents themselves, all I held near and dear.
> Far abroad, all alone, I'm borne overseas
> with the doleful kingfishers as my companions—
> because of your troubles, simply so I could help you win
> the contests with the oxen and Earthborn men, safe and sound.
> And lastly, the Fleece. When the truth had come out, you won
> that by my folly, too, while I showered tragic disgrace

upon women. So I proclaim that as your daughter, wife,
and sister, I travel with you to the land of Hellas.
In every way, then, stand by to protect me.
Don't leave me too far away when you go visiting kings.
Fight for me, plain and simple. Shore up justice
and divine law. We both consented to it. Otherwise,
this instant take your sword and slash my neck right through,
so that I may reap a reward that fits my mad lust.
Cruel wretch! If this king whom you both trust
with your dreadful pact decrees that I go to my brother,
how will I face my father? With a grand reputation?
What punishment or harsh penalty will I not suffer
in torment for the terrible deeds that I have done?
And will you gain the homecoming that is dear to your heart?
May Zeus's wife, queen of all, your glorious boast, never
bring that to pass! And may you remember me someday,
ravaged by cares. May the Fleece vanish into the netherworld
of Erebus, like a dream, carried off on the breeze.
May Furies of my vengeance chase you from my country at once.
How much anguish I've suffered due to your callousness!
Moral law prevents my curses from falling to the ground
unfulfilled, since you've broken a mighty oath, you brute!
But you can be sure that all of you will not blithely sit
and mock me for long on the strength of your treaties." (4.353–90)

In both texts, she recaps the contests at Colchis and mentions Jason's broken oaths; her betrayal of her family; her resulting bereftness, displacement, and reliance on Jason; and her reputation, both now and in the future. Lombardo and Polsley encourage our recognition of Euripides's intertext with the deft sentence, "I showered **tragic** disgrace upon women" (4.366–67), and in the tragedy, Medea also comments on her impact on the reception of womankind. Outside of the Apsyrtus episode, Apollonius's Medea, like her Euripidean counterpart, wrestles with the idea of Greek cultural identity and uses an embroidered garment to lure a victim (Apsyrtus, the princess) to their death (stay tuned for more on that garment and others).

Props and Costumes

This Introduction started with the same idea that launched the Argonauts and the *Argonautica*: the Fleece. Though neither the Argonauts nor their readers encounter the Fleece until the early part of the fourth book, Apollonius's thirty-odd mentions of it in Books 1–3 keep expectations high. When Jason finally gets his hands on it, the item does not disappoint. It is radiant and epic-sized:

> So too Jason
> lifting up the massive Fleece in his hands,
> and his cheeks and brows flushed with a flame-red glow
> reflected from the shimmering mass of wool.
> It was about as big as the hide of a yearling stag,
> that hunters call a brocket, the Fleece golden above,
> heavy, and thickly flocked. As the hero strode along,
> the sheen was reflected up from the ground.
> He wore it over his left shoulder, and it reached
> down to his feet, but every now and then
> he gathered it up in his hands, terribly afraid
> some god or man might try to take it away. (4.165–76)

Apollonius amplifies its exoticism by using so unusual a word for "stag" that scholiasts felt the need to define it; Lombardo and Polsley's "brocket" recreates this effect for most modern Anglophones. The Fleece makes one more physical appearance in the poem at Drepane, the island home of the Phaeacians, where Medea fulfills the wish the *Odyssey*'s Nausicaa did not: she marries the hero who arrived on her home shore. It is no traditional wedding, however, but a sexual rendezvous hastily planned by Arete intended to legitimize their marriage and give Alcinous diplomatic cover for defending them. The rendezvous happens in a cave, on a couch the Argonauts spread with the Fleece "so that the marriage would be honored and become the subject of song" (4.1155–56). The *Argonautica*—particularly this passage—*is* the song. It is a strange honor that Apollonius ends this "song" with the detail that it wasn't Jason's first choice and that both partners were anxious, leading to a moment of poetic melancholy:

> No, we forlorn mortals
> might walk sure-footed the road of delight
> but bitter sorrow always keeps pace with our joy. (4.1179–81)

Glory Projected: An Introduction to Apollonius's Argonautica

Teased as the prize and then materializing as an alluring and eerie talisman, the Fleece is last seen as a key prop in an unsettling cave boudoir. Apollonius's descriptions of the Fleece put it firmly in the mind's eye of the readers. Vivid description of a physical object real or imagined (an artwork in particular), a rhetorical trope we now call ekphrasis, had been popular since Achilles's shield in Homer's *Iliad* but hit its vogue in the Hellenistic era, with authors even competing to determine whose description of a given work was most lifelike. The two Fleece passages engage many facets of the trope: attention to color and lighting effects, inclusion of movement and sound, and internal viewers who react to the object. Jason, in the passage above, keeps gathering up the Fleece anxiously. The Argonauts marvel and are eager to touch it (4.178–81). The nymphs who bring flowers to the cave react to it with longing and trepidation (4.1160–62). But the very first reaction we see to the talisman comes in a splendid simile immediately preceding its description:

> *A maiden catches on her fine-spun cloak*
> *the light of the full moon as it rises above*
> *the high roof of her chamber, and her heart is glad*
> *as she observes the beautiful glow.*
>   So too Jason
> *lifting up the massive Fleece in his hands,*
> *and his cheeks and brows flushed with a flame-red glow*
> *reflected from the shimmering mass of wool.* (4.162–68)

Jason is glad to see the Fleece. The simile hints that it is joy like that of a bride-to-be, for the word used for "maiden" is *parthenos*, which evokes marriageability (for context, just a few lines earlier, Medea was called a *korē*, a less specific word for "young woman"). This simile feminizes and domesticates Jason even as it renders him a viewer of the Fleece and a reflection of it, literally reflecting its light. When, just after this simile, he hoists it onto his shoulder and it covers his whole height, he becomes a different sort of reflection—a doublet of the magic ram, about to carry a child across the sea away from a murderous parent and to safety (after a fashion). Considering the two Fleece scenes, grove and cave, we begin to glimpse Apollonius's engagement with the deeper intellectual and cultural concerns that undergird ekphrasis, such as the difference between reality and representation and the collusion of allure and mendaciousness. Ultimately, which shiny artifact are we interpreting: The Fleece? The hero Jason?

Glory Projected: An Introduction to Apollonius's Argonautica

The *Argonautica*? Or the *Argonautica* interpreting Jason interpreting the Fleece? Let us bear in mind, too, that Jason's acquisition of the Fleece had long been a common theme in Greek vase painting, suggesting that visual artists were as captivated with the representational allure of the Fleece as was Apollonius.

Apollonius includes two other important coats that work together, and together with the Fleece, to entangle different parts of the whole epic in ways that prompt the reader to revisit and rethink earlier episodes. Clothing is occasionally mentioned in the text; for example, Polydeuces takes off a "finely woven mantle" (*eustipton pharos*) and Amycus his "dark, two-ply cloak" (*lōpē*) before their boxing match at the beginning of Book 2 (2.28, 30–31). But when summoned to an audience with Queen Hypsipyle in Book 1, Jason dons a special cloak:

> Jason had already buckled around his shoulders
> a double-folded purple mantle that Pallas Athena
> had woven and given to him when she first laid down
> the Argo's keel-struts and taught the hero
> how to measure timbers with rule and line.
> You could more easily stare at the rising sun
> than fix your eyes on that robe's crimson blaze.
> It was indeed bright red in the middle but its edges
> were purple, with many scenes artfully interwoven. (1.702–10)

The cloak's origin, crafted by the goddess of craft even as she was crafting the first ship, suggests that it holds layers of meaning behind what is immediately apparent. What is immediately apparent is that it is special: majestic purple with a crimson center and literally stunning to the eyes. The familiar language of ekphrasis appears in the attention to light and color and the presence of a model viewer, internal or hypothetical: in this case, us as readers. And here we see the cloak (and Jason wearing it) as the sun. Just after the lengthy description of the "scenes artfully interwoven," Apollonius offers further interpretive guidance in the form of a simile:

> And he went up to the city like a brilliant star,
>
> *a star seen by young women from their chambers,*
> *gazing at it as it rises above the rooftops*
> *through the dark air, charming their eyes*

Glory Projected: An Introduction to Apollonius's Argonautica

> *with its beautiful, ruddy glow, and causing*
> *one of them to rejoice, lovesick as she is*
> *for a boy who is now far away amid strangers*
> *and to whom her parents plan to wed her one day.*
>
> So too the hero ascended to the city. (1.759–67)

Again, Jason is like a star with a ruddy glow (compare the "crimson blaze" above) and charms the eyes of the one who looks. But now, in the simile, the internal viewer of the star = Jason = cloak is a lovesick maiden on the eve of marriage, *parthenos* in the Greek text. The maiden recalls Atalanta, mentioned five lines earlier as a woman Jason left behind; anticipates Hypsipyle in the immediate context; and looks forward to the simile from Book 4 (described above) comparing Jason looking at the Fleece to a maiden looking at her cloak in the moonlight.

The heart of the cloak ekphrasis is a description of the scenes artfully interwoven into it: the Cyclopes finishing up a thunderbolt for Zeus (flashing light); Amphion and Zethus magically building the walls of Thebes; Aphrodite holding Ares's shield, which mirrors her face; a violent raid on the land of King Electryon of Mycenae; the chariot race of Pelops and Hippodameia; Apollo avenging his mother's rape by Tityos; and Phrixus on the magical ram, listening to it. The cloak description is busy with ekphrastic signature details such as shifting light, sound, artistic self-consciousness, and embedded interpreters, recommending it to Hellenistic readers' refined tastes (evidence in fact exists of actual contemporary cloaks embroidered with mythological tableaus). We might ask, Why these scenes? So did one ancient reader, a scholiast who read the montage as an allegory for the cosmic order and human affairs (schol. to 1.763–64a). In this respect, it recalls the shield of Achilles in Homer's *Iliad* 18, which also includes snapshots revealing the wondrous scope of the universe from a human perspective. Jason's literal investiture in divinely manufactured gear renders this an "arming scene" and him an Achilles on the verge of his *aristeia*, destructive and glorious. Yet, where Achilles goes on to defeat Hector, Jason achieves a victory of bedroom diplomacy.

The other focal garment is not mentioned until Book 4. It is a purple woven mantle (a peplos) that plays a role in the epic's most shocking episode, the murder of Apsyrtus. Medea and Jason use the cloak as a token of goodwill to lure Apsyrtus into a private meeting with Medea, whereupon Jason will ambush him. Apollonius describes it using ekphrastic strategies now familiar to us:

Glory Projected: An Introduction to Apollonius's Argonautica

> So the two of them agreed, weaving a guileful web
> for Apsyrtus. They assembled many gifts
> suitable to present to guests and among them,
> a sacred, crimson robe of Hypsipyle. The Graces
> had woven it with their own hands for Dionysus
> on the island of Dia, and he later gave it to Thoas,
> his son, who in turn left it for Hypsipyle,
> and she presented it, along with many other gifts,
> to Jason, for him to wear. You could never satisfy
> your desire to touch it or even to gaze at it.
> And a divine fragrance wafted up from the fabric
> ever since the king of Nysa lay down upon it,
> drunk with wine and nectar, as he embraced
> the lovely breast of the daughter of Minos
> after Theseus abandoned her on the island of Dia
> when she had followed him from Cretan Cnossus. (4.420–35)

Though this cloak is splendid to the eye (crimson, divinely woven, such that "You could never satisfy your desire to touch it or even to gaze at it"), its greater meaning comes not from its physical description but from its pedigree. The Graces made it for Dionysus, whence it passed to Thoas, then Hypsipyle, then Jason. It is steeped in abandonment, betrayal, and attendant violence. Working backward through this pedigree, Jason's receipt of the cloak from Hypsipyle is mentioned only here and is least problematic, though his departure grieves her sorely. Thoas's story is elaborated in Book 1 as part of the back story of the Lemnian women. In response to their husbands' infidelities, the Lemnian women murdered all Lemnian men—guilty and innocent alike—except for King Thoas, whom Hypsipyle spared but exiled (1.591–618). Apollonius's readers would no doubt connect the murderous revenge of the scorned Lemnian wives with what they knew of Jason's future from Euripides's *Medea*. Importantly, when Hypsipyle herself tells Jason the island's story (1.779–821), though she says she will speak the truth (1.782, Greek *nēmertes*, "unerringly"), she tells Jason they sent the men away, "glossing over the murder of Lemnos's men" (1.820–21). (Interestingly, in her description of the societal chaos caused by the men's infidelity, Hypsipyle elaborates on tension among step- and half-siblings and their different mothers, a phenomenon that scholars call "amphimetric strife" and which is particularly relevant to dynastic politics of the Hellenistic era and to Medea's Euripidean "future.")

xxxiii

Glory Projected: An Introduction to Apollonius's Argonautica

Further back in its pedigree, this crimson peplos was the cloth on which Dionysus bedded Ariadne. This anticipates the boudoir function of the Fleece later in Book 4 and, more importantly, reminds the reader of Medea's cousin Ariadne. Jason mentions Ariadne in his first conversation with Medea in Book 3, when the two meet at the Temple of Artemis:

> "Once upon a time the maiden daughter of Minos,
> Ariadne, took compassion, and rescued Theseus
> from grisly contests. Pasiphae, daughter of Helios,
> gave birth to her. But when Minos's anger had eased, she
> joined Theseus on the ship and left her homeland behind.
> Even the immortal gods themselves loved her,
> and as a sign a crown of stars, which they call Ariadne's crown,
> rolls along in the midst of the sky all night long,
> among the constellations of the heavens. So too
> you will have thanks from the gods, if you save
> such an impressive band of chieftains. Surely, judging
> from your lovely form, you excel in compassion." (3.1005–16)

Jason means to secure her help, curiously by hinting at what admiration she will gain from it; in this way, Apollonius nods to Euripides's Medea, ever attentive to her standing among men and gods. Jason leaves out of this comparison exactly *how* Ariadne rescues Theseus from grisly contests. She does it by helping Theseus kill her brother, the Minotaur. He also notably omits the rest and most famous part of Ariadne's story: that Theseus abandons her soon after on an island and sails away. Medea reveals to Jason that Ariadne is her relative and is well-known ("And tell me of this maiden you named, whoever she is, the well-known daughter of Pasiphae. She is a relative of my father," 3.1085–87). At this prompt, Jason drops the comparison ("Why do I tell you of . . . the far-famed Ariadne, daughter of Minos?" 3.1109–11), and Medea does too ("nor will I compare myself to Ariadne," 3.1121–22), but Apollonius does not let the comparison go when he mentions the peplos in Book 4. Abandonment, betrayal, and violence (here, fratricide) are woven into this fabric.

One final note on the peplos: this is the same type of garment Euripides's Medea uses to trick and then poison Jason's new bride (*Medea* 786). Apollonius is a genius with these details.

Glory Projected: An Introduction to Apollonius's Argonautica

Gods and Monsters

In the 1963 sword and sandal film *Jason and the Argonauts*, director Don Chaffey and special effects master Ray Harryhausen offered dazzling visuals of the myth's most fantastic elements: its gods and monsters. The gods appear on screen early and often, intervening in activities on Earth (such as when Triton holds the Symplegades apart so the Argo can pass through) and conniving from Mount Olympus. Jason even visits them there to discuss his plight in a strongly self-referential scene: relatively tiny, Jason literally stands on the game board the gods have been using to play out scenarios of his quest while the relatively huge gods gather around to gaze at him as if at a spectacle. As the gods, so the filmmaker, each in control of their world, here benignly. When Jason confesses, "I wouldn't have believed a mortal could ask the help of the gods, much less visit them," Zeus and Hera smile; Zeus praises Jason, and Hera offers tangible advice. Harryhausen's monsters in the film offer dread counterpoint to the gods, likewise situating the heroes *as humans* in their world. The dusky, muscular, winged Harpies who vex Phineus evoke the demons of apocalyptic art. The seven-headed hydra emerges chthonic and serpentine from its lair. It begets an army of skeletons, creatures beyond death whom the Argonauts must face. Talos, brazen and terrifying, appears early in the film as a statue brought to life by Hercules's recklessness. Analogous to the Olympians with their board game, Harryhausen's signature technique of using clay models and stop-motion photography plays into the commentary on filmmaking-as-world-building.

Apollonius's treatment of gods and monsters consistently invites the reader to ponder (the) cosmic order from various perspectives. Homer's readers will recognize the narrative role the gods play in *Argonautica* as they watch, discuss, and intervene in the human stage. *Argonautica*'s gods do likewise, such as here when they watch the Argonauts' departure along with other audience members:

> On that day all the gods looked down from the sky
> upon the ship and the might of the half-divine heroes,
> the bravest of all men who then sailed the sea.
> Nymphs on the highest peaks of Pelion marveled
> as they gazed at the work of Itonian Athena
> and the heroes themselves plying the oars.
> And from the mountaintop down to the sea
> came Cheiron, son of Philyra, dipping his feet

Glory Projected: An Introduction to Apollonius's Argonautica

> into the white surf, and as he waved his broad hand
> again and again he cried out to them as they sped on,
> wishing them a swift journey and a safe return home.
> With him was his wife, who, cradling in her arm
> Peleus's son, Achilles, showed the babe to his father. (1.531–43)

This passage in Apollonius neatly configures a range of supernatural viewers, each defined by their viewing (and critical) distance: the gods from heaven, farthest away and most omniscient; the nymphs (lesser deities) from a nearby mountain peak—a broad but defined vantage point, since wood for the Argo came from Mount Pelion; and semidivine Cheiron, who had actually taught Jason and so gets a surfside seat for the sendoff. Throughout the epic, gradations of divinity situate and comment upon humans in the universe.

Scenes of the Olympians reacting, discussing, and plotting are the most familiar to readers not only as staples of Homeric epic but also in the sense that the gods' behavior mimics human behavior. The opening scene of Book 3 is a *locus classicus* for the phenomenon; Hera, Athena, and Aphrodite chat and maneuver among each other like Alexandrian ladies at court (for example, Gorgo and Praxinoa in Theocritus's *Idyll* 15, headed to a festival). Aphrodite's exasperation with petulant Eros resonates with any reader who has ever cared for a young child. Such familiarity bothered some ancient thinkers, such as Xenophanes of Colophon in the sixth century BCE, who complained that it rendered the gods reprehensibly small. Perhaps so, and the scene invites criticism not only of the gods' household foibles but also of their motivations and attitudes toward humans. Hera's opening salvo to Athena is that they devise a scheme "to spirit the Golden Fleece of Aeetes away to Hellas, or to cajole him, coaxing him with soft words," while Athena reveals that her own scheming was "to help the heroes' courage" (3.13–14, 20). At Hera's suggestion, they land on a different plan: to outsource the scheming to Medea by inciting her love for the hero:

> "Come, let us go to Cypris. Let's both accost her,
> urge her to order her son, if he will obey, to target
> the daughter of Aeetes, the sorceress, with his arrows,
> and bewitch her with love for Jason. Her shrewd designs
> might enable him to carry the Fleece back to Hellas." (3.24–28)

Two aspects of this speech raise concerns for the reader interested in theodicy: first, Hera is willing to involve Medea, an innocent party and a risky one; and second, she renders Athena, Aphrodite, and Eros as accomplices, thus tangling responsibility for the things Medea and Jason will later do, good and awful alike. The ethics of involving Medea come into sharper focus when we learn in Book 4 that Hera knows Medea's love is doomed; there, she reveals that Medea is destined to be Achilles's bride in the underworld. Hera uses Medea to benefit Jason, but this short-term benefit will have long-lasting disastrous consequences for him. Medea's involvement leads to Jason's doom, and Hera knows it. Hera's involvement of accomplices lends the scene a tragic rather than epic perspective; Euripides's Medea and Jason in fact argue at length precisely about who or what should take credit or blame for Jason's quest. Tangled divine responsibility goes along with confusion about the gods' overall plan, especially since Zeus's role is understated. In *Argonautica*, it is Hera who takes the lead, though even her motives are unclear: she is angry at Pelias (1.15, 3.60–62) and fond of Jason (3.62–64). Zeus's will is not completely absent, though; Apollonius reminds the reader periodically that the quest is Zeus's required atonement for the sacrifice of Phrixus (2.1188–90, 3.327). The gods' will is inscrutable.

This inscrutability is by their own design, as we learn from the prophet Phineus:

> "Listen, then. It is not lawful for you to know exactly
> about everything. But what the gods permit, I will not hide.
> I was a reckless fool before, when I divulged Zeus's will
> in full sequence from beginning to end. He wishes
> to reveal his decrees himself, an oracle at a time,
> leaving men yet in need of the gods' complete purpose." (4.300–305)

The limits of human knowledge are the dominant theme of the Phineus episode. The Argonauts encounter Phineus in Bithynia on the south coast of the Black Sea. The episode begins with his back story: he was a prophet by the gift of Apollo who "had no respect at all for Zeus himself, foretelling exactly the god's sacred will" (2.169–70), so Zeus cursed him with blindness, perpetual old age, and the harassment of the Harpies, winged monsters who foul any food he would eat. Even before he tells them why his guidance is incomplete (the passage above), he gives them incomplete guidance. When the Boreads take pity and seek to help him, they ask why he has been punished with the Harpies' persecution, for they don't want to incur divine wrath themselves; "though we long to help you, our hearts are bewildered," they say (2.238). Phineus ignores their question but swears the oath they request: "No divine wrath will strike you in return for aid you render me" (2.251–52). Yet when the brothers come close to catching the Harpies "and would have torn them to bits, heaven's will notwithstanding" (2.272–73), an observant third party (the goddess Iris) has to intervene to protect the boys:

> "Sons of Boreas, it is not right that you strike the Harpies,
> the hounds of mighty Zeus, with your swords. I myself
> will swear to you: they shall no longer draw near to Phineus." (2.277–79)

Phineus's oath is accurate in letter—the Boreads meet no harm, in the end—but not in spirit. He certainly gives at best an incomplete response. Does he mislead them deliberately? Is this part of his post-punishment capitulation to withhold something from truth-seekers, "leaving men yet in need of the gods' complete purpose" (2.305)? In the context of Phineus's necessary omissions and misdirection, the attentive reader might well stop short at the last piece of divine knowledge he shares with Jason:

> ". . . keep in mind the wily support you enjoy
> from the Cyprian goddess, for the glorious outcome
> of your undertaking rests entirely on her." (2.416–18)

The glorious outcome of this quest does indeed rest on the Cyprian goddess (though as we noted above, not on her alone), but so too does its dreadful aftermath.

Amid the unreadable will of the gods, Apollonius offers alternative ways of grasping the nature of the universe and humans' role within it. One of these is a recurring exploration of cosmic origins. Even a casual dip into *Argonautica* is likely to include an aetion, or origin story for some visible phenomenon or practice in the current day. Apollonius's learned explanations of this or that local ritual or place-name speak to the Alexandrian intellectual milieu. His cosmologies are the universal counterpart to those local aetia. The first cosmology comes in the learned song of Orpheus in Book 1, which comprises an account of the formation of the universe drawn from the philosophy of Empedocles (fifth century BCE, positing strife and love as primal forces) followed by a version of the succession myth drawn from Hesiod (eighth century) and Pherecydes (sixth century), among others. Apollonius had access to the Library, after all. The cosmologic thread is picked up in the ekphrasis of Jason's cloak, which begins with a representation of the Cyclops forging Zeus's thunderbolt; Zeus, not yet armed, is precisely where Orpheus's song left off. Elsewhere we read of Cronus's castration of his father Ouranus (4.998–99), early challenges to Zeus's supremacy (Typhoeus at 2.36–40 and 2.1206–12, Prometheus at 2.1246–56 and cf. 3.856–70, not-yet conceived Achilles at 4.808–12), or the birth of other gods (Dionysus at 4.1147–50, Athena at 4.1325–26). At other moments, the text focuses on the universe's physical structure, such as Argus's exposition in Book 4 of primeval navigable waterways north and south unknown to the much younger Greeks (4.249–89), or the toy Aphrodite uses to secure Eros's help with Medea in Book 3:

". . . the dazzlingly beautiful plaything of Zeus—
the toy his dear nurse Adrasteia made for him
in his wide-eyed infancy, in the Idaean cave—
a ball, well-rounded, a better novelty than any toy
you could get from the hands of Hephaestus.
Its sections are formed of gold, and around each of them
wind two circular strips of webbing. Its seams are hidden,
with a dark blue spiral running over all of them.
If you toss it up in your hands, it casts a blazing trail
through the air, like a star. I will give it to you." (3.124–33)

Eros's toy reflects the scientific thinking of many Presocratics for whom the cosmos was a sphere (Empedocles, Parmenides) as well as contemporary interest in the heavens (Aratus, Eratosthenes of Cyrene, cf. the "Lock of Berenice"). Perhaps there existed even crafted models representing various understandings of universal structure. Yet even this philosophical, scientific representation of the cosmos is yoked to divine agency: it is the plaything of godlings.

Despite the evident and divinely ordained gulf between men and gods in the text, the *Argonautica* persistently offers examples of clear communication and even permeability between the realms. Minor gods prove graspable in the text. The sea-god Glaucus at the end of Book 1, for example, rises from the deep to tell the Argonauts to give up searching for Heracles, for Heracles is destined for greater things (1.1305–22). But most examples of the lesser divinities' clear assistance are found in Book 4. Thetis advises the Argonauts not to delay attempting the passage through Scylla and Charybdis (4.857–75). Though she communicates only with Peleus, she is clear and direct and promises divine

Glory Projected: An Introduction to Apollonius's Argonautica

aid, which does in fact appear. When Libya's guardian goddesses advise the Argonauts to compensate their mother for carrying them, Jason does not understand the advice (4.1349). However, Peleus correctly interprets that they need to portage the Argo for a time (4.1386–95). Next, Orpheus, "earnestly beseeching" the Hesperides, asks them to "manifest yourselves openly to us who long for you" (4.1444, 1437). They do so and reveal to the Argonauts where to find potable water: Heracles just the day before cleaved open a spring (4.1464–74). Finally, with Orpheus paving the way by dedicating a tripod to local deities and Euphemus making a direct request for information ("give honest answers to our questions," 4.1588), Triton offers the wandering Argonauts "kindly advice" (4.1607) about where to exit the large salt lake named for him and how to navigate thence toward Greece.

It is possible, then, for humans to seek and receive divine help when the distance from human to god is not quite so great. The text's fascination with more proximate deities also emerges in repeated mention of the process and possibility of deification, an idea that resonated with Apollonius's Alexandrian monarchs. The obvious example is Heracles, whose apotheosis Glaucus promises in Book 1:

> "He is destined
> to complete a full twelve labors for insolent Eurystheus,
> at Argos, and to dwell with immortals, abiding with them,
> if he should accomplish a few toils more." (1.1310–13)

Apollonius keeps Heracles fresh in the readers' minds throughout the epic, even after he goes missing, as the Argonauts track or anticipate the mighty hero's wanderings all over the world. We have seen Heracles as a foil for Jason in terms of their heroic quality. He is also an emblem of one possible fate for heroes: true immortality, as opposed to the immortality granted through song alone. The other example is Polydeuces, Leda's son by Zeus (his twin Castor was held to be fathered by the mortal Tyndareus; see Apollonius's cagey language in the catalog at 1.140–44). In the boxing match against Amycus, the poet refers to him as "a true son of Zeus" (2.41) and after his victory, the Argonauts sing a song honoring him (2.152). The word Apollonius uses is *hymnos*, which need not refer to a song to the gods but certainly suggests a status elevated even beyond the heroic. The Mariandyni, enemies of Amycus, "[welcome] Polydeuces as if he were a god" (2.751), and then their king Lycus takes Polydeuces a step closer to divine:

Glory Projected: An Introduction to Apollonius's Argonautica

> "Moreover,
> for the sons of Tyndareus, I will set up a lofty temple
> atop the Acherusian summit. It shall draw the eyes
> of all sailors on the sea, even from very far away,
> and seafarers will pray for the pair's favor. Afterward
> I will also set apart for them, as for the gods,
> rich fields of finely tilled ground in front of the city." (2.803–9)

The important part here is that Lycus not only wants to honor Polydeuces ritually, but he also expects something in return. Heroes can become gods, and then they can help other heroes. The poet teases this fate for Jason and his Argonauts at the end of the text by hymning them: "Be gracious, race of blessed heroes! And may these verses be sweeter to chant year after year among men" (4.1809–10). One suspects that Apollonius was following the lead of Ptolemy II Philadelphus, who adopted cult worship during his lifetime in the manner of Egypt's ruler-gods.

The monsters Jason encounters similarly explore what it means to be human in the world. Though the first three books include impressive monsters—the Harpies, the dragon that guards the Fleece, Aeetes's fire-breathing bulls, and the Earthborn—the monsters of Book 4 are of particular cosmological interest here since in that book, Jason is also exploring the outermost reaches of the known world. First are Circe's beasts on Aeaea. Though Medea has heard of the island (she is Circe's niece), Jason confesses the Greeks have never even heard of it (3.1084–85, 1104–5). When the Argonauts arrive there in Book 4, they look with amazement at Circe and her creatures:

> And creatures, not like wild beasts, but not humans either,
> with an assortment of limbs, were thronging about,
> as sheep in a fold follow the shepherd.
> Earth herself had once engendered such species,
> composed of various limbs, from the primordial slime
> when she had not yet solidified beneath a rainless sky
> nor been relieved of moisture by the scorching sun,
> and before Time combined these forms and gave them order.
> Such were unformed monsters that followed her now.
> The heroes were seized with amazement . . . (4.677–86)

These differ from the beasts of Homer's Circe, which resemble pigs but retain human intellect, though not memory (*Odyssey* 10.250–61, Lombardo transl.). Apollonius

Glory Projected: An Introduction to Apollonius's Argonautica

imagines elemental creatures, a precursor to humankind—and note, too, the attention to the origins of the physical cosmos and the resonance with Empedocles's early creatures. These creatures are not, of course, the Argonauts—Jason orders them to stay behind. Nor, of course, are they Odysseus's men, who in narrative time exist a generation later. They are unidentified, casting Circe as a divine creator, a model monster maker, a distant ancestor to Ray Harryhausen. The witch hints that she could, if she wished, refashion the lovers into primordial beasts ("I will design no further ruin for you," 4.752). But she takes pity and, in fitting response to the crime Jason and Medea have committed against Apsyrtus, Circe sacrifices a sow who has just given birth and sprinkles the suppliants with the blood to clean their miasma and restore them to the human community. Circe won't, however, aid the pair against her brother Aeetes. The whole episode ruminates on what defines humanity vis-à-vis animals: intentional creation or evolved design, guilt and responsibility, and relationship with family and/or the broader community.

Second is Talos, the bronze giant who guards Crete. Like Circe's beasts, he is a relic from the distant past and evocative of archaic cosmologies (notably Hesiod's myth of ages):

> He was the sole remainder of the race of bronze,
> men sprung from ash trees, sons of the gods,
> and Zeus gave him to Europa to be guardian of Crete,
> striding around the island three times a day
> on his feet of bronze. His entire body was bronze,
> and he was invulnerable, except that under
> one ankle's sinew lay a blood-red vein
> covered only with the thinnest layer of skin,
> which would prove to be the critical difference
> between life and death. (4.1665–74)

Though Apollonius tells us Talos was born of ash trees, his metallic body, non-blood circulation, and automated circuit of Crete suggest a more mechanical identity. Indeed, earlier Greek texts understood him as a sort of robot created by Hephaestus, who had made other automata (see, e.g., Simonides of Ceos). A vase painting contemporary with Simonides shows Jason using a tool to remove a bolt from Talos's ankle (Beazley 5362). Robots were of keen interest to Greek philosophers, who imagined how they might contribute to utopias by erasing the need for slave labor. By Apollonius's day, engineers had devised working automata, such as a sort of cuckoo clock designed by Ctesibius of Alexandria (third century BCE) and parade float from the reign of Ptolemy II Philadelphus (Apollonius's patron), which was a statue in the shape of Nysa that stood, poured out milk, and sat again without any human intervention (Athenodorus *Deipnosophistai* 5.198ff.). In Apollonius's text, Medea alone takes out Talos by distracting his gaze with phantom images such that he carelessly nicked his ankle and ichor bled out. Apollonius reacts to the monster's demise with a comment on its meaning for humanity:

> Father Zeus, amazement wells up in my mind
> when I see that dire destruction befalls us
> not only from bodily wounds and disease,
> but can afflict us even from a distance! So too Talos,
> despite his bronze structure, yielded the victory
> to the power of Medea the sorceress. (4.1701–6)

Talos's death makes Apollonius wonder about the vulnerability of living things—even those made of bronze, even bloodless—and about what makes them living in the first place. Harryhausen's Talos, a bronze statue come to life, is not so far from Apollonius's in the deeper contemplation about what makes a man.

On the Cutting Floor

The rich texture of this poem—its density of descriptive detail, narrative pacing, background music, and colorful characters—is the work of a master artist marshaling all available resources for the task. One of these resources is the benefit of a text to edit; unlike Homer's orally composed epics (a feat that confounds the mind), Apollonius had time to choose what to keep and what to cut. One striking feature of this text is the author's willingness to insert himself into it. Apollonius makes his editing process visible in the text, such as when he refuses to disclose the secret rites at Samothrace, into which the Argonauts were initiated ("Of these rites I will make no further mention . . . the mysteries of which it is forbidden for me to sing," 1.912, 914–15; and cf. Hecate's rites, 4.240–42). The flip side of this is when he apologizes for disquieting content, such as the location of the sickle Cronus used to castrate his father Ouranus ("forgive me, Muses, I don't tell the old tale willingly," 4.997–98). The expressed tension between what he can say and should say advertises Apollonius's skill and

Glory Projected: An Introduction to Apollonius's Argonautica

authorial integrity that fits the scope of the epic material, especially in a belated age marked by scholarly critical distance from it.

As for that distance, *Argonautica* includes many moments in which we readers find ourselves directly addressed by an author willing to reveal his own thinking. At times, the effect is that as readers, we are pulled into the world of the poem and invited to feel its scenarios, as at the death of King Cyzicus at the end of Book 1:

> Nor did the king escape his fate
> and return to the bed in his bridal chamber.
> No, Aeson's son Jason leaped upon Cyzicus
> and struck him in the middle of his chest,
> shattering his sternum around the spear-point
> and sending him rolling onto the sand,
> fulfilling his fate. No mortal may escape that;
> no, we are hedged in on every side.
> When he thought he had escaped bitter death
> at the hands of the Argonauts, Fate ensnared him
> that very night as he did battle with them. (1.1033–43)

The sharing of our human, universal mortality generates pity for Cyzicus and allows us to imagine our own lives as something heroic. At other times, Apollonius expresses his own reaction to the story on the page, such as his inability to fathom the reasons for Medea's watershed decision to go with Jason at the beginning of Book 4:

> Speak now, divine Muse, and in your own voice recount
> the laborious schemes the Colchian maiden now wove.
> My own soul quavers with speechless bemusement
> as I try to decide whether she left the Colchians
> out of sheer panic or love-stricken grief. (4.1–5)

This passage and others in which Apollonius seeks the Muses' help emphasize his (and our) distance from the heroes and their choices. The hymnic language that closes the epic likewise maintains a gap between what was and what is. As Apollonius mentions the Argonauts' joy at the end of their trials, he prays a sweet immortality for his verses. It has been so, and may it be so:

> Be gracious, race of blessed heroes! And may these verses
> be sweeter to chant year after year among men. (4.1809–10)

Translators' Preface

Apollonius, as he wishes us to know, is a master of meticulousness, erudite technicalities, and layered complexities. He quickly presents himself as a consummate intellectual, striving to assert a solid place in the epic tradition and to convey the depths of his ability and learning. In the process of reading, we are on a journey with the narrator as much as with his heroes. With pedantic asides and sweeping landscapes, he constantly reminds us that he is the heroic captain of the voyage, and his voice will not be shut out. To succeed, we must meekly, yet courageously, travel with him as our guide through deadly perils and possible pitfalls.

The analogy of this voyage reflects the process of translation, as well. Apollonius poses challenges and affords opportunities. During our journey with him, we feel that we have come to know him more personally, and have become increasingly more familiar with his keen sense of details (albeit at times admittedly frustrating, and taxing the translators' knowledge of ancient geography) and his deep desire to outdo his epic predecessors. Indeed, we have come to expect Apollonius to express himself; we could not help but appreciate the freedom of his epic's space and scope and of Apollonius's determined narratorial identity, emphatic and precise.

In that spirit, we have endeavored to preserve Apollonius's voice and personality in making his expedition more stylistically and linguistically approachable for the reader. Names are simplified in some cases (e.g., as with Aphrodite for Cypris), although proper names are generally retained, as are similes and patronymics. The geography is crafted to be faithful for the Argo and the reader but not overly cumbersome, and we have incorporated internal glosses to accommodate subtleties of both genealogy and geography. The reader may detect the sense of a natural rhythm that emerges as the epic unfolds; despite our early decision not to adapt the epic into English dactylic hexameter, Apollonius has an insistent voice, one that tries to go over Homer himself. As a result, the Argo's voyage is not simply an expedition but an engaging experience, one that we are privileged to share with all others who join the adventure.

Suggestions for Further Reading

Apollonius worked in an environment of intense and interdisciplinary research; the same can be said for modern scholarship concerning his work. For a broad introduction to Hellenistic literature and its contexts, anglophone readers should consult Kathryn Gutzwiller's *Guide to Hellenistic Literature* (Blackwell 2007) and relevant chapters in Blackwell's *Companion to Hellenistic Literature* (ed. J. Clauss and M. Cuypers, 2010) and Brill's *Companion to Apollonius Rhodius* (ed. T. Papanghelis and A. Rengakos, 2008).

Fans of the *Argonautica* will find the work of Richard Hunter indispensable, particularly the set of essays *The "Argonautica" of Apollonius: Literary Studies* (Cambridge 2009). In this book, Hunter offers chapters on Jason as a hero, the love story and Medea, the gods, Apollonius's literary style, the Hellenistic context, and the reception of his epic in Vergil's *Aeneid*.

The following titles explore those themes and others:

Beye, C. R. 1969. "Jason as Love Hero in Apollonios' *Argonautika*." GRBS 10: 31–55.

Cameron, Alan. 1995. *Callimachus and His Critics*. Princeton: Princeton University Press.

Clare, R. J. 2002. *The Path of the Argo. Language, Imagery and Narrative in the "Argonautica" of Apollonius Rhodius*. Cambridge: Cambridge University Press.

Clauss, James J. 1993. *The Best of the Argonauts: The Redefinition of the Epic Hero in Book 1 of Apollonius's "Argonautica."* Berkeley and Los Angeles: University of California Press.

Feeney, Denis. 1991. *The Gods in Epic: Poets and Critics of the Classical Tradition*. Oxford: Oxford University Press.

Hulse, Peter. 2015. "A Commentary on the *Argonautica* of Apollonius Rhodius, Book 4.1–481." PhD diss., University of Nottingham.

Hunter, R. L. 1989. *Apollonius of Rhodes "Argonautica" Book III*. Cambridge: Cambridge University Press.

Hunter, R. L. 2015. *Apollonius of Rhodes "Argonautica" Book IV*. Cambridge: Cambridge University Press.

Knight, V. 1995. *The Renewal of Epic: Responses to Homer in the "Argonautica" of Apollonius*. Leiden: Brill.

Suggestions for Further Reading

Lovatt, Helen. 2021. *In Search of the Argonauts. The Remarkable History of Jason and the Golden Fleece.* London: Bloomsbury.

Mori, Anatole. 2008. *The Politics of Apollonius Rhodius' "Argonautica."* Cambridge: Cambridge University Press.

Murray, Jackie. 2005. "Polyphonic Argo." PhD diss., University of Washington.

Nelis, Damien. 2001. *Vergil's "Aeneid" and the "Argonautica" of Apollonius Rhodius.* ARCA, Classical and Medieval Texts, Papers, and Monographs, 39. Cambridge: Francis Cairns.

Phillips, Tom. 2020. *Untimely Epic: Apollonius Rhodius' "Argonautica."* Oxford: Oxford University Press.

Thalmann, William G. 2011. *Apollonius of Rhodes and the Spaces of Hellenism.* Oxford: Oxford University Press.

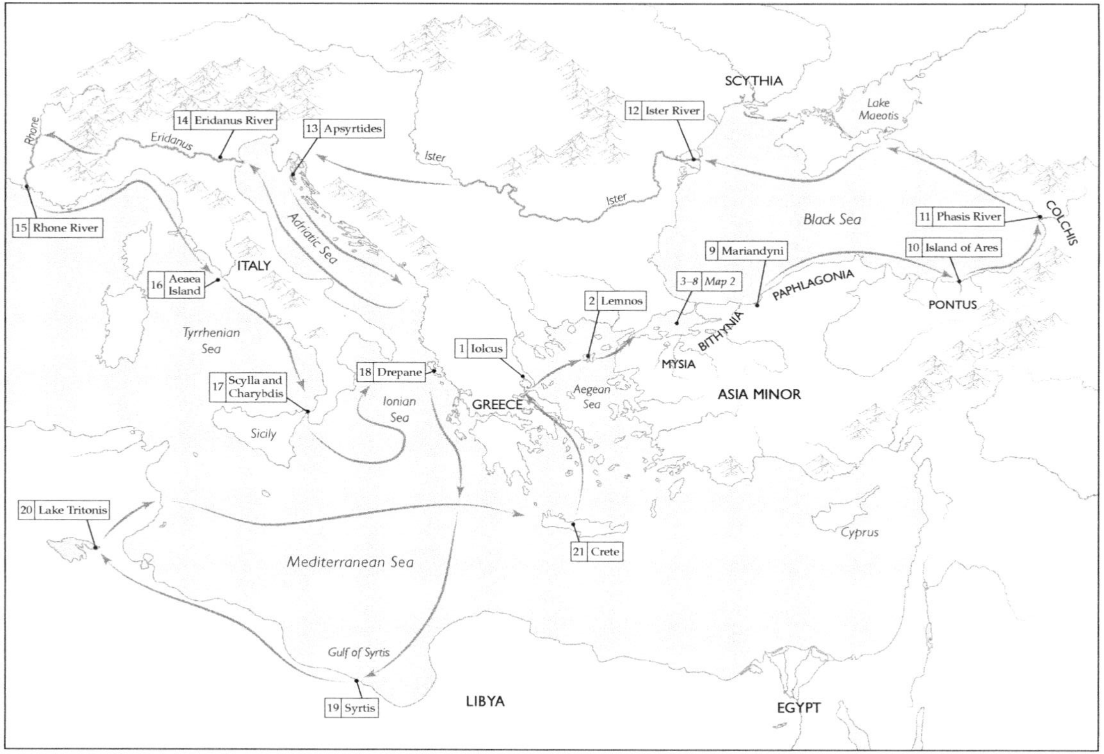

Map 1: Route of the Argo

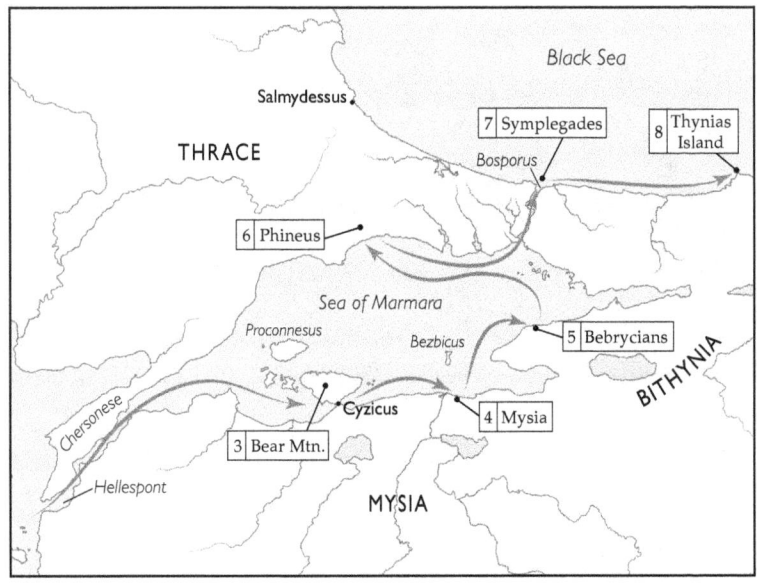

Map 2: Detail

Argonautica

BOOK ONE

Invocation of Apollo; Pelias and Jason

 Beginning with you, Apollo, I will recall the glory
of the ancient heroes who, commanded by Pelias,
rowed the Argo down through the Pontus
and the Clashing Rocks in their quest
for the Golden Fleece.
      Pelias had heard
from an oracle that a grim doom
awaited him—to be murdered at the hands
of a man approaching with only one sandal.
Not long after, this prophecy was fulfilled
when Jason crossed the Anaurus's wintry stream,   10
extricating one sandal from the mudflats there
but leaving the other deep in the floodwater.
He came to the banquet Pelias was offering
to his father Poseidon and all the other gods,
but paying no honor to Pelasgian Hera.
The king spotted him immediately and, pondering,
devised for Jason a troublesome voyage
so that he might lose his homecoming either at sea
or at the hands of enemies in a foreign land.
His ship, as bards of old tell us, was built by Argus   20
under the guidance of Pallas Athena.

Catalog of the Argonauts

 But now I will recount the names of the Argonauts,
and of their ancestors, and tell of their long voyages
and heroic deeds as they wandered the sea.
May the Muses' voices be heard in my song!

 Orpheus is first on our roster, born to Calliope
and Thracian Oeagrus near Pimpleia's summit.

Book One

Men say his music charmed the mountains'
rugged rocks and their coursing rivers.
The wild oaks that grow at Zone　　　　　　　　　　　　　30
on the shore of Thrace still stand as tokens
of his magic, trees that under the spell of his lyre
he led down from Pieria. Such was the poet
Jason welcomed aboard at Cheiron's behest,
Orpheus, lord of Bistonian Pieria.

Next came Asterion, born to Cometes
on the shores of the swirling Apidanus.
He lived in Peiresiae near Mount Phylleia
where the Apidanus and the bright Enipeus,
flowing from afar, finally merge their streams.　　　　　　40
Next, from Larisa, came the son of Eilatus,
Polyphemus, who in his younger days fought
among the Lapiths when they battled the Centaurs.
His limbs now were heavy with age,
but his martial spirit remained as of old.

Nor was Iphiclus, Jason's uncle, left behind in Phylace,
for Jason's father, Aeson, had married Iphiclus's sister,
and his kinship demanded that he be in the ranks.

Nor did Admetus, lord of Pherae's sheepfolds,
stay behind in the shadow of Chalcodonia's peak.　　　　　50

Nor did Hermes's crafty sons, Erytus and Echion,
stay home in the rich wheatfields of Alope,
and venturing forth with them was their kinsman Aethalides,
whom Eupolemaia, Phthian Myrmidon's daughter,
bore near the streams of Amphrysus. The two others
Antianeira, daughter of Menetes, bore.

From fertile Gyrton came Coronus, a brave man,
but not braver than his father, Caeneus,
who, the poets say, perished when he single-handedly

routed the Centaurs, who could neither bend nor kill him. 60
Unbroken and unyielding he passed beneath the earth,
overwhelmed by an avalanche of massive pine trees.

Titaresian Mopsus came too, whom more than any others
Apollo taught augury from the flight of birds.

Eurydamas, son of Ctimenus, came too, whose dwelling
was in Dolopian Ctimene near Xynia's waters.

And Actor sent from Opus his son Menoetius
to join the company of the best of heroes.

Eurytion, Irus's son, joined the company too—
Actor's grandson—and strong Eribotes, Teleon's son. 70
Third with them was Oileus, unmatched in courage
and peerless in pursuit of foes scattered in flight.

From Euboea came Canthus, sent by Canethus,
son of Abas. He was eager to fight
but would not return to Cerinthus, fated as he was
to wander with Mopsus, a seasoned seer with whom
he would perish wandering in farthest Libya.
For no fate is too remote for mortals to meet:
they were buried in Libya as far from the Colchians
as the distance between the rising and setting sun. 80

Clytius and Iphitus journeyed with him.
Oechalia's rulers, sons of ruthless Eurytus,
to whom the archer Apollo once gave his bow
and who perished challenging the donor with it.

Next came the sons of Aeacus, not together
nor from the same place. They had settled in exile
far from Aegina after foolishly killing their brother Phocus.
Telamon lived on the Attic island, Peleus in Phthia.

Book One

Next, from Cecropia, came the warrior Butes,
son of Teleon, and Phalerus with his ashen spear, 90
dispatched by his father, Alcon. Even though he had
no other sons to care for him in his old age,
he sent his beloved, only son, so that he might
shine like a beacon among all the great heroes.

Theseus, though, foremost of all of Erechtheus's sons,
was kept unseen by an invisible bond
beneath the land of Taenarus, for he had
taken that road along with Peirithous.
The two of them would surely have lightened
the labor of all the rest of the heroes. 100

Tiphys, son of Hagnias, went out from Thespis.
He knew how to predict rising seas, how to foretell
storm-winds from the sun and stars, and how to predict
the best time to sail. Tritonian Athena herself
had recruited him, and he was a welcome comrade.
The goddess herself had designed the swift ship,
and Arestor's son Argus had helped her build it,
the most excellent ship ever rowed on the sea.

Next came Phlias from Araethyrea,
where he lived the good life thanks to his father, 110
Dionysus himself, by the springs of Asopus.

From Argos came Bias's sons, Areius and Talaus
along with mighty Leodocus, all born from Pero,
Neleus's daughter. Melampus the Aeolid
endured much for her in the house of Iphiclus.

And Heracles? We know that the great-hearted hero
did not ignore Jason's desire to have him.
No, when he heard that the heroes were gathering
and had himself reached Lyrcaean Argos from Arcadia
on the road that he traveled carrying the boar 120

that had browsed in Lampeia's thickets
near Erymanthia's swamplands, he put down
from his back the animal, bound with chains,
at the entrance to the market-place of Mycenae,
and set out against the will of Eurystheus.
With him went Hylas, the brave young hero
who would bear his arrows and guard his bow.

Next was a descendant of godlike Danaus:
Nauplius, son of Clytonaeus and grandson of Naubolus,
who was sprung from Lernus, an offspring of Proetus.   130
Amymone, daughter of Danaus, having wed Poseidon
gave birth to Nauplius, supreme among sailors.

Idmon was last of the Argives to board.
Although he had learned his fate from augurs,
he still came, to ensure his good reputation.
He was not really Abas's son. Apollo himself
begat him to be among the illustrious Aeolids
and taught him himself the prophetic arts,
how to read the birds and sacrificial flames.

And Aetolian Leda sent forth from Sparta   140
Polydeuces and Castor, adept charioteers,
twins she gave birth to in the house of Tyndareus.
She did not attempt to keep them from going,
but was of a mind worthy of the bride of Zeus.

The sons of Aphareus, Lynceus and Idas,
came from Arene, exuding great strength,
and Lynceus excelled in keen sight also,
if it is true, he could see what was beneath the earth.

And Periclymenus, eldest of godlike Neleus's sons
born at Pylos, joined the crew also. Poseidon himself   150
had given him immeasurable strength and the ability
to assume whatever shape best suited him in battle.

And from Arcadia came Amphidamas and Cepheus,
sons of Aleus, inhabitants of Tegea, Apheidas's realm.
Third was Ancaeus, sent by his father, Lycurgus,
their older brother. Lycurgus remained in the city
to care for Aleus, who was now growing old.
Ancaeus wore the skin of a Maenalian bear
and his right hand gripped a double-edged axe,
for his grandfather had hidden his armor   160
in the hope of preventing his grandson's departure.

Augeias, reputed to be the grandson of Helios,
was also there. He ruled the Eleans and gloried
in his wealth. His great desire was to see
the land of the Colchians and Aeetes, their ruler.

Asterius and Amphion, Hyperasius's sons,
came from Pellene, the Achaean city founded
by their grandfather on Aegialus's brows.

Next, from Taenarus, came swift-footed Euphemus,
whom Europa, mighty Tityos's daughter,   170
bore to Poseidon. He could skim the grey sea
on the tips of his toes, and never wet the soles of his feet.

Two other sons of Poseidon came. Erginus was one,
from gloried Miletus; the other, Ancaeus,
was from Parthenia, sacred to Imbrasion Hera,
both boasting of skill at sea and in war.

Next, from Calydon, came Oeneus's son,
mighty Meleagrus, and Laocoon,
Oeneus's brother, though not by the same mother,
for a maidservant bore him. In his old age Oeneus   180
sent him to protect his son. This was how Meleagrus
joined this band of heroes while still in his youth.
No other had been better, I think, except Heracles,
if he had waited one more year and been trained

among the Aetolians. And his uncle Iphiclus,
son of Thestius, a skilled warrior both hand-to-hand
and with a javelin, was his companion.

With him came Palaemonius, ostensible son
of Olenian Lernus, but really of Hephaestus,
which was why his feet were crippled. But his physique   190
and bravery were such that no one would scorn,
and he was one of the heroes who won fame for Jason.

The Phocians were represented by Iphitus,
son of Naubolus, grandson of Ornytus.
He once hosted Jason when he went to Pytho
to consult the oracle about his voyage,
entertaining him then in his own halls.

Next were Zetes and Calais, sons of Boreas
whom Oreithyia, Erechtheus's daughter,
bore to the storm-god on Thrace's icy frontier,   200
where the god snatched her away as she
whirled in a dance by the river Ilissus.
He carried Oreithyia far from Cecropia
to what men now call Sarpedon's Rock,
near the river Erginus, enfolding her
in clouds of dark mist as he had his way with her.
Now Zetes and Calais beat the dusky wings
that grew on their ankles as they rose in the air,
a wonder to see, wings flecked with gold scales,
and the long, dark hair that swirled around   210
their heads and necks fluttered in the wind.

Neither did Acastus, son of mighty Pelias,
want to stay behind in his heroic father's palace,
nor did Argus, minion of Pallas Athena.
They too were ready to be on the roster.

Book One

All these were assembled to serve Aeson's son Jason.
The locals called all the heroes Minyae, for most of them,
and all the bravest, believed that they were sprung
from the blood of the daughters of Minyas.
Jason himself was the son of Alcimede,   220
whose mother was Clymene, daughter of Minyas.

Jason and Alcimede's farewell

When the servants had made ready everything
a fully equipped ship about to voyage forth needs,
the heroes made their way through the city
and down to the shore where the vessel was docked,
a beach that men call Magnesian Pagasae.
A great crowd of people rushed there as well,
but the heroes gleamed like stars among clouds,
and someone seeing them in their armor would say:

"Lord Zeus, what is Pelias thinking? To what land   230
far from Hellas is he sending off these heroes?
They'd burn down Aeetes's palace in a single day
if he refused to deliver up the Fleece.
It's a hard journey, but has to be undertaken."

That's what they were saying throughout the city.
The women, though, would lift their hands to the sky
and pray to the gods for the heroes' safe return.
One of them lamented to her companion in tears:

"Poor Alcimede, evil has come to you, albeit late,
and your life is ending stripped of its splendor.   240
Aeson also, so unfortunate a man. Better for him
if he were buried wrapped in his funeral shroud,
oblivious to all this bitter suffering.
If only the murky billows had overwhelmed
Phrixus and the ram when young Helle perished!
But the baneful portent was spoken in a human voice
only to torture Alcimede hereafter."

Book One

So the women spoke as their heroes departed.
A crowd of servants, both male and female,
now gathered around Jason's mother, all of them   250
smitten with grief. And with them his father,
sad and old, groaned as he lay there, wrapped in blankets.
Jason did what he could to ease their suffering.
Then he ordered the manservants to gather up
his weapons for war, and in grievous silence they did so.
But his mother clung to him, ceaselessly weeping,

as an abandoned maiden weeps, throwing her arms
around the neck of her white-haired nurse,
a maiden who has no others to care for her
as she lives a dreary life with her stepmother   260
who abuses her with a constant barrage of insults;
and as she weeps her heart is frozen with sorrow
and she cannot sob forth her burden of grief.

So too Alcimede, and as she wept embracing her son
she poured forth her sorrow in words such as these:

"Ah, would that on the very day when—oh, the misery!—
I heard King Pelias's dire directive,
I had given up my life, and forgotten my troubles!
Then you would have buried me with your own dear hands,
O my son. That was the one last wish I hoped for from you. 270
Now I, once so highly admired by Achaean women,
will be forsaken in my empty halls, like a female slave—
unhappy wretch—wasting away yearning for you,
the reason for my lavish splendor in days gone by,
you, my only son, the reason I first undid my sash,
and the last, since Eileithyia begrudged me another child,
resenting me far more than any other woman.
Alas for my delusion! Never, not even in a dream,
did I have even the slightest premonition
that Phrixus's escape would be the ruin of me!"   280

Book One

Moaning in this way, Alcimede wept, and her women folk,
standing beside her, lamented. But Jason
spoke to her gently with these soothing words:

"Please, Mother, don't keep piling up heartbreak.
Your tears won't avert any misery. No,
you will simply heap one grief on another.
The gods dole out devastating sorrow to mortals.
Even though you feel deep distress in your heart,
have the courage to bear your share of grief.
And take heart from Athena's divine prophecies, 290
since Apollo has given propitious oracles,
and take heart from the support of our chieftains.
Now stay here with your handmaids, in peace, at home,
and don't be a bird of ill omen for the ship.
My clansmen and servants will follow me there."

Having said this, he began to walk out of the house.

Apollo leaving some scented shrine to set out for
sacred Delos or Claros or Pytho, or to broad Lycia
near the stream of Xanthos
                            will give you some idea
of how Jason moved through the crowds of people 300
as they cheered and shouted. He was met by Iphias,
priestess of Artemis, patron goddess of the city,
who kissed his right hand but lacked the strength to speak,
eager though she was. The crowd surged on,
and she was left behind, as the old often are by the young,
and the hero soon had moved far ahead.

Preparations for the journey

When he had left
the well-constructed streets of the city,
he came to the beach at Pagasae, where he was greeted
by his crewmen assembled near the ship. When they saw
Acastus and Argus barreling down from the city, 310

12

they marveled that they had come against Pelias's will.
Argus, son of Arestor, wore around his shoulders
a hairy bull-hide that reached down to his feet;
Acastus, a beautiful double-folded mantle
that his sister Pelopeia had presented to him.
Jason held back from asking them about every detail,
but ordered all to be seated for an assembly.
They seated themselves on the folded sails
and the mast that still lay on the ground, and Jason,
son of Aeson, addressed them all with goodwill: 320

"All of the gear a vessel needs is here in good order,
ready for us to embark. There is no need to delay
on that account. We're only waiting for a tailwind.
We all want to return to Hellas after our voyage,
and we are united in reaching the land of Aeetes.
So putting selfishness aside, choose the best man here
as our leader, the best to settle our internal disputes
and to deal with all our foreign alliances."

At this, the young heroes all turned their eyes
toward Heracles, the great hero, sitting in their midst, 330
and with one shout, they approved him as their leader.
But he simply stretched forth his right hand and said:

"Let no one give this glory to me. I won't be persuaded.
I will not allow any other champion to stand up either.
Let the man who assembled us command our forces."

Thus high-hearted Heracles, and they all assented.
And Jason rose up, the warrior glad at heart,
and made this speech to the approving throng:

"To be sure, if you trust me with your glory,
let nothing else hinder our departure. 340
Let us now appease Phoebus with sacrifices
and then prepare a feast. Until my servants' arrival,

Book One

my chief farm-hands who will bring chosen oxen,
we'll haul the ship down to the sea, rig the tackling,
and draw lots to determine our benches for rowing.
Meanwhile, let's build out on the beachhead
an altar for Apollo, god of embarking,
whose oracle promised he would show me the way,
guiding our course through the sea, as long as I offered
sacrifice to him before this voyage for Pelias." 350

Having said this, he was the first to start working,
and they rose to their feet in obeisance.
Then they piled their clothes on a smooth stone ledge
above the surf line, cleansed by a storm surge long before,
and got to work. First, at the command of Argus,
they girded the ship with a sturdy, braided rope,
stretching it tight all around, so that the planking
would be compressed by the bolts and would withstand
the force of the waves. Next they dug a trench quickly,
as wide as the ship, and at the prow, as far as it would extend 360
into the sea when they pulled the craft down.
Then, after digging even deeper in front of the stem,
they laid in the furrow a row of polished rollers,
and tilted the ship down onto the first few
so that she would glide down on top of them. Then,
on both sides of the deck, reversing the oars,
they tied them to the thole pins, so they would project
about a cubit in length. Then the heroes stood
on both sides at the oars and strained forward
with hands and chest both. Tiphys then leapt on board 370
to urge them to push at just the right moment.
As he shouted at them from the top of his lungs,
they leaned into it, shoving with all of their strength,
and heaved the ship from her place, then digging in
with their feet, they forced her onward. Pelian Argo
responded at once, and both sides shouted
as they rushed ahead. The rollers groaned from its friction
with the weighty keel, giving off a dark smoke

as the vessel glided into the sea. But the heroes
stood firm, hauling her back as she surged forward.   380
They fitted the oars in their pins, and stored the provisions.

When all this had been done with careful attention,
they drew lots to determine the seating assignments,
two men to each bench; but the middle bench was reserved
for Heracles and Ancaeus, who hailed from Tegea,
and not determined by lot. And by universal assent
they appointed Tiphys as the Argo's helmsman.

Sacrifice to Apollo

Next, they piled up stones near the sea to build an altar
to Apollo, under the names of Actius and Embasius—
god of the shore and god of embarcation—   390
and quickly laid above it dried olive-wood logs.
Meanwhile, Jason's herdsmen had driven up two oxen,
which two of the younger crewmen dragged near the altar.
Others brought a water basin and barley, and Jason prayed,
invoking Phoebus Apollo, the god of his fathers:

"Hear me, Lord, who dwell in Pagasae and Aesonis,
the city named for my father. When I consulted
your oracle at Pytho, you promised to guide my journey,
for you were the instigator of this expedition.
Guide the ship there and back to Hellas with my comrades   400
safe and sound. We who return, all the voyage's survivors,
will again offer illustrious sacrifice of bulls on your altar.
And I will escort to Pytho and Ortygia gifts beyond counting.
Accept now, Far-Shooter, this offering of ours
which we present to you here as fare for safe passage.
Lord Apollo, may I loosen the hawsers under your guidance
and may a kindly breeze blow us over a tranquil sea."

As Jason prayed he cast the barley meal. Then Heracles
and proud Ancaeus cinched their belts, readying themselves
to slaughter the steers. Heracles brought his club down   410

in the middle of one steer's head, and the animal
collapsed then and there. Ancaeus struck the other's neck
with his bronze axe, shearing through the sinews,
and it fell headlong onto both of its horns.
Their companions quickly severed the victims' throats,
skinned the hides, cut out the sacred thighbones,
and covering them with layers of fat, burned them
on a wood fire. Jason poured out undiluted libations,
and Idmon, the seer, rejoiced as he observed the flames
gleaming all around the sacrifice, and the smoke   420
spiraling up in dark columns, all good omens,
and he pronounced the will of Leto's son, Apollo:

"It is heaven's will and fate itself that you will come back
with the Golden Fleece. But both in journeying forth
and returning, you will encounter trial after trial.
My own hateful fate, however, decreed by a god,
is to die far away on the mainland of Asia.
Even so, and though I learned my destiny
before I came here, I have left my fatherland,
so that my embarcation may bring my house fame."   430

Hearing this prophecy, the young heroes rejoiced
that they would return, but grieved for Idmon's fate.

Now, as the sun was sloping down the sky, and the fields
were just being shadowed by the rocky crags,
the heroes spread fronds thickly on the sand
and lay down in rows above the surf line. Near them
was spread an abundance of food and sweet wine
that the cupbearers had drawn off in vessels.
The men began to tell stories to one another in turns,
such tales as youths tell when they are amiably   440
enjoying themselves at the feast and the drinking bowl.
But Jason, at loose ends, was brooding over events,
and seemed to be preoccupied and somewhat depressed.
Idas sensed this, and in a loud voice addressed him:

"Son of Aeson, what are you mulling over?
Come on, out with it, man! Are you overcome with fear,
fear that confounds cowards? With my spear as witness,
the spear that wins for me glory in war
that far exceeds what is won by any other—
Zeus does not lend me as much strength as my spear does—   450
no calamity will be lethal, no venture wasted
with Idas as ally, not even if a god opposed you.
That's what you can expect in your man from Arene."

He spoke, and holding a goblet filled to the brim,
he drank off the undiluted sweet wine, drenching
his lips and ruddy cheeks. The whole company
raised a loud ruckus, and Idmon faced him down:

"Are you possessed? You're bringing premature destruction
upon yourself. Has the undiluted wine
gone to your head, puffing you up to your ruin,   460
and provoking you to dishonor the gods?
There are various words that a man may use
to encourage his companion, but your language
was simply rash. Aloeus's sons once flouted their gods
with talk like that. Your valor is no match for theirs,
but all the same they were slain by the swift arrows
of Leto's son Apollo, mighty though they were."

Idmon finished, and Aphareian Idas laughed out loud,
and looking at him up and down, lashed out like this:

"Come on now, and use your oracles to prophesy this: 470
Are the gods going to bring me the same sort of doom
that your father foretold for the sons of Aloeus?
And think this over: How are you going to escape from my hands
if you're caught making prophecies that shift like the wind?"

Such was Idmon's retort, and the strife would have continued
if their companions, and Jason himself, hadn't restrained them

with cries of indignation. And then Orpheus,
lifting his lyre with his left hand, began to sing.

He sang how the earth, the sea, and the sky,
once mingled together in a single form, 480
were split from each other by ruinous strife;
and how the stars and the moon and the circling sun
always maintain their celestial positions;
and how the mountains arose, and the resounding rivers,
together with their nymphs, came into being,
and all of the creeping things upon earth.
And he sang how Ophion and Eurynome,
Ocean's daughter, first ruled snow-capped Olympus,
and how they fell into the waters of Ocean
after one yielded to Cronus, the other to Rhea, 490
who then ruled together over the blessed Titans,
while Zeus, a young child with childish concerns,
still lived in the Dictaean cave; and the Cyclopes,
themselves born of Earth, had not yet armed him
with the thunder and lightning that give Zeus renown.

He ended there, stilling his lyre and immortal voice.
But even after he had finished they sat in silence,
leaning forward, listening for more,
so enchanted were they by the music's spell.
Not long after they mixed libations to Zeus, 500
all in due order, poured them upon the fire's embers,
and prepared for sleep in the darkness of night.

Departure from Iolcus

When Dawn's bright eyes saw the peaks of Pelion
and the cliffs were being soaked by the wind-ruffled sea,
Tiphys awoke and was soon rousing his companions
to board ship and make ready for rowing.
Then the harbor of Pagasae and Pelian Argo herself
gave voice to an eerie cry, urging the men to set forth.

Book One

The ship had been built with a divine beam
brought by Athena from an oak in Dodona 510
and fitted into the deck's upper planking.
The crew of heroes went to the benches
previously assigned to each man for rowing
and sat with weapons and armor close at hand.
In the middle sat Ancaeus, and with him Heracles
in all his might, with his club close at hand,
and as he tread the planks the ship's keel subsided.
Then, the hawsers loosened, they poured wine on the sea.
But Jason turned his tear-filled eyes away from his homeland.

Young men, either in Ortygia or Pytho 520
or by the waters of Ismenus, will set up a dance
in honor of Phoebus Apollo, and round his altar
beat their feet quickly to the sound of a lyre.

So too now, to the music of Orpheus's lyre,
they beat the surging sea with the blades of their oars,
and on both sides of the ship the dark brine seethed,
roaring and boiling under the heroes' might.
Their weapons gleamed in the sunlight as the Argo
sped on its way, and its long, brilliant wake
trailed far behind, like a path through a meadow. 530
On that day all the gods looked down from the sky
upon the ship and the might of the half-divine heroes,
the bravest of all men who then sailed the sea.
Nymphs on the highest peaks of Pelion marveled
as they gazed at the work of Itonian Athena
and the heroes themselves plying the oars.
And from the mountaintop down to the sea
came Cheiron, son of Philyra, dipping his feet
into the white surf, and as he waved his broad hand
again and again he cried out to them as they sped on, 540
wishing them a swift journey and a safe return home.
With him was his wife, who, cradling in her arm
Peleus's son, Achilles, showed the babe to his father.

When they had left the harbor's curving coastline behind,
through the skill of Tiphys, whose hand on the tiller
guided them securely into open water, they duly set up
the tall mast in the mast-box, secured it with forestays,
tightening them on both sides, then hauled the folded sail
to the top-mast and let it unfurl down. As a shrill wind
picked up, they fastened the ropes around the polished pins.   550
As the ship ran quietly along the Tisaean headland,
Orpheus, son of Oeagrus, plucked the strings of his lyre
and, keeping time, sang a song about Artemis,
daughter of glorious Zeus, savior of ships at sea
and patron goddess of Iolcus's maritime mountains.
And schools of fish, both large and small, followed
the ship and the music, frolicking in the seaways.

Countless sheep will follow their shepherd,
after they have had their fill of grass in the meadow
as he leads the way back to the fold, and as he goes   560
he pipes a gay shepherd's song on his shrill reed pipe.

So too these fish followed the ship as a breeze blew it onward.

And now the Pelasgians' foggy land, with all its wheatfields,
sank out of view. Speeding ahead they skirted the rugged flanks
of Mount Pelion, and soon the Sepian promontory
dropped away, and Sciathus appeared ahead in the water,
while farther off, Peiresiae came into view,
as did Magnesia's calm shore on the mainland,
and the tomb of Dolops. Here the wind shifted against them
and they put in for the evening. At nightfall   570
they sacrificed sheep in honor of the hero
while the sea swelled and churned. They spent two days
on that shore, and on the third day spread the ship's sail
and set forth again. And men even today
refer to that beach as Argo's Departure.

Setting out from there they sailed past Meliboea,
skirting a stormy headland. The following morning
they saw Homole close by, angled toward the sea,
and soon after reached the mouth of the Amyrus River.
They saw Eurymenae from there and the scoured ravines   580
of Ossa and Olympus. Then, running all night
with a tailwind, they reached the slopes of Pallene
beyond Canastra's cliffs. Running into the dawn,
Thracian Mount Athos loomed up before them,
its highest peak overshadowing Lemnos
and distant Myrine, even though it lies as far off
as a shipping vessel might reach sailing 'til noon.
All that day, until darkness came on, the breeze blew fresh,
filling the taut sails. But at sunset the wind died down,
and they had to row to Lemnos, the Sintian island.   590

Hypsipyle and the women of Lemnos

All of the men here had been ruthlessly murdered
by the island's women, an outrageous transgression
triggered by the men having hatefully rejected
their wedded wives in favor of a passion
for the women they had captured when they raided Thrace,
this due to Aphrodite's terrible anger
for their having denied her due honor. Ill-starred women,
their ravenous jealousy led to their ruin. Not only
did they kill their husbands for being unfaithful,
but they slew all of the men on the island as well   600
to avoid paying any retribution for murder.
Of all the women, Hypsipyle alone spared one,
her aged father, Thoas, king of the Lemnians,
sending him off to drift on the waves in a hollow chest
with some hope of survival. Fishermen hauled him ashore
on the island of Oenoe (in later times called Sicinus,
the name of the son Oenoe bore to Thoas).
The women's work then—tending the cattle
and plowing the fields—they found easier

than the domestic work of Athena that had been their lot.　　610
Still, they often gazed out over the boundless sea
with fear in their hearts that the Thracians might come.
So when they saw the Argo being rowed to the island
they crowded out from the gates of Myrine
in full battle gear and poured onto the beach
like raving Bacchants, thinking the Thracians had come.
Hypsipyle, Thoas's daughter, donned her father's gear,
and down they streamed, in speechless fear and dismay.

Meanwhile the captains had sent Aethalides
down from the ship. He was their chief messenger　　620
and carried the wand of Hermes, his father,
who had given him an unfailing memory
of all things. And even now, even though he has entered
Acheron's indescribable whirlpools,
has oblivion overrun his soul, but his everlasting fate
is to forever be changing place, at times
to be counted among those who dwell underground,
and at times among the living in the light of the sun.
But why should I go on and on about Aethalides?
At that time, toward dusk, he persuaded Hypsipyle　　630
to welcome the newcomers, but when the next day dawned
they had still not loosened the ropes to the north wind's breath.

The women of Lemnos now streamed through the city
at Hypsipyle's command. And when they had gathered
in a great assembly, she spoke among them in urgent tones:

"Come, my friends. Let us present these men with a store
of delightful gifts that will satisfy their hearts—suitable supplies
for fitting out a ship at sea, provisions of food and sweet wine—
so that they stay well outside our towers and do not come
to know us too closely by going to and fro furnishing　　640
their ship's needs, and then spread a wicked and widespread
report of us. We've carried off a mighty feat, but one that
none of them would approve, if they learned of it.

Book One

This is the plan that seems best suited for us now.
But if any of you has better counsel, let her rise to speak,
for that is why I've summoned you here to this conference."

She spoke and sat down on the stone seat of her father.
Then up stood her beloved nurse, Polyxo,
old and frail, limping on shriveled feet
and leaning on a staff, eager to address them. 650
Four virgins, unwedded women with downy white hair,
were seated near her. Standing in the assembly
she raised her head from her cupped back and said:

"Let us send gifts to the strangers, as Hypsipyle herself wishes.
It is indeed better to give them. But how do you propose
that we enjoy any of life's benefits if the Thracian army
marches against us in full force? Or any other enemy,
as often happens among mortal men? Even as it is,
this company now has come on us unexpectedly. And if
one of the blessed gods should avert that disaster, 660
countless other woes worse than warfare lie before us
when our present older generation of women fades away
and you younger childless women reach abhorrent old age.
How will you make a livelihood then, poor wretches?
Do you think that your oxen will spontaneously yoke
themselves to the plow, break up the soil in fresh furrows,
and conveniently reap a sudden harvest at year-end?
Without a doubt, though the Fates of death yet shrink back
from claiming me, I believe that likely within the year,
I'll already lie draped in a burial robe of earth 670
and will have received my due share of funeral gifts,
before the onset of such a crisis. But I urge you
younger women to ponder these matters with care.
As it is, a path of escape lies ready before you,
if you commit your homes, the whole of your livestock,
and your glorious city into the strangers' care."

Polyxo spoke, and the assembly roared with approval.
Then Hypsipyle rose again and said in reply:

23

Book One

"Since everyone favors this plan of action,
I will dispatch a messenger down to the ship." 680

She then turned to Iphinoe and said:

"Go, Iphinoe. Hurry to meet this man,
whoever commands this expedition,
and entreat him to come to our land
so that I may inform him of our people's pleasure.
And if they so desire, encourage them with all goodwill
to enter our land and city at once, without fear."

Having said this she dismissed the assembly
and started for home. And so Iphinoe
came to the Minyae, who asked why she had come, 690
and she replied quickly with words such as these:

"The maiden Hypsipyle, daughter of Thoas, sent me
to come here to summon the ship's captain,
whoever is leading the expedition,
so that she may inform him of our people's pleasure.
If you so desire, she encourages you with all goodwill
to enter our land and city at once."

Her speech was well received. The Argonauts surmised
that Thoas was dead, and that his beloved daughter,
Hypsipyle, now ruled. They hurried Jason off 700
and prepared to be on their way soon themselves.

Jason had already buckled around his shoulders
a double-folded purple mantle that Pallas Athena
had woven and given to him when she first laid down
the Argo's keel-struts and taught the hero
how to measure timbers with rule and line.
You could more easily stare at the rising sun
than fix your eyes on that robe's crimson blaze.
It was indeed bright red in the middle but its edges

were purple, with many scenes artfully interwoven. 710
On it were the Cyclopes seated at their work,
forging a thunderbolt for Zeus. It was almost finished,
but already brilliant, needing only one more ray,
which they were now beating out with their iron hammers
as it seethed and sputtered with flames on the anvil.

On it too were Antiope's twin sons,
Amphion and Zethus, and Thebes nearby,
as yet without towers, as they worked quickly
to lay its foundations. Zethus was shouldering
a steep mountain crag, and behind him Amphion 720
played loud and clear on his golden lyre,
as a rock twice as large followed his footsteps.

Next was fashioned rich-haired Aphrodite,
wielding Ares's buckler, her tunic loosened
beneath her left arm and on the other side
her image clear in the shield's polished bronze.

There was woven in also a wooded pasture,
and around the grazing cattle the Teleboans
and the sons of Electryon were battling,
the latter defending themselves, and the raiders 730
vying to despoil them. The dewy meadow
was drenched with their blood, and the hordes
were having their way with the herdsmen.

And there were two racing chariots inwoven,
Pelops shaking the reins of the one in front,
and at his side was Hippodameia.
Myrtilus was urging his steeds in pursuit,
and with him Oenomaus had gripped his spear
but fell when the axle broke off from the hub
just as he was about to pierce Pelops's back. 740

Book One

And a young Phoebus Apollo, the Archer God,
was wrought on the cloak, shooting at Tityos,
who was dragging his mother by her veil,
Tityos, born to divine Elare, but it was Earth
who gave him a second birth and nursed him.

And woven in it too was Phrixus, the Minyan,
as if he were listening to the ram, which seemed
to be speaking. Gazing at them in silence
you would cheat your soul in the hope of hearing
words of wisdom from them, and gaze long with that hope.   750

Such were the gifts from the Itonian goddess,
Pallas Athena.
               And in his right hand Jason
held a javelin that Atalanta once gave him
as a gift of hospitality in Maenalus
when she met him there. She was glad to do so,
eager as she was to join the adventure.
But Jason himself opposed this, out of fear
that strife might arise because of her love.

And he went up to the city like a brilliant star,

a star seen by young women from their chambers,   760
gazing at it as it rises above the rooftops
through the dark air, charming their eyes
with its beautiful, ruddy glow, and causing
one of them to rejoice, lovesick as she is
for a boy who is now far away amid strangers
and to whom her parents plan to wed her one day.

So too the hero ascended to the city.

When they had passed through the gates
the city's women folk crowded behind them,
fascinated by the stranger, who went straight ahead,   770

his eyes fixed on the ground until he reached
Hypsipyle's splendid palace. When he appeared
the maidservants opened the paneled doors.
Iphinoe led him quickly through a veranda
and had him sit on a glistening chair
facing her mistress. And Hypsipyle,
though averting her gaze and blushing modestly,
addressed him craftily with these wily words:

"Stranger, why are you lingering like this and waiting
so long outside our towers? Our men don't dwell in the city.   780
They sojourn in Thrace, on the mainland, where they plow
the wheatfields. I shall tell you the truth of all our hardship,
so you'll know well for yourselves. When my father, Thoas,
ruled over the city, then our citizens used to sail away
from home on raids. They would sack the houses
of the Thracians who lived on the opposite shore,
and they returned with heaps of spoils, and young women, too.
But it was all the cunning plan of a baneful goddess,
Cypris. She struck them with ruin and poisoned their hearts,
for they loathed their lawful wives, and, yielding to folly,   790
they chased away the women they hated and took to bed
women captured at spear-point. We held out a long while,
hoping they'd change back to their old ways, though late.
But the foul misery, always worse, grew twice as bleak.
Lawful children were dishonored in their own homes,
while a bastard generation arose in their place.
Thus unwed girls and widowed mothers, as well,
were left to wander about the city, neglected.
No father cared in the slightest for his own daughter,
even if he witnessed her brutal death at the hands   800
of a vicious stepmother. Sons did not defend their mother
against shamefully scandalous treatment, as before,
nor did brothers have a care in their hearts for a sister.
But in their homes, dances, gatherings, feasts, and banquets,
their thoughts were reserved for the women they'd taken.
Then some god planted epic courage in our hearts

no more to welcome them back from Thrace to our towers,
so that they'd be inclined either to regard what is right
or to leave and go elsewhere, along with their captives.
Then they begged us for all young boys left in the city   810
and taking them, too, went back to where they remain
even now, in the farmlands of snow-covered Thrace.
So, then, stay here and lodge with us, and if you wish
to settle—and if it pleases you—then you'll surely have
the privilege and power of my father, Thoas.
And I'm certain you'll find no fault with our land.
Our rich harvest exceeds all other islands in the Aegean.
Now quickly, go to your ship. Tell my words to your friends,
and tarry no longer outside of our city."

So she spoke, glossing over the murder   820
of Lemnos's men. And Jason answered her:

"Hypsipyle, we are very grateful for the help
you are offering to us in our time of need.
I will return to the city after I have reported
all this to my men. But rule of the island
must remain yours. I do not refuse out of scorn,
but because grievous trials drive me on."

Jason said this, touched her right hand,
and quickly turned to go back, surrounded
by countless young women dancing for joy   830
until he passed through the gates. And then
they came to the shore in smooth-rolling wagons
laden with many gifts. By then Jason had related
to his men everything Hypsipyle had said.
The women lost no time leading the men
back to their homes to be entertained there,
for the Cyprian goddess had aroused in them
a sweet desire, all for the sake of Hephaestus,
so that Lemnos, his island, might again
be inhabited by men and so escape ruin.   840

Book One

Jason then set out for Hypsipyle's palace,
and the others to wherever fortune led them,
all except Heracles, who had decided,
along with a few chosen comrades, to stay with the ship.
The city became festive with dancing and banquets,
and the air was filled with smoke from sacrifices
honoring both Cypris and Hera's son Hephaestus.
Day after day the sailing was delayed,
and they would have lingered there longer,
had not Heracles assembled his crewmates   850
apart from the women and lit into them:

"Are you possessed? Are we barred from our homeland
for killing our kin? Or have we come here from there
looking for wives, scorning our women back home?
Are we going to settle here and plow Lemnos's cropland?
We'll gain no grand fame loitering like this
with foreign women, nor will some god, answering our prayers,
take a fleece on the hoof and just give it to us.
Let's each of us get back to business and leave Jason behind
in Hypsipyle's bed until he's populated Lemnos   860
with his offspring and attained great glory."

He upbraided the lot of them, and not a man
dared look him in the eye or utter a word in response.
The assembled crew immediately began
to prepare for departure, and when the women realized
what they intended they came running in pursuit.

Bees pouring out of their hive in a rock
to gather nectar from beautiful lilies
in a dewy meadow as they flit about
from one blossom to another
                          will give you some idea   870
of how these women poured forth and clustered
around the men with loud lamentation,
saying goodbye with both caresses and words,
and praying to the gods for their safe return.

Book One

Jason and Hypsipyle's farewell

Hypsipyle too prayed, grasping Jason's hands,
tears flowing for the loss of her lover as she said:

"Go, and may the gods deliver you and your crew
unharmed, bringing the Golden Fleece to the king,
as you earnestly wish. This island and my father's scepter
will be here for you, if you choose to come back later,   880
on your return. And you could easily rally scores of men
from other cities. But you'll not have this aspiration,
nor do I myself foresee that it will come to pass.
Yet when you're away and when you've reached home,
remember Hypsipyle. Leave me a mandate which I can fulfill,
gladly, if the gods should permit me to be a mother."

And Jason, with deep appreciation, replied:

"Hypsipyle, may all these things prove fitting
in the eyes of the gods, just as you recount them.
But uphold a nobler opinion of my character,   890
since it is perfectly enough for me merely to dwell
in my native country, owing to Pelias's courtesy.
Only let it please the gods to release me from trials!
Still, if it's not my fate to make the return journey
and to sail from afar back to the land of Hellas,
and if you should give birth to a male child,
then when he becomes a young man, send him
to Iolcus in Pelasgus, to bring relief
to my father and mother in their distress—
that is, if he finds them yet living at all—   900
and that they may then find tender care
by their own hearth, in their own halls, far from the king."

He finished, and then boarded the ship, followed by
the rest of the heroes. Sitting in order
they took hold of the oars, and after Argus

Book One

had loosened the cables from the surf-pounded rock,
they beat the seawater white with their oars.
That evening, at Orpheus's bidding, they put in
at Samothrace, island of Electra, Atlas's daughter,
in order to be initiated into the secret rites there, 910
and so sail more safely over the chilling sea.
Of these rites I will make no further mention,
but bid farewell to the island and the deities
who dwell therein and administer the mysteries
of which it is forbidden for me to sing.

They rowed away eagerly over the brooding depths,
with Thrace on one side and Imbros to the south,
and at sunset reached the Chersonesus's headland.
There they raised their sails to a strong south wind
and entered the coursing stream of Helle, 920
daughter of Athamas. By dawn the sea to the north
was behind them, and by the next evening
they were running along the Rhoetian coastline,
with the land of Ida on the starboard side.
Sailing past Dardania, they moved on to Abydus
and then left Percote behind them,
the beach of Abarnis, and divine Pityeia.
And during that night, the ship being propelled
by both sail and oar, they passed completely through
the deep purple eddies of the Hellespont. 930

The Doliones and the Earthborn

There is a steep island in the Propontis,
not very far from the Phrygian mainland,
with rich wheatfields sloping down to the sea.
An isthmus jutting out from the mainland
lies so low it is prone to be flooded.
The isthmus has two shores lying beyond
the Aesepus River, and the locals there
call the island Bear Mountain. Some of the inhabitants
are fierce and violent, Earthborn Giants,

Book One

    phenomenal beings, a wonder to their neighbors.   940
They each have six strong hands to raise,
two from their stout shoulders and four below,
fitted close to their horrible ribs.
The Doliones also live in the isthmus,
ruled by Cyzicus, son of Aeneus, whom Aenete,
daughter of noble Eusorus bore,
but the Earthborn monsters left them alone
because they were protected by lord Poseidon,
the Doliones' own primeval ancestor.

    To that isthmus the Argonauts drove on, propelled   950
by the winds from Thrace, and a fair haven
received them. There, at the advice of Tiphys,
they disposed of their small anchor stone,
leaving it under the spring of Artacie,
and found a heavier one that better suited their needs.
The original anchor, according to the oracle
of Archer Apollo, was later duly placed
by the Ionians, sons of Neleus, as a sacred stone
in the temple of Jasonian Athena.

    Then the Doliones, and Cyzicus himself,   960
came out to greet them, and when they learned
who they were and what their quest was
they welcomed them with due hospitality
and persuaded them to row a little farther
and tie up their ship at the city harbor.
There, on the beach, they built an altar
to Ecbasian Apollo and offered sacrifice.
The king himself gave them all the sheep
and sweet wine they needed, for he had heard
that whenever a godlike band of heroes   970
might come to his land, he should greet them
courteously, and have no thought of war.
His beard, like Jason's, was still a soft wisp,
and he had no children as yet to rejoice in,

his wife, fair-haired Cleite, daughter of Merops,
being still untouched by the pangs of childbirth.
He had just recently brought her home,
after paying priceless gifts, from her father's house
over on the mainland, but even so left his bridal chamber
to prepare a banquet for the strangers, casting aside   980
all fear from his heart. They asked each other questions,
one of them inquiring about the goal of the voyage
and Pelias's commands, the others inquiring about
the surrounding cities and peoples, and the wide Propontis.
More he could not tell them despite their desire to know.
The next morning they climbed great Mount Dindymum
to see for themselves all the seaways, and then
brought their ship from where they had anchored it
into Chytus, the harbor. And the path they followed
still is referred to as the Path of Jason.   990

But then the Earthborn ones from the other side
stormed down the mountain and, heaving crags,
blocked up the mouth of the vast Chytus River
where it met the sea, like men laying an ambush.
Heracles, though, had been stationed there
with the younger heroes, and he quickly drew back
his recurve bow and started bringing down the monsters
one at a time. They responded by lifting
more huge boulders and hurling them down.
These dread creatures had no doubt been nurtured   1000
by Zeus's wife, Hera, as one of Heracles's trials.
But now the rest of the warrior heroes returned,
before reaching the summit, to slaughter the Earthborn
with arrows and spears, until they laid them all low
in their furious charge into battle,
                         like woodcutters
casting long tree trunks they have hewn with their axes
into rows on a beach, so that they may dry in the sun
and hold bolts securely.
                  So too these monsters
near the entrance of the foam-flecked harbor

Book One

  lay stretched out in a row, heaps of them bending   1010
  chests and heads into the saltwater waves, their limbs
  spread on the beach; and others with their heads
  on the sandy shore and their feet deep in the brine,
  both groups ready prey to birds and fish at once.

  This fearful contest behind them, the heroes
  loosened the ship's hawsers, spread the sail open,
  and moved ahead through the heaving water.
  All day long the ship ran ahead under sail,
  but when darkness fell the shifting wind drove them
  back to the hospitable Doliones' land.   1020
  They stepped ashore in the darkness, and the boulder
  around which they hastily tied their hawser
  is known to this day as the Sacred Rock.
  No one noticed that it was in fact the same island,
  nor could the Doliones see in the blackness of night
  that the heroes had returned, thinking instead
  that Pelasgian warriors, Macrians, had landed.
  So they strapped on their armor and laid into them.
  Ashen spears clashing against shields, they fell
  on each other like hissing fire that falls on dry brush   1030
  with cresting flames, and the din of battle
  fell upon the Doliones with a terrible fury.
  Nor did the king escape his fate
  and return to the bed in his bridal chamber.
  No, Aeson's son Jason leaped upon Cyzicus
  and struck him in the middle of his chest,
  shattering his sternum around the spear-point
  and sending him rolling onto the sand,
  fulfilling his fate. No mortal may escape that;
  no, we are hedged in on every side.   1040
  When he thought he had escaped bitter death
  at the hands of the Argonauts, Fate ensnared him
  that very night as he did battle with them.
  And many other heroic Doliones were slain.
  Heracles killed Telecles and Megabrontes;
  Acastus killed Sphodris; Peleus killed Zelus

and Gephyrus swift in battle. Telamon's spear
brought down Basileus, Idas slew Promeus
and Clytius Hyacinthus, and Castor and Pollux,
Tyndareus's sons, killed Megalossaces and Phlogius. 1050
Then Oeneus's son killed bold Itomeneus
and Artaceus, a leader of men. All of these
the local inhabitants still honor as heroes.
The others all fled in terror, like doves before hawks,
rushed together toward the gates, and the city was filled
with loud screams and groans when the grim battle turned.

At dawn both sides realized their fatal error,
and the Minyae were overwhelmed with grief
when they saw before them Cyzicus, son of Aeneus,
fallen in the dust and blood. For three whole days 1060
they lamented, pulling out their hair, Minyae
and Doliones both. Then three times 'round his tomb
they marched in bronze armor, performed rites,
and celebrated funeral games, as was due and proper,
on the grassy plain where even today
his funeral mound rises and can be seen by men.

Nor did Cleite, his bride, survive her husband,
but surmounted one evil with another more awful,
fastening a noose 'round her neck. Her death was mourned
even by the nymphs of the grove, and the tears they shed 1070
were transformed by the goddesses into a spring
which they call Cleite, the illustrious woman's name.
That day was the Doliones' most terrible day
ever sent by Zeus, both for the men and the women.
None of them dared even to taste food, and in their grief
they trudged through life eating their food uncooked.
And even now, when the Ionians in Cyzicus
pour annual libations for the dead, they grind their meal
for the sacrificial cakes at the community's mill.

Book One

Sacrifice to Rhea

After this, rough weather for twelve days and nights 1080
kept them from putting out to sea. But the next night,
when all of the chieftains were sound asleep,
and Acastus and Mopsus, son of Ampycus,
kept watch, there hovered over Jason's tawny head
a halcyon prophesying in shrill tones
surcease from the storm-winds. Then some god
made it turn aside and fly up, only to settle
on the ornament gracing the stern of the Argo.
Then Mopsus touched Jason as he lay wrapped
in soft sheepskins, roused him awake, and said: 1090

"Son of Aeson, you must climb up rugged Dindymum
until you reach the shrine. There appease the mother of all gods,
who is beautifully enthroned. The raging squalls shall cease
their violence. This command is what I heard shortly ago
from the halcyon, the sea-bird that flitted about in the sky
above you as you slept, and that revealed all to me.
By her will exist the winds, sea, and whole earth below,
as well as the snow-capped seat of Mount Olympus,
and when she ascends from the mountains to mighty heaven,
Zeus himself, Cronus's son, gives way to her. Likewise too 1100
the other blessed immortals revere the wondrous goddess."

Thus Mopsus, welcome words for Jason to hear.
He rose from his bed with joy, woke all his comrades,
and recounted the prophecy. The younger men
quickly drove oxen from their stalls and began to lead them
to the mountain's summit. Others untied the hawsers
from the sacred rock and rowed to the harbor.
From there the heroes climbed the mountain,
leaving a few men on the ship. As they ascended,
the Macrian cliffs and the facing Thracian coast 1110
seemed close at hand. So too the Bosporus's misty mouth
and the Mysian hills, while on the other side

the Aesepus River was in plain view, along with
the city and Nepeian plain of Adrasteia.

In the upland forest there was a sturdy vine-stump
that grew into a very old tree, which they cut down
to be the sacred image of the mountain daemon.
Argus planed it skillfully, and they installed it
on that craggy mountainside in a grove of oaks,
which of all trees sink their roots deepest.   1120
Near it they piled stones to fashion an altar,
wreathed themselves with oak leaves, and attended
to the sacrifice, invoking the most venerable
mother of Dindymum, whose home is in Phrygia,
and Titias and Cyllenus, sole dispensers of doom
and who weigh fates for the Idaean mother,
namely the Idaean Dactyls of Crete,
whom Anchiale, clinging with both hands
to the land of Oaxus, bore in the Dictaean cave.
Jason prayed over and over, beseeching the goddess   1130
to avert the storm-winds as he poured libations
on the sacrifice's flames. And at the same time
Orpheus orchestrated the youths dancing
in full armor, their swords clashing on shields
to drown out the ill-omened wails of lament
the people were sending up in grief for their king.
And so from that time on the Phrygian people
have propitiated Rhea with tambourine and drum.
And that gracious deity, it seems, was moved
by these sacrifices. Favorable omens appeared: 1140
the trees shed abundant fruit, and about the dancers' feet
the earth produced flowers from the tender grass.
Wild animals left their woodland lairs
and came up to the dancers wagging their tails.
And the goddess worked yet another miracle.
Until then no water flowed on Dindymum,
but now an endless stream began to run down
from the arid peak, and in later time the locals

called that stream the Wellspring of Jason.
And they prepared a feast to honor the goddess 1150
on Bear Mountain, singing hymns of praise
to most august Rhea. Then at dawn the winds
died down, and they rowed away from the island.

The Mysians and the disappearance of Hylas

Then a spirit of competition arose
among the chieftains, to see who would be last
to stop rowing, for the sea was smooth,
lulled to rest under the windless air.
Trusting this calm they propelled the ship forward,
and as she coursed through the brine
not even Poseidon's storm-footed steeds 1160
could have kept up with them. But when the sea
was hit by violent gusts rising from the river
as evening came on, they were exhausted and stopped,
the weary rowers pulled along now only by the might
of Heracles's arms that made the ship's timbers quiver.
But as they pressed on to reach the Mysian mainland
and could see the mouth of the Rhyndacus River
and the tomb of Aegaeon, close to Phrygia now,
Heracles, plowing the sea-surges' furrows,
had his oar snap in two. He fell off to one side, 1170
half of the oar still gripped in his hands,
the rest swept away by a receding wave.
He sat up in silence, glaring around him,
not accustomed to having his hands idle.

At the hour when a plowman or fieldman returns
gladly to his hut, hungry for dinner, and at the entrance
bends his weary knees, dirt-caked, and looking at his hands
worn with labor, curses his belly—at that hour
the heroes arrived at the homes in the Cianian land
near Mount Arganthonian and the mouth of the Cius. 1180
The Mysians, who lived there, welcomed them warmly

and gave them needed supplies, sheep, and plentiful wine.
Then some brought dried wood, and others from the meadows
an abundance of leaves to be strewn for beds,
while still others were twirling sticks to kindle a fire.
And some, after sacrificing at dusk to Apollo Ecbasius,
were mixing wine in a bowl to prepare for a feast.

Zeus's son Heracles though, leaving his comrades
to prepare the feast, went into a forest
to make ready an oar that would fit his hand.   1190
Wandering around he found a pine tree unburdened
by too many branches or leaves, but more like the trunk
of a lofty poplar, both in length and thickness. He laid
his quiver and bow on the ground, took off his lion-skin,
and with his bronze-sheathed club loosened the pine
from the ground. Then, grasping the trunk with both hands
at the bottom, he pressed his shoulder against it,
and using his great strength he lifted it from ground,
deep-rooted as it was, along with great clods of earth,
and,
    just as when an unexpected blast of wind   1200
strikes down from sky in the stormy season
when baleful Orion is setting, wrenching a ship's mast
from its stays, along with its wedges,
                            so too Heracles
hoisted the pine. Then he picked up his bow and arrows
and his lion-skin and club, and headed back to the ship.

Meanwhile, Hylas had set out with a bronze pitcher
looking for a spring, so that he might quickly draw water
for the evening meal and have everything in order
for his lord's return.   Heracles nurtured the boy in this way
from early childhood when he carried him off   1210
from the house of his father, Theoidamas, a good man,
whom the hero had pitilessly killed in an argument
about a plow ox. Theoidamas was plowing fallow land

when ill fate struck him. Heracles, looking for a pretext
to attack the Dryopians because they occupied land
to which they had no right, commanded Theiodamas
to give up his ox. But these tales distract me
from the theme of my song.
                              So Hylas came to the spring
that the people there call Pegae. The local nymphs
were holding their dances just then, for it was the custom   1220
of all the nymphs who haunted that lovely headland
to sing hymns to Artemis by night. Those who haunted
the mountains and glens were far off just now,
but a certain water-nymph, just surfacing
in the spring's lovely water saw the child close up,
saw his cheeks' rosy glow, his sweet boyish grace
in the light of the full moon beaming from the sky.
Cypris made her heart flutter, and in her confusion
she could scarcely keep her wits about her.
But just as he dipped his pitcher in the stream   1230
and the rushing water made the bronze vessel ring,
she laid her left arm on the back of his neck,
yearning to kiss his tender mouth, and with her right hand
in the crook of his arm she drew him down into the eddy.

The boy's only comrade to hear his cry
was Polyphemus, son of Eilatus, as he went down the path
toward Pegae, expecting the return of Heracles,
and as soon as he heard it, he rushed toward the cry.

A wild beast in the forest hears the bleating of sheep,
and burning with hunger he runs toward the sound,   1240
yet does not fall onto the flock, for the shepherds already
have penned up the sheep, and in his frustration
he wears himself out groaning and roaring.
                                               So too Polyphemus
groaned as he wandered about, his voice rife with misery.
Then, unsheathing his great sword he started in pursuit,
fearing the boy might be preyed on by wild beasts,

or that being alone he might have been ambushed,
an easy mark for men now carrying him off.
As he rushed along like this, brandishing his sword,
he met Heracles on the path, recognizing him   1250
as he hurried through the darkness down to the ship,
and, heart racing, blurted out what had happened:

"Sir, I'm the first to bring you this bitter news.
Hylas set out for the wellspring and has not returned.
Either he has been kidnapped by robbers,
or beasts are tearing him apart. I heard him yelling."

When Heracles heard him say this, sweat ran down
his temples, and the black blood boiled in his chest.
In his rage he threw the pine down and darted
headlong down the path wherever his feet took him.   1260

A bull stung by a gadfly stampedes along,
leaving behind meadow and marshland,
ignoring herdsman and herd. Stopping at times,
he lifts his great head and bellows, bitten
by the malevolent bug.
                    So too Heracles,
quivering with rage, would run without resting,
and then cease from his labor and shout into the distance.

The fates of Heracles and Polyphemus

But soon the morning star rose above the highest peaks,
and the wind swept down, prompting Tiphys
to urge the men to board ship and catch the breeze.   1270
They embarked with a will, drew up the anchors
and hauled the hawsers astern. The sails bellied out
in the wind, and they were soon sailing
far from the coast and past the Poseidian headland.
It was not until the cheerful morn, rising in the east,
shone in the sky, and the paths stood out clearly,

and the plains gleamed with dew, that it dawned on them
that they had unwittingly left those men behind.
Fierce quarrels broke out, and a violent tumult arose
because they had abandoned their bravest companion. 1280
And Jason, bewildered by this predicament,
never said a word, neither this nor that,
but just sat there depressed, eating his heart out.
Telamon grew angry at this, and said:

"Sit like that, then, and take it easy since you
thought it was fine to leave Heracles behind.
This was all your idea, so his glory would not
outshine yours throughout Hellas—if the gods
grant us a homecoming. But what good are words?
I'll go myself, alone, with none of your comrades 1290
who have helped you devise this treachery."

With that he rushed upon Tiphys, son of Hagnias,
his eyes flashing fire, and they would have turned back
then and there to the land of the Mysians, driving
through the deep sea and unrelenting storm-winds.
But the two sons of Thracian Boreas restrained Telamon
with harsh words, a reckless act, staying the search
for Heracles, who would make them pay for it later.
(For when they were returning from the funeral games
for Pelias, he killed them on the island of Tenos, 1300
and burying them there erected two columns,
one of which became a great wonder in that
it moves whenever the north wind blows.
But all of this was to happen in later times.)

Now Glaucus rose before them from the deep sea,
the sage spokesman for Nereus, the Old Man of the Sea,
and lifting up his shaggy head and chest from his flanks
he laid hold of the ship's keel and spoke to the eager crew:

Book One

"Why do you strive to take valiant Heracles to Aeetes's city,
contrary to the counsel of mighty Zeus? He is destined   1310
to complete a full twelve labors for insolent Eurystheus,
at Argos, and to dwell with immortals, abiding with them,
if he should accomplish a few toils more. Cease your pining
for him, then. Polyphemus, for his part, is fated to labor
at the mouth of Cius, among the Mysians, by founding a city
famed far and wide. Afterward he shall fulfill his destiny
in the sprawling land of the Chalybes. But Hylas,
beloved by a nymph, has been made her husband,
for whose sake the two wandered away and were left."

He spoke, and then plunged into the restless waves,   1320
and the dark water foamed in eddies around him
and dashed against the ship's hull as it moved through the sea.
The heroes all cheered, and Telamon, son of Aeacus,
hastened over to Jason and, taking the hero's hand
in his own, put his arm around him and said:

"Son of Aeson, don't be angry with me if I was rash
and got carried away by my folly. Grief overcame me
and drove me to scornful, imperious words.
But let's commit my fault to the breezes,
and return to our former warm friendship."   1330

And Jason, choosing his words carefully, answered:

"My friend, you denounced me vilely, and that's a fact,
openly declaring that I wronged an admirable man.
No matter. Know full well that I won't cultivate anger,
although it is true that earlier I was vexed.
After all, it wasn't over flocks of sheep or goods
that you became so inflamed with rage,
but a man who is your trusted friend. I hope
that if a like situation were ever to befall me,
you'd fight another man on my behalf, too."   1340

Book One

He spoke, and as of old, they sat down together.

As for Polyphemus, he was destined, by the will of Zeus,
to found a city among the Mysians named after the river;
and the other, Heracles, would eventually go back
and toil at the labors enjoined by Eurystheus.
But now he threatened to devastate the Mysian land
if they did not uncover for him Hylas's doom,
whether dead or alive. So the Mysians gave pledges,
choosing the people's noblest sons and swearing
they would never stop searching. And so even now   1350
the people of Cius ask about Hylas, Theiodamas's son,
and give thought to well-built Trachis, the city where
Heracles settled the youths sent from Cius as pledges.

A freshening wind propelled the ship all day
and all night, but there was not a puff of air
when dawn rose. They spotted a beach jutting out
from a bend in the coast that looked very broad,
and by the time the sun rose they had rowed to land.

Book Two

Amycus and the Bebrycians

Here were the ox-stalls and farmstead of Amycus,
the Bebrycians' arrogant king, born of a nymph,
Bithynian Melie, and Poseidon Genethlius.
He was the haughtiest man alive, and had an outrageous law
that no one could leave his land before challenging him
in a boxing match. He had already dispatched in this way
many of his neighbors. Now he went down to the ship
and disdained to ask them the purpose of their voyage,
or even who they were, but spoke to them as follows:

"Listen, you sea-going vagrants. It's only right you know   10
our law says that no stranger who comes to the Bebrycians
may leave until he has put up his fists in a bout with me.
So pick out your bravest warrior and stand him up here
to fight me in boxing. But if you trample on my decrees,
you can be sure that everything will go against you."

Thus Amycus in his arrogance, and they seethed with anger
when they heard it, Polydeuces most of all.
He stepped forward as his comrades' champion, and said:

"Restrain yourself and your ugly violence,
whoever you are. We'll comply with your laws.   20
I myself am perfectly willing to take you on."

He spoke bluntly. But his opponent glared at him
with rolling eyes,
    like a lion hit by a spear
when hunters surround him in the mountains,
and though pressed by a throng, pays no attention to them,

*but keeps his eyes fixed on the man who struck him first
but did not kill him.* Then Tyndareus's son laid down
his finely woven mantle, beautifully wrought
by one of the Lemnian women who had given it to him
as a token of hospitality. And the king cast off his dark,   30
two-ply cloak, with its clasps, and the knotted
olivewood crook that he carried. Then they both
looked around and agreed on a spot close by,
and told their comrades to sit in two lines on the sand.

The boxing match of Amycus and Polydeuces

The two men were not at all alike in build or stature.
Amycus seemed like he was born of baleful Typhoeus
or from Earth herself, the sort of monster she birthed
in primeval times in her wrath against Zeus.
But the son of Tyndareus shone like a star in heaven
whose beams are most beautiful in the evening sky,   40
a true son of Zeus, his cheeks still downy,
his eyes bright and glad, but his might and temper surged
like that of a wild beast. He held his hands out
to see if they were pliant as ever and not stiff
from the toil of rowing. Amycus made no such trial,
but stood apart in silence, his eyes fixed on his foe,
seething with desire to butcher the heart in his breast.
Between them stood Lycoreus, Amycus's second,
who now placed at their feet two pairs of gauntlets
constructed of dry and very tough rawhide.   50
The king addressed Polydeuces arrogantly:

"Choose whichever pair you like. I'll give it to you
willingly, without casting lots, so you can't blame me later.
Tie the gloves on your hands. You're going to learn yourself
and share with another man that I am the best
at splitting dry ox-hide and staining men's cheeks with blood."

He spoke, and his opponent did not taunt him in return,
but with a slight smile picked up the gauntlets that lay at his feet.
Castor and great Talaus, Bias's son, quickly tied them
onto his hands while speaking words of encouragement.   60
Aretus and Ornytus seconded Amycus, little knowing
they would never do this again for their ill-fated master.

When they had squared off, they raised their gauntleted hands
in front of their faces and attacked each other in deadly strife.
The Bebrycian king then,
                    *as a rough wave on the sea
rises in a swell against a swift ship, but her shrewd pilot
barely escapes the impact just as the billow
starts to break over the bulwark,*
                            pursued Tyndareus's son,
trying to overwhelm him and give him no respite.
But the hero, never wounded, skillfully countered   70
his foe's every attack, and as the punches flew
quickly observed where his foe could not be attacked
and where he was vulnerable, this while holding his ground
and returning blow for blow.
                        *Shipwrights hammering
a vessel's timbers to fit into honed clamps keep pounding
one board after another as the blows resound in turn.*

This was how their cheeks and jaws crashed and thudded,
along with a loud clattering of teeth. Nor did they stop
punching each other until they both started gasping.
Standing a little apart they wiped the voluminous sweat   80
from their foreheads, exhausted, panting for breath.
Then they charged each other again, like two bulls
fighting furiously over a grazing heifer. Then Amycus
reared up on tiptoe, as if he were about to slay an ox,
and swung his weighted fist down upon his rival,
but the hero pivoted aside from the attack
and received a glancing blow on his shoulder.
Then, closing in and slipping his knee behind the king's,

Book Two

he struck him suddenly above the ear, crushing
the bones in his skull, and the king fell in agony   90
upon his knees. The Minyan heroes cheered
as Amycus's life-force poured out all at once.

Battle against the Bebrycians

The Bebrycians did not stint their king. They took up,
en masse, rough clubs and spears, and charged Polydeuces.
But his comrades, swords drawn, stood in front of him,
and first Castor split the skull of a man as he charged,
the two parts falling down, one on each shoulder.
Polydeuces killed Mimas and huge Itymoneus,
kicking one beneath his breast with a sudden leap
and sending him into the dust, and striking the other   100
with his right hand above the left eyebrow,
tearing away the eyelid and leaving the eyeball bare.
Then Oreides, one of Amycus's audacious men,
wounded Talaus, Bias's son, in the side
but did not kill him, the bronze just grazing the skin
as it slid under his belt but not penetrating flesh.
In the same way Aretus clubbed Iphitus, Eurytus's son,
who was not yet destined to die, as Aretus himself was,
soon to be cut down by Clytius's sword. Then Ancaeus,
Lycurgus's fearless son, grabbed his huge axe,   110
and gripping in his left hand a dark bear hide,
plunged furiously into the Bebrycians. With him
the sons of Aeacus charged forward, accompanied by
the warrior Jason himself.
                     Grey wolves will attack
on a winter's day and terrify countless sheep, unnoticed
by the keen-scented dogs and the shepherds themselves;
and glaring around they seek what prey to attack
and carry off, while the sheep huddle together
and trample each other.
                    So too the Argo's heroes
terrified the haughty Bebrycians.
                        And as shepherds   120

or beekeepers smoke out a huge swarm of bees in a crag,
and the bees murmur and drone cooped up in their hive
until, choked by the dusky smoke, they finally fly out
far from the rock,
     so too the Bebrycians held on
no longer, but dispersed inland throughout the country,
spreading the news about Amycus's death, unaware
that more trouble was upon them. For at just that time
their vineyards and villages were being destroyed
by Lycus's and the Mariandyni's hostile spears,
now that their king was dead. These two tribes   130
were always at odds about the ore-bearing land,
and now the enemy was ravaging their homesteads and farms,
while the heroes were driving off their herds of sheep.
You could hear one of them say to another:

"Imagine what they would have done, the cowards,
if a god had somehow brought Heracles here.
If he were here I think, and no doubt about it,
there would have been no boxing bout at all.
No, when the king came to announce his rules,
our hero, club in hand, would quickly have forced him   140
to forget his arrogance along with his edicts.
Yes, and we heedlessly left him deserted on shore
and went sailing over the sea. With him gone
we'll surely realize our calamitous folly."

So he spoke, but all this happened by the will of Zeus.
They spent the night there tending to the injured,
offered sacrifice to the gods, then prepared a great meal,
and no man fell asleep by his bowl or during the oblation.
They wreathed their brows with the bay that grew by the shore
close to where their ship was tied up, and as they chanted   150
in tune with Orpheus's lyre, the windless shore was charmed
by their song honoring Polydeuces, son of Zeus.

Book Two

When the sun rising from distant lands illumined
the dewy hills and awakened the shepherds
they untied the hawsers from the trunk of the bay tree
and stowed on board all needed provisions.
Then with the wind at their back they threaded their way
through the eddying Bosporus. But then a mountainous wave
rose up before them, cresting above the clouds,
so high you would say they could never escape 160
a calamitous death, for it hung amidship like a great cloud,
and yet could sink away if it met with a skillful pilot.
And so with Tiphys at the helm they escaped unscathed,
although with great dismay. And the next day they tied up
on the coast across from the Bithynian land.

Phineus and the Harpies

Phineus, son of Agenor, lived there by the sea,
enduring the greatest suffering of all mankind
due to the gift of prophecy Apollo had granted him.
He had no respect at all for Zeus himself,
foretelling exactly the god's sacred will. 170
So Zeus afflicted him with a lingering old age,
stole from his eyes the sight of heaven's sweet light,
and did not allow him to enjoy the dainty food
brought by his neighbors when they came to learn
heaven's decrees. The Harpies would come then
and with their crooked beaks snatch the food
out of his hands and mouth. Sometimes they would leave
not a morsel of food, sometimes just a little
so that he might live to suffer even more torment.
And they shed a foul stench over everything, 180
discouraging anyone from bringing the food to his mouth
or even stand at a distance; so disgusting was the smell
of the leftover scraps. But as soon as Phineus heard
the crew's voices and their tramping feet, he knew
they were the men at whose coming, the oracle
had foretold, he would finally enjoy his food. He rose

from his bed like a lifeless dream and, hunched
over his staff, groped along the walls as he
edged his way to the door on his withered feet,
his whole body trembling from weak old age.　　　　　　　　190
His dry skin, crusted with dirt, was all that held
his bones together. He limped from the hall
and reclined at the courtyard's entry, enveloped
by a hazy stupor, the earth reeling beneath him
as he lay weakly in a speechless trance.
When they saw him there they gathered around him
and wondered. At last he drew a labored breath
from deep in his chest and spoke prophetically:

"Listen, most valiant of Hellenes, if it is truly you
whom Jason leads after the Fleece on the ship called Argo,　　200
at a cold-blooded king's command. Surely it is you.
My mind still knows all things through its divinations.
Leto's son, I thank you, Lord, despite my grave afflictions.
By Zeus, god of suppliants, highest terror to wicked men,
for the sake of Phoebus, I beg you, and of Hera herself—
and above all other gods, under her care you have come—
help me. Save a hapless man, a wretch, from ruin.
Don't callously sail away, leaving me behind in this state.
Not only has the fury Erinys trampled my eyes
and do I drag on old age to its dreary, tedious end,　　　　　210
but besides all these evils, the bitterest evil of all still looms
over me. The Harpies, swooping down from an unseen
den of ruin, snatch food right out of my mouth.
And I have no plan for recourse. But when I crave
a meal, it would be easier to escape my own thoughts
than them; they fly so swiftly through the air.
If they do leave me so much as a scrap of food,
it reeks of mold. Its violent stench is excruciating,
beyond suffering. No mortal could bear to be near it
for even a moment, not even if his heart was wrought　　　220
of unbreakable steel. But Necessity, bitter and ravenous,
forces me to stay, and staying to feed my confounded belly.

Book Two

It is ordained that the sons of Boreas put a stop to these plagues.
And they are not strangers, who will be my defenders,
that is, if I am indeed Phineus, once acclaimed among men
for my wealth and prophetic art, and if my father was Agenor,
and if, when I ruled among the Thracians, I took Cleopatra
their sister home as my wife, with wedding gifts."

Hearing this, each of the heroes was filled with sorrow,
and none more so than the two sons of Boreas.   230
Wiping away their tears they came up to Phineus,
and Zetes, placing his hand on the pitiful old man, said:

"Poor wretch, I think no other mortal has a worse plight
than yours. Why has such grinding torment latched on to you?
Have you committed a mortal sin against the gods,
a foolish offense through your prophetic arts,
and evoked their mighty wrath against you?
Though we long to help you, our hearts are bewildered
if Fate truly has honored us like this. To mortals
the rebukes of the immortals are abundantly clear.   240
We refuse to hold off the Harpies when they come,
in spite of our fervor, until you swear that for this act,
we will not be estranged from the gods."

When Zetes finished, the old man, opening his blind eyes
and lifting them up, replied in this way:

"Silence. Don't entertain these thoughts in your mind, son.
May Leto's son be my witness, who graciously taught me
skills of divination. Be witness, too, the unlucky
doom which falls to me, and this blinding cloud upon my eyes,
and the deities below—and may they deal with me   250
harshly if I die in such perjury—no divine wrath
will strike you in return for aid you render me."

When they heard Phineus's oath, the two young heroes
were eager to help him. Working quickly,

they prepared a feast for the old man, a final prey
for the Harpies. Then they took their stand close by,
ready to cut them to pieces when they swooped down.
Phineus had barely touched the food when the creatures
blasted down from the clouds like lightning, yelling,
with a ferocious passion for food. The heroes saw them   260
but no sooner had they shouted and charged than the Harpies
gulped everything down and sped away far over the sea,
with the two sons of Boreas, swords drawn, in hot pursuit,
empowered by Zeus with indefatigable strength.
Without Zeus's help, they never could have kept up,
for the Harpies would outfly the west wind's blast
both when they came to Phineus and when they left.

Hunting hounds on the track of horned goats or deer
high on a mountainside and straining to catch up
will snap their jaws in vain when they are close.   270

So too Zetes and Calais, closing in fast, just grazed
the Harpies with their fingertips and would have
torn them to bits, heaven's will notwithstanding,
when they had caught up with them at the Floating Islands,
had not swift Iris seen them and leaped down the sky
from heaven above and held them back, saying:

"Sons of Boreas, it is not right that you strike the Harpies,
the hounds of mighty Zeus, with your swords. I myself
will swear to you: they shall no longer draw near to Phineus."

Having said this she swore by the waters of Styx,   280
the greatest oath and most awesome a god can swear,
that the Harpies would never again approach the house
of Phineus, son of Agenor, since it was so fated.
Persuaded by the oath, the heroes turned back to the ship,
and because of this, what once were called the Floating Islands
came to be called the Strophades, the Islands of Turning.
Both the Harpies and Iris departed, the former

to their lair in Minoan Crete, but the goddess
ascended to Olympus on her soaring wings.

Meanwhile the heroes carefully scrubbed down 290
the old man's skin and sacrificed choice sheep
they had made off with after despoiling Amycus.
And when they had laid out a huge feast in the hall,
feast they did, and with them Phineus ate
to his heart's content, as if in a dream.
When they had their fill of food and drink, they stayed up
all night, waiting for Boreas's sons to return.

Phineus's prophecy

The old man himself sat with them, near the hearth, foretelling
how their voyage would go, their mission accomplished:

"Listen, then. It is not lawful for you to know exactly 300
about everything. But what the gods permit, I will not hide.
I was a reckless fool before, when I divulged Zeus's will
in full sequence from beginning to end. He wishes
to reveal his decrees himself, an oracle at a time,
leaving men yet in need of the gods' complete purpose.
First, once you've left me, you'll see the two Cyanean Rocks
in the straits of the sea. I suppose no one has slipped
through them freely. They have no roots to anchor them
underneath, but they clash against each other time and time
again, and a seething surge of seawater towers overhead 310
and breaks against the rocky shore with a mighty crash.
I bid you, therefore, to obey my instructions, if in truth
you plot your path shrewdly, with respect for the gods.
Do not bring doom upon yourself, causing your death
through sheer folly, and do not rush on, bowing to whims
of impulsive youth. Leave the first attempt to a bird,
a dove, releasing it from the ship. If it escapes safely
by flying through the rocks to the sea beyond,
then no longer refrain from the path, but grip the oars

Book Two

firmly in your hands and cleave the straits of the sea, 320
since your light of deliverance will not be in prayers
so much as in the strength of your hands.
Best, then, to forsake all other efforts, and to toil on
with stout hearts. I do not forbid you from praying first
to the gods. But if the dove flies on its wings only to perish
midway through, turn back, since it is far better to yield
to the gods. You could not escape the wretched doom
of the rocks, not even if the Argo were wrought of iron.
Unhappy men, do not dare to transgress my divine edicts,
though you think me three times more repulsive than I am 330
to the sons of Ouranus, or even more hated than that.
Do not dare to defy the omen by sailing your ship
any farther. However matters turn out, thus they are.
But if you should elude the Clashing Rocks unscathed
and come to Pontus, now keep the land of Bithynia
on your right. Sail on, wary of breakers, until you round
the swift-flowing river Rhebas and the dusky shore
and reach the harbor of the island of Thynias.
A short voyage over the sea from there will bring you
ashore at the Mariandyni's land, on the opposite coast. 340
Here a path descends into the depths of Hades.
Overhead stretches the jutting headland of Acherusia,
while below the eddying Acheron cuts through the headland
itself, and pours its waters from a massive ravine. Nearby
you will travel past many hills of the Paphlagonians.
The Eneteian Pelops was this people's first king,
and they proudly profess to be of his bloodline.
There is a headland lying opposite Helice the Bear.
Facing north, it is steep on all sides. They call it Carambis.
Boreas's stormy blasts are ripped in two to pass over it, 350
it towers into heaven so loftily, turned toward the sea.
Rounding it you'll find vast Aegialus stretched out before you,
and at its edge, where the coast juts out, the waters
of the river Halys gush out with a ghastly, terrible roar.
After it, flowing nearby, the smaller Iris rolls into the sea
with white eddies. On that side a massive, monstrous bluff

Book Two

protrudes from the land. At its mouth, the Thermodon
flows into a calm bay under the Themiscyreian headland
once it has drifted through the sweeping continent.
Here is the plain of Doeas. Near to it are the three cities 360
of the Amazons, and next, supremely wretched of men,
the Chalybes. Theirs is a ruthless, stubborn land.
Strenuous laborers, they toil away at working iron.
Their neighbors beyond the Genetaean promontory
of Zeus, god of hospitality, are the Tibareni, a people
with abundant flocks of sheep. On their borders, in turn,
the Mossynoeci inhabit the forested mainland and foothills.
Trees are materials for their wooden homes, built in towers,
and for the stout towers, too, which they call mossynes,
and from which the people have their own name. 370
Passing them by, you will beach on a smooth island,
after resorting to countless clever schemes to drive off
scores of ravenous birds which haunt the desert island.
On it Otrere and Antiope, the queens of the Amazons,
built a stone temple of Ares when they set out to war.
A help beyond words will come to you there
from the cruel sea. Having your best interests in mind,
then, I advise you to hold fast and to stay there. But
what need to sin again by using my gift of prophecy
to describe everything from beginning to end? 380
Beyond the island and the mainland opposite
reside the Philyres. Beyond them are the Macrones
and, in turn, the untold tribes of the Becheiri. Next
to them live the Sapeires. The adjoining territory
belongs to the Byzeres, and at last beyond them reside
the belligerent Colchians themselves. But press on
in your ship until you reach the sea's deepest reaches.
There at the Cytaean mainland, from the faraway
Amarantian mountains and Circaean plain,
the swirling Phasis rolls its broad stream into the sea. 390
Sailing to the mouth of that river, you will observe
the tower of Cytaean Aeetes and Ares's shady grove,
where a dragon, a monster dreadful to look upon,

glares in all directions at once with penetrating eyes,
guarding the Fleece that is spread wide atop an oak.
Sweet sleep never subdues his pitiless eyes;
no, neither by day nor by night."

                              Thus Phineus,
and as they listened they were seized with fear.
They sat a long time in silence, until at last
Jason, in a quandary at their plight, spoke: 400

"Old man, already you've come to our journey's end,
and offered a sure token, one we can trust for a safe passage
through the detestable rocks to Pontus.
But whether we'll return home to Greece again
after we've escaped in our flight from these dangers,
that is counsel I should also welcome from you.
What should I do? How will I retrace through the sea
a course so formidably grueling,
being an untrained captain with an untrained crew?
To say nothing of the fact that Colchian Aea   410
lies on the very edges of Pontus and of the world."

When Jason had finished, the old man said in reply:

"My son, when you first slip through the deadly rocks,
take heart, since a god will guide you by another course
from Aea. There will be guides aplenty on the way to Aea.
But friends, keep in mind the wily support you enjoy
from the Cyprian goddess, for the glorious outcome
of your undertaking rests entirely on her.
Now ask nothing more about these matters from me."

As Agenor's son finished the twin sons of Boreas   420
shot down from the sky and stood on the threshold.
The heroes stood up when they saw them arrive,
and Zetes, still breathing hard after his exertion,
spoke among his eager audience, telling them

Book Two

how far they had driven the Harpies, how Iris
had forbidden their killing them, and how the goddess
graciously gave them pledges, and how the creatures
had plunged into a cavern in the Dictaean cliffs.
They were all pleased to hear this, as was Phineus himself,
and Jason, with a wealth of goodwill, was quick to say: 430

"There's no doubt, Phineus, that some god, burdened
by your dismal circumstances, brought us here from a land
far away so that Boreas's sons could be your saviors.
And, I expect, if he also granted your blind eyes daylight,
I'd rejoice as much as if I were sailing back homeward."

Thus Jason, but Phineus, with downcast eyes, responded:

"Son of Aeson, that is beyond recovery. No cure remains,
for my seared eyes are devastated and past all hope.
Instead, may a god grant me death straightaway,
and once dead I'll partake of all splendid glories." 440

Then the two of them engaged in conversation,
and before very long early born Dawn appeared.
Then Phineus's neighbors gathered around him,
the ones who used to visit him and bring him food.
And the old man gladly delivered his prophecies
to all his visitors, and thereby freed them from worry,
and so during their visits they tended to his needs.
Among them was Paraebius, dearest to Phineus.
And the old man was happy with all of the strangers
now in his house, for the seer himself had long said 450
that a band of heroes traveling from Hellas
to Aeetes's city would tie up their ship
in the Thynian land and by the will of Zeus
would stop the Harpies from ever returning.
All of the others the old man pleased with words of wisdom,
but bade Paraebius remain with the Argonauts
and then sent him to bring back the choicest of sheep.
When he had left, Phineus addressed the heroes gently:

"My friends, not all men, it seems, are utterly lawless
or oblivious to kindness. And so this man, too, 460
of such character as he is, came here to learn his fate,
for when he had labored and toiled to his very utmost,
then the necessities of life, incessantly growing,
would wear him down. Day after day dawned
more despicably, with never a respite from his toil.
But he was paying the grim reparations for his father's sin,
for when his father was alone, felling trees in the mountains,
he dismissed the prayers of a nymph, a hamadryad.
She tearfully tried to soften him with passionate words,
begging him not to cut down the stump of an oak 470
that shared her age, and in which she had lived
for many continuous years. Yet he hewed it down,
recklessly, driven by the arrogance of his youth,
and so the nymph rendered her pointless death
a future curse to him and his children. When he came,
I knew of his offense, yes, and I urged him to build an altar
to the Thynian nymph and to offer expiatory sacrifices
upon it, pleading to avoid his father's fate. Here,
since he escaped the god-sent calamity, he has never
forgotten or spurned me. Only with difficulty do I send 480
him from my door, and that with him unwilling,
he is so eager to be near me in my distress."

Phineus said these things, and soon his friend arrived,
leading a pair of sheep from the flock. Then Jason
and Boreas's two sons rose at the old man's bidding.
Acting quickly they prayed to Apollo, lord of prophecy,
and offered sacrifice there as the sun was setting.
The younger heroes prepared a mouth-watering feast.
And after they had eaten they all went to their rest,
some near the ship's hawsers, others in groups 490
throughout the house. And at dawn the Etesian winds
blew strongly, the winds that, at Zeus's command,
blow equally throughout every land.

The story goes that Cyrene once tended sheep
in the marshy meadows along the Peneus
in days gone by, her virginity and an unstained bed
being dear to her. But one day, as she guarded
her flock by the river, Apollo carried her off
far from Haemonia and placed her among
the nymphs in Libya near the Myrtosian height.   500
It was there that she bore to him Aristaeus,
known to the Haemonians as Hunter and Shepherd.
Love prompted him to make her a nymph there,
a long-lived huntress, and he brought his son,
while still an infant, to a cave to be nurtured there
by Cheiron. And when he had grown to manhood
the Muses gave him a bride and taught him the arts
of healing and prophecy, and made him shepherd
of all their flocks that grazed in Phthia
on the Athamanteian plain and around steep Othrys   510
and the sacred stream of the Apidanus River.
But once, when Sirius, the Dog Star, in the summer sky
scorched the Minoan islands with its heat,
with no respite for the inhabitants, they summoned
Aristaeus, at Apollo's command, to stop the plague.
At his father's command, Aristaeus left Phthia
and settled in Ceos. There he gathered together
the Parrhasians, who are descended from Lycaon,
and dedicated a great altar to Zeus Icmaeus,
and on the mountain offered sacrifices to Sirius,   520
the Dog Star, and to Cronus's son, Zeus himself.
And this is why the Etesian winds from Zeus
cool that land for forty days, and to this day in Ceos,
priests offer sacrifice before the Dog Star rises.

That is the story, but the Argonauts stayed there
out of necessity. And every day the Thynians,
as a courtesy to Phineus, sent them countless gifts.
Later they built an altar on the facing shore,
dedicating it to the Twelve Olympians. They laid
offerings on the altar, boarded their swift ship,   530

and prepared to row. Nor did they forget to bring
a trembling dove. Euphemus caught her
and brought her aboard, quivering with fear.
Then they untied the two hawsers from the land.

The Clashing Rocks

Athena did not fail to notice their launching.
She immediately stepped onto a light cloud
that would waft her along, mighty though she was,
and rushed down to the sea, with benevolent thoughts
for the oarsmen.
    As when a traveler roaming far
from his homeland, as we humans, gathering   540
our courage, often do, and no land is too distant,
every possible route is clear to his view, and he sees
in his mind his own home, and all the routes
over land and sea, and thinking fast, now this way,
now that, he strains his eye,
                so too Athena,
shooting down to land on Thynia's bleak shore.

Their winding route led to a narrow strait
enclosed on both sides by rugged cliffs.
A deep eddying current slapped against the ship
as they moved fearfully on. And now the thudding   550
of the crashing rocks assaulted their ears,
the sound echoing from both sea-washed shores.
Then Euphemus, holding the dove in his hand,
started to climb onto the prow, and the crew,
at Tiphys's command, rowed with all their might
to propel the Argo between the two rocks.
As they rounded a bend, they saw the rocks opening
for the very last time. Their spirit ebbing away,
Euphemus released the dove. As it darted forward
they all raised their heads to look. The dove flew   560
between the two rocks, which rushed back together
and crashed as they collided face to face.

Book Two

The sea-spume shot up and massed like a cloud;
awesome thunder rolled across the sea,
and the sky's dome roared all around them.
The caves beneath the rugged cliffs roared
as the seawater came gushing in, and the white foam
from the clashing waves shot up high above the cliff.
Then the swirling current whirled the ship around,
as the rocks clipped off the tips of the dove's tail-feathers,   570
but she flew away unharmed. The rowers shouted,
and Tiphys commanded them to row
with all their might, for the rocks were moving apart again.
They trembled as they rowed, until the backwash
drove them between the rocks again. Then sheer dread
seized them all, for inescapable destruction
loomed above them. The broad Pontus could be seen
both to the right and left, when all of a sudden
an enormous wave reared up, arching before them
like the face of a cliff, and at the sight of it   580
they bowed their heads down, for it appeared
poised to crash down along the ship's whole length
and completely overwhelm them. But Tiphys
quickly eased the ship's labor with the oars,
and the massive wave rolled away under the keel,
raising the Argo's stern, lifting her high
and away from the rocks. Then Euphemus,
touring the benches, urged all his shipmates
to row as hard as they could, and with a shout
they thrashed at the water. But as far as the ship   590
responded to the rowers, she leaped back twice as far,
and the oars bent like bows against the heroes' might.

Then a huge, arching wave swept down upon them,
and the ship plunged like a cylinder through the cavernous sea,
but the swirling current still held her between the two rocks
that shook and thundered, confining the wooden vessel.
Then Athena shoved back one rock with her left hand,
and with her right hand pushed the ship through.

Then she flew through the air like a fletched arrow.
And yet the still clashing rocks, as the ship passed, 600
shore off her stern-ornament. The crew being unscathed,
Athena soared up to Olympus, and at that moment
the rocks became rooted in a single spot forever,
an event that had been destined by the immortals
as soon as a manned ship passed through them unscathed.
The heroes could breathe again after their chilling fear,
the great expanse of sea and sky clear in their eyes.
They felt they had been saved from Hades. And Tiphys said:

"I hope that both we and the ship have escaped
once and for all. No one is due the credit more 610
than Athena is, who breathed her divine strength
into the ship when Argus bolted it tightly together.
The Argo cannot be caught. It's divinely decreed.
Son of Aeson, you should no longer dread so much
the dictates of your king, since a god has granted
us flight through the rocks. Phineus, Agenor's son,
said that the toils to come will be easy to accomplish."

He spoke, and proceeded to speed the ship through the sea
past the Bithynian coast. And Jason gently responded:

"Tiphys, why do you soothe me this way, in my grief? 620
I made a mistake, acted like a fool.
I was helpless, caught up in my abject delusion.
When Pelias issued his command, I ought to have straightaway
refused this mission, right there on the spot,
even if it meant I was doomed to death, torn limb by limb.
As it is, I'm beset by unbearable angst, bewildering terror,
dreading the thought of sailing through the icy-cold sea-waves
and dreading the moment when we'll set foot on the mainland.
I'm hemmed in on all sides by implacable foes.
At the close of each day, I pass the endless nights in anguish 630
ever since, for my sake, we first gathered together,
always mulling over every detail. Yet you prattle publicly,

without a single care, completely untroubled,
concerned merely for your own life, your own desires.
Still, I'm not distraught for myself, not in the slightest!
No, but for others' sake, this man and that one, and then for you,
and for the rest of my companions—this is my undying worry,
whether I can bring you back safely to the land of Hellas."

Thus Jason, testing the heroes. They responded by shouting
words of good cheer. This warmed his heart, and he went on: 640

"Friends, my heart swells with courage at your valor.
Yes, even if I were to traverse the gaping trenches of Hades,
I'd no longer let gripping fear overtake me,
since you stand steadfast despite the grim horrors that engulf us.
But since we've sailed away from the Clashing Rocks,
I trust that we'll never face a similar fear in the future,
if in fact we proceed according to Phineus's guidance."

His words quieted them down, and they fell to the oars,
quickly passing the Rhebus with its swift current,
the peak of Colone, the adjoining black headland,   650
and the mouth of the Phyllis, where Dipsacus once hosted
Athamas's son, Phrixus, when he was flying on the ram
from the city of Orchomenus. Dipsacus was the son
of a meadow-nymph, contented to live with his mother
by his father's river, tending his flocks by the shore.
They soon sighted his shrine and sailed past it quickly,
passed the river's broad banks, and Calpe's deep current,
rowing all day long and through the windless night.

As plow oxen labor to cleave the moist soil,
sweat pouring down their flanks and neck, their eyes rolling   660
right and left beneath the yoke, their hot breath
coming in gasps as they toil all the day long,
planting their hooves deep in the earth,
                            so too
these heroes kept dragging their oars through the brine.

Apollo's epiphany

When the immortal light has not yet fully returned,
nor is it still utterly dark, but a subtle glow has spread
over the night sky, the time when people wake up,
the twilight hour as it is called, they pulled into the harbor
of Thynias, a desert island, and, thoroughly exhausted,
ascended to the shore. And to them there appeared   670
Apollo, son of Leto, on his way from Lycia
to the Hyperboreans, that innumerable folk.
His golden locks flowed in clusters over his cheeks
as the god moved along; he held in his left hand
a silver bow, and a quiver hung from his shoulders
and along his back. Beneath the god's feet the whole island
trembled, and the waves surged high all along the beach.
The men were helpless with awe when they saw this,
but no one dared to meet the god's beautiful eyes.
They just stood there with their eyes to the ground   680
as he passed through the air and far onto the sea.
Finally Orpheus, addressing them all, said:

"Come, let's call this island the Sacred Island
of Apollo of the Dawn, since he has manifested himself
to our eyes at the break of day, and we will sacrifice
what offerings we can, building an altar on the shore.
If he later grants us a safe return to the Haemonian land,
then we will lay the thighs of horned goats on his altar.
As it is now, I urge you to appease him by offering
the savory steam of sacrifices and libations.   690
But be gracious, our king, gracious in your appearing!"

Orpheus said this, and they quickly constructed
an altar out of stones. Then they scoured the island
in search of a fawn or a wild goat, animals that often
will pasture in woodlands. Apollo provided
a quarry for them, and with sacred ritual
they wrapped the thigh bones in fat and burned them

Book Two

on the consecrated altar, calling on Apollo,
Lord of the Dawn. And around the flaming altar
they set up a dancing-ring, chanting, "All hail   700
to Apollo, Apollo the Healer." And with them
Orpheus, son of Oeagrus, chanted as he played
his Bistonian lyre how once below Parnassus's peak
Apollo shot with his bow the monster Delphyne
when he was still young and beardless, still reveling
in his long, fine hair. Be gracious, O Lord.
May your locks be forever unshorn, ever unravaged,
as is only right. And no one but Leto
may ever stroke them with her dear hands.
And the Corycian nymphs, daughters of Pleistus   710
took up the glad refrain, chanting "Healer,"
the lovely refrain of the Hymn to Phoebus.
Having celebrated the god with dancing and singing,
they swore an oath, pouring sacred libations,
that they would always help each other and be of one mind,
touching the sacrifice as they swore. And even today
a temple sacred to Concord stands in that place,
a temple the heroes themselves built honoring the goddess.

When the third morning dawned with a fresh west wind
they sailed away from that lofty island. On the other side   720
they sailed past the mouth of the Sangarius River,
past the fertile fields of the Mariandyni,
past the stream of Lycus and Lake Anthemoeisis,
the ropes and tackle quivering as they sped on.
The wind dropped that night, and they were glad to reach
the Acherusian peninsula and the harbor there
surrounded by cliffs that face the Bithynian Sea.
Below are rocks scoured smooth by the seawater
rolling in like thunder. Above, a canopy of plane trees
crowns the topmost peak. Leading inland, a hollow glen   730
slopes gently away, where there is a cave of Hades
overarched by trees and stones. An ice-cold breath
issues continually from its chill depths, forming
a glistening frost that melts under the high noon sun.

There is never silence on that bristling headland, but rather
the constant murmuring of the resounding sea
and the rustling of leaves in the wind from that cave.
Here too is the outpour of the Acheron River,
which crashes down through a hollow ravine
and drains away into the eastern sea. In later days   740
the Nisaean Megarians named it Sailors' Salvation,
when they planned to settle in the Mariandyni's land,
and the river saved them along with their ships
from a violent storm. It was along this route
that the heroes took the Argo through the Acherusian gorge
and came to shore on the other side as the wind fell down.

Lycus and the Mariandyni

It was not long before they were noticed by Lycus,
lord of that land and of the Mariandyni people,
who had already heard of the heroes killing Amycus,
and for that reason considered themselves allies.   750
They welcomed Polydeuces as if he were a god,
flocking around him, for they had long been enemies
of the haughty Bebrycians. So they went up to the city
and with all goodwill spent the day preparing
a feast in Lycus's palace and cheerfully talking.
Jason told him the name and lineage
of each of his comrades, told him what Pelias
had enjoined upon them, how they were welcomed
by the women of Lemnos, what they did at Cyzicus,
how they reached the Mysian land and Cius,   760
where, all against their will, they left Heracles behind.
And he told them everything that Glaucus said,
and how they killed Amycus and the Bebrycians,
of Phineus's suffering and his prophecies,
how they escaped from the Cyanean Symplegades
and encountered Apollo on the island close by.
He told the whole story, and Lycus was enchanted
in his very soul, but he grieved that Heracles
had been left behind, and said to them all:

Book Two

"Friends, what a man of whose help you are deprived 770
as you cleave the long path to Aeetes! I know full well,
for I saw him right here in the halls of Dascylus, my father,
when he came on foot through the continent of Asia
fetching the belt of war-minded Hippolyte. He found me
a young man, the down first appearing on my cheeks.
Then, competing in the games that were held in memory
of my brother Priolas—slain by the Mysians, and to this day
mourned with the people's most heartbreaking dirges—
in the boxing contest he vanquished the mighty Titias,
who outmatched all our youths in beauty and strength, 780
and he knocked his teeth to the ground. At one fell swoop,
too, he subdued for my father the Mysians and Phrygians,
who live with their lands adjoining ours, and he won
the tribes of the Bithynians, land and all, even as far as
the mouth of the Rhebas and peak of Colone. Besides them,
the Paphlagonians, Pelops's race, yielded just as they were,
all those around whom the Billaeus's dark water breaks.
But now the Bebrycians and the insolence of Amycus
have stolen what's mine, since Heracles lives far away.
For a long time they've been slicing away swaths of land, 790
to the extent that they have set their boundaries
at the meadows of the deep-flowing Hypius. For all that,
they have paid the price, and that by your doing. It was,
I think, not without the gods' goodwill that Tyndareus's
son waged war against the Bebrycians when he did,
on this day that he killed their notorious king.
So, then, whatever I am able to pay you in return,
be sure I will pay it gladly, as is right for weaker men
to do when stronger men undertake to help them first.
To attend all of you and accompany you on your voyage, 800
I am sending Dascylus, my son. If he goes, you are sure
to find men well-disposed as you sail along, all the way
to the mouth of the river Thermodon itself. Moreover,
for the sons of Tyndareus, I will set up a lofty temple
atop the Acherusian summit. It shall draw the eyes
of all sailors on the sea, even from very far away,
and seafarers will pray for the pair's favor. Afterward

I will also set apart for them, as for the gods,
rich fields of finely tilled ground in front of the city."

And so all that day they delighted in the banquet. 810
But at dawn they hastened down to the ship,
and Lycus himself, after he had presented them
with many gifts, accompanied the heroes,
and sent forth with them his son from his home.

The deaths of Idmon and Tiphys

It was here that Idmon, son of Abas, met
his destined fate, nor did his soothsaying save him
from what had been ordained. In the meadow
near the reedy river there lay a white-tusked boar,
cooling his flanks and huge belly in the mud,
a deadly monster dreaded even by the nymphs 820
who haunted the marsh but was known to no man.
He was feeding in the swamp as Abas's son walked along
the high banks of the muddy river when the boar
bolted out from its unseen lair, leaped out
from the reeds, and charging Idmon gashed his thigh,
severing ligaments, muscle, and bone.
The hero collapsed to the ground with a cry
that his comrades answered as they flocked together.
Peleus quickly took aim at the vicious boar
as he fled back to the swamp and then turned around 830
for another charge, but it was Idas who got off a shot,
and the boar fell impaled upon his sharp spear.
They left the boar on the ground where he had fallen,
and carried Idmon, breathing his last, back to the ship,
where he died in the arms of his grieving comrades.

They now put off any thought about further voyaging,
and grieved for three whole days for their beloved friend.
On the next day they buried him with the greatest respect,
with the people and King Lycus himself
taking part in the rites. As is due to the deceased, 840

Book Two

they slaughtered innumerable sheep at his grave.
And so a funeral mound was built in that land,
and as a marker for future generations there stands
the trunk of a wild olive tree, its green leaves flourishing,
a little below the Acherusian headland. And if I must,
directed by the Muses, tell the true story, Apollo
ordered the Boeotians and the Nisaeans
to worship him as guardian of their city,
and to build that city around the ancient trunk
of a wild olive tree; but instead of honoring   850
the pious Aeolid Idmon the people there instead
honored Agamestor, a local hero.
                             And who was it
who died next? For the heroes now constructed
a second barrow for a dead comrade. The story goes
that Tiphys, son of Hagnias, died, no longer destined
to sail any farther. For then and there a brief illness
laid him to rest far from his homeland, just after
the crew had honored the dead son of Abas.
Their grief was unbearable. They threw themselves down
on the shore, helpless, silent, wrapped in their cloaks,   860
with no thought of food or drink, utterly disheartened,
for now they had lost all hope of return.
And in their grief they would not have journeyed on,
had not Hera infused extraordinary courage
into Ancaeus, whom Astypaleia bore to Poseidon
near the waters of Imbrasus, Ancaeus,
a highly skilled pilot, who now said to Peleus:

"Son of Aeacus, how is it good to neglect our venture
by lingering on in a foreign land? It's not so much
for my skill in warfare that Jason takes me with him   870
far from Parthenia in search of the Fleece, as much as
for my experience with ships. For my part, let none fear
as far as the ship is concerned. Other knowledgeable men
are here, as well. Not a one of them will impede our voyage,
no matter whom we choose as helmsman. Quickly now,

reassure the men of all of this, and stir their hearts
to remember our project with boldness."

Hearing this, Peleus was greatly heartened,
and he lost no time in addressing them all:

"Poor wretches, why do we nurse futile grief like this? 880
Those men have perished, suffering their allotted fate.
But among us there are still helmsmen in our company,
and many of them. So let's waste no more time on our task.
Rouse yourselves to action, and cast off your sorrow."

Jason's response was hardly optimistic:

"Son of Aeacus, where are these helmsmen of yours?
For the crewmen in whom we formerly exulted
are even more crestfallen than I, utterly dismayed.
And so I foresee baleful ruin for us, along with our dead,
if we're condemned never again to reach the city 890
of Pelias, that murderous criminal, or never again
to pass beyond the rocks to the land of Hellas.
An evil doom will enshroud us here, on this very spot,
leaving us to grow old for nothing, in utter disgrace."

But Ancaeus, motivated by the goddess,
lost no time undertaking to pilot the Argo.
And after him Erginus, Nauplius, and Euphemus
showed that they too were eager to steer,
but the others restrained them, seeing that
many of their comrades had chosen Ancaeus. 900
So on the twelfth day they boarded at dawn
since a strong westerly wind had started to blow.
They rowed out quickly through the Acheron River,
and then trusting to the wind spread their sails wide
and started cutting through the waves under a clear sky.
They soon passed the mouth of the Callichorus River,
where they say that Bacchus, the Nysaean son of Zeus,

when he had left India and came to dwell in Thebes
held orgies and dances in front of a cave
inside of which he passed the solemn nights unsmiling.   910
From that time on the neighbors called the river
Callichorus and the cave Resting Place.

Next they spotted the tomb of Sthenelus, Actor's son,
who, returning from the war against the Amazons
as a comrade of Heracles, was hit by an arrow
and died there on the beach. They stayed there a while,
for Persephone herself sent forth the soul
of Actor's son, who had been weeping with desire
to see, ever so briefly, men like himself. And sitting
on the edge of the tomb he gazed at the ship,   920
looking like he did when he went to war,
on his head a beautiful helmet with four ridges
gleaming with a blood-red crest. And then he returned
into the immense gloom. They saw this and marveled,
and Mopsus, son of Ampycus, speaking as a prophet,
urged them to land and appease him with libations.
They quickly furled the sail, tied up the ship,
and there on the shore paid obeisance to Sthenelus's tomb,
pouring libations to him and sacrificing sheep.
Besides these offerings they built an altar to Apollo,   930
savior of ships, and burned fat thigh bones. And Orpheus
dedicated his lyre, which is why the place is called Lyra.

As soon as the wind freshened they boarded ship,
unfurled the sail and made it taut to both sheet-lines.
Then the Argo moved as swiftly over the sea
                                   *as a hawk
soars high through the sky entrusting its outspread wings
to the wind and is borne on swiftly in unswerving flight,
floating in the clear sky on motionless pinions.*

Book Two

Voyage past Sinope and the Amazons' harbor

Before long they passed by the stream of Parthenius
as it melds with the sea, a most placid river   940
in whose pleasing waters Artemis, daughter of Leto,
bathes after the hunt before ascending to heaven.
Then they ran on through the night without ever stopping,
passing by Sesamus, lofty Erythini, Crobialus, Cromna,
and forested Cytorus. And then as the sun rose
they rounded Carambis, then rowed the length
of Aegialus all day long and well into the night.

Before long they made landfall on the Assyrian shore,
where Zeus himself gave a home to Asopus's daughter,
Sinope, and allowed her to keep her virginity,   950
ensnared by his own pledges. Longing for her love,
he had promised to grant her whatever her heart's desire
might be, and she cleverly asked for virginity.
She tricked Apollo, who longed to bed her,
in much the same way, and besides these two gods
she outwitted also the river-god Halys,
and no mortal had ever made love to her either.
In that same place there still lived the sons of Deimachus
of Tricca: Deileon, Autolycus, and Phlogius,
ever since they wandered far away from Heracles,   960
and when they noticed the assemblage of heroes
they went out to meet them, declared who they were,
and that they no longer wished to remain in that place.
So as soon as Argestes, the northwest wind, blew,
they boarded the Argo and, along with the heroes,
left behind the Halys and the nearby Iris River
and the Assyrian delta. Then on that very same day,
they rounded the headland that guards the Amazons' harbor.

Melanippe, a daughter of Ares, had set out from here once
and was caught by Heracles, who had been lying in wait.   970
Hippolyte gave him her glittering warrior-belt

to ransom her sister, and he released his captive unharmed.
In this headland's bay, at the mouth of the Thermodon,
they beached their ship, the sea being too rough to sail.
No other river branches out into so many great streams,
four less than a hundred if one would count them all,
and all from a single stream that flows down to a plain
from what men say are called the Amazonian Mountains.
From there it spreads inland straight through hilly terrain,
from where its many branches go winding on   980
this way and that, some close to each other, some at a distance,
many nameless ones swallowed up by the sand,
but the main channel, mingled with a few more,
explodes with foam into the Inhospitable Pontus.
They would have lingered there and fought the Amazons,
a battle that would have entailed considerable bloodshed,
for the Amazons, who dwelled on the Doeantian plain,
were not gentle and had no sense of justice,
a hubristic people who cared only for war,
for they were the children of Ares and Harmonia,   990
the nymph who bore him war-loving daughters
after their marriage in the Acmonian forest.
But the northwest wind started to blow again,
sent by Zeus, and with it they left the curving beach
where the Themiscyreian Amazons were arming themselves,
for they didn't live gathered in cities, but scattered
all over the land in three separate tribes.
In one part lived the Themiscyreians, ruled at that time
by Hippolyte; in another the Lycastians;
and in a third the javelin-armed Chadesians.   1000

On the next day, at nightfall, they reached the land
of the Chalybes, who neither plow with oxen,
nor grow fruit in orchards, nor pasture flocks
in dewy meadows. What they do is mine the iron-rich land
and sell the ore as their livelihood. Morning never dawns
without sooty labor amid bleary smoke and flames.

Next they rounded the headland of Genetaean Zeus
and sped safely past the Tibareni's land.
When women give birth here, their husbands
lie in bed groaning, their heads swathed, while their wives 1010
feed them and prepare for them baths after childbirth.

Then they arrived at the holy mountain in the land
where the Mossynoeci live in wooden huts
called mossynes, whence that people's name.
Their laws and customs are strange. Public behavior
is conducted in their homes, but what we do in our houses
they do outdoors in the middle of the street
without any blame. They have no respect at all
for the marriage bed, but like herd-feeding pigs
they make love with women on the open ground 1020
without any embarrassment. Their king resides
in the highest hut of all, dispensing justice,
poor man, for if he issues mistaken judgments
they lock him up starving for the rest of the day.

Ares's island and the birds

Passing them by they cut through the water with oars,
skirting the island of Ares throughout the day.
At dusk even the light breeze fell, and it was then
that they spotted, darting through the air, one of the birds
sacred to Ares that inhabit that island. Shaking its wings
as it flew above the fast-moving ship, she shot down at it 1030
a sharp feather that struck Oileus's shoulder.
The oar dropped from his hands when he was hit.
His comrades were amazed at the winged projectile.
Eribotes, seated nearby, drew the feather out, untied
the strap from his sword-sheath, and bound up the wound.
Then another bird swooped down, but the hero Clytius,
Eurytus's son, drew back an arrow on his curved bow
and shot. The bird whirled around and fell near the ship.
Amphidamas, son of Aleus, had this to say:

Book Two

"We are near to the island of Ares, as you yourselves   1040
also know from the sight of these birds. I expect arrows
will not serve us much for landing the ship. Let us instead
devise another plan to help us, if you do intend to land,
keeping in mind what Phineus commanded, for not even
Heracles, when he came to Arcadia, could prevail
with bow and arrow to drive out the birds that floated
in the Stymphalian lake, as I witnessed for myself.
But he shook a bronze rattle in his hands while he stood
on top of a giant mountain peak, and raised such a clamor
that they fled far away, screeching in frenzied terror.   1050
So now let us, too, concoct some similar scheme.
I myself will share with you what I have devised
after giving the matter some prior thought.
Set your high-crested helmets on your heads, and
half of you take turns rowing, while half of you fortify
the ship using your polished spears and shields.
Then all of you at once shout with a tremendous roar,
so that they panic at the unfamiliar tumult
and bobbing crests and the spears lifted up high.
And if we do reach the island itself, then raise   1060
a monstrous din by clashing your shields."

The heroes all approved Amphidamas's suggestion.
They put on their heads their gleaming bronze helmets,
the red crests rippling. They took turns at the oars,
half of them rowing while the others covered the ship
with shields and spears.
                    A man roofing his house with tiles
to serve both as decoration and protection from rain
will fit them tightly together, one after another.
                                   So too
they roofed over the ship with their overlapping shields.

And as a clamor arises from men charging ahead   1070
when two lines of battle collide,
                            so also the shout
that rose up from the ship. They saw none of the birds yet,

but when they made land and clattered their shields
innumerable birds rose in flight all around them.

When the son of Cronus sends down from the clouds
a dense hailstorm on a city, the people in their houses
hear the clattering on the roof but sit at ease
since the stormy season has not caught them by surprise
and they have reinforced their roofs.
                                       So too with these birds,
showering the heroes with feathered shafts as they darted 1080
over the water to the mountains beyond.
                                                What then
was Phineus thinking when he suggested
the divine band of heroes make land in that place?
What kind of welcome help was about to arrive?

The rescue of Phrixus's sons

The sons of Phrixus were sailing to Orchomenus
from Aea, coming from Cytaean Aeetes
on a Colchian ship in order to take possession
of the prodigious wealth of their father,
who enjoined this voyage when he was dying.
And now they were very near to that island, 1090
but Zeus had ordered the north wind to blow
and signal with rainfall Arcturus's rising.
All day long the god was making the leaves quiver
high on the mountain, breathing gently upon them,
but at night he swept down hard on the water,
and with howling blasts made the sea surge high.
A dark mist shrouded the sky and none of the stars
shone through the enveloping murky gloom.
And so the sons of Phrixus, soaked to the skin
and trembling with fear of a horrific doom, 1100
were carried helplessly along, their sails snatched away
by the powerful wind, their hull broken in half
by the force of the breakers. The four men, prompted

by the gods above, held onto a huge beam, one of many
that were flung here and there when the ship broke apart.
The wind and the waves brought the men to the island
in deep distress, within an inch of death.
And then the rain stormed down upon the sea
and the island, and all the country opposite,
where the arrogant Mossynoeci lived, and the waves flung   1110
the sons of Phrixus and the heavy beam
upon the island's beach in the dead of night.
The downpour from Zeus ceased when the sun rose,
and the two bands of men approached each other.
It was Argus who was the first to speak:

"We beg you, by Zeus the beholder, whoever you are,
show kindness, and offer help in our desperate need.
Savage tempests, falling upon the sea in a brutal storm,
thoroughly shattered all the planks of the sorry ship
we sailed in as we cut our path, embarking on business.   1120
Therefore we implore you as suppliants, if you will listen,
to give us even mere coverings for our bodies, and
to receive us warmly, showing pity for men who are
of the same age as you and in wretched distress.
But for Zeus's sake, for he is the god of hospitality
and strangers alike, respect suppliants and strangers!
Both suppliants and strangers belong to Zeus,
and doubtlessly he beholds even us in his gaze."

And Jason, surmising that Phineus's prophecies
were being fulfilled, prudently replied: 1130

"We'll furnish you with all these things immediately,
with sincere goodwill. But come, tell me truly, what country
you reside in, what sort of business prompts you to sail
over the sea, and what your noble names and lineage are."

And Argus, overwhelmed by his troubles, answered:

Book Two

"Aeolus's grandson Phrixus reached Aea from Hellas,
as I assume you yourselves have heard before, no doubt in detail.
Phrixus, who came to Aeetes's citadel, riding on a ram
which Hermes had rendered golden. Even now
you may still see the Fleece. He then sacrificed the ram   1140
at its own suggestion, above all to Cronus's son Zeus,
the god of fugitives. Aeetes received him in his palace
and gave him as wife his daughter Chalciope,
without asking gifts of betrothal, and with a merry heart.
On both sides, we are of his lineage. But at length
Phrixus died, an old man, in the home of Aeetes,
and we, with immediate respect for our father's orders,
are traveling to Orchomenus for Athamas's possessions.
And if you truly are eager to know our names,
this is Cytissorus, this is Phrontis, and this is Melas.   1150
As for me myself, you may call me Argus."

When he said this, the heroes exulted at their meeting
and attended to them, filled with amazement.
Then Jason, as was only fitting, replied:

"Certainly, then, you're our kinsmen on my father's side,
as you plead for our friendly assistance in your wretched hardship,
for Cretheus and Athamas were brothers, and I am
Cretheus's grandson, traveling with these comrades
from that same Hellas to the city of Aeetes.
But we'll discuss these matters more thoroughly later.   1160
For now, put on some clothing. I find it divinely inspired
that you've come into my care in your desperate need."

Jason said this and gave them clothing out of the ship.
Then they all went together to the temple of Ares
to sacrifice sheep. Hurrying now, they stood 'round the altar
which was outside the roofless temple, an altar
constructed of pebbles. Fixed in the middle
was a sacred black stone to which the Amazons prayed.
It was not right for them, coming from the opposite coast,
to sacrifice sheep and goats on this altar, but they did   1170

slaughter horses from their teeming herds. The sacrifice over
and the feast prepared, Jason spoke among them again:

"Truly, Zeus sees everything. We men never escape
his gaze, not for a moment, at least those who are pious and just.
Just as he saved my father from my murderous stepmother
and granted him countless riches besides,
in the same way, too, he kept you alive and well
throughout this death-dealing storm. And once aboard this ship,
you'll have freedom to sail wherever you like,
whether to Aea or divine Orchomenus's wealthy city, 1180
for Athena built this ship, cutting its timbers with her bronze tools,
near Pelion's summit. Argus joined in its construction.
But a savage sea-swell mercilessly shattered your ship
before you even neared the rocks that clash together
day after day in the narrow sea-straits. Even so,
hasten to help us in our ambitious mission
to fetch the Golden Fleece and bring it back to Greece.
Be our guides on the voyage, since my quest is meant
to appease the demand for Phrixus's bloodshed,
and to avert Zeus's anger against the sons of Aeolus." 1190

Soothing words, but they reacted with horror,
surmising that they would not find Aeetes obliging
if they wanted to abscond with the ram's Golden Fleece.
Then Argus, troubled that they should want to do this, said:

"My friends, so far as our strength is a benefit to you,
you will never be deprived of the help, not in the slightest,
when any need arises. But Aeetes is remarkably endowed
with lethal ferocity, and so I'm filled with dread by this voyage.
He boasts that he is Helios's son, and tribes of Colchians,
past counting, live all around, and he could rival Ares 1200
in his fearsome war-cry and mighty strength. To be sure,
to snatch the Fleece from Aeetes's clutches is no easy feat,
with such a monstrous serpent guarding the perimeter,
deathless and sleepless—Earth herself brought forth
the beast on the shoulders of Caucasus, on the site

of Typhaon's rock. They say that is where steaming gore
dribbled in hot drops from Typhaon's head, struck
by a thunderbolt sent from Zeus, son of Cronus,
for lifting his burly hands in rebellion against the god.
This is how he was when he reached the mountains   1210
and the plain of Nysa, where he lies to this day,
submerged beneath the depths of the Serbonian lake."

Their cheeks grew pale when they heard how demanding
this enterprise was. Peleus attempted
to cheer them up with words such as these:

"Trusty friend, don't harbor such grim fear in your heart.
We aren't so short on valor that we cannot be a match
for Aeetes when it comes to a trial of arms. No, I think
that we who are sailing there are versed in warfare,
as well, our blood drawn nearly from the blessed gods.   1220
So if he will not give us the Golden Fleece, as a friend,
then I expect the Colchians will not benefit him."

In this way they conversed, addressing each other,
until, satisfied with the feast, they went to sleep.
When they rose at dawn a light breeze was blowing.
When they raised the sails the wind blew stronger,
and they soon left behind the island of Ares.

That evening they came to the island of Philyra,
where Cronus, son of Ouranus, when he reigned
on Olympus over the Titans, and Zeus   1230
was still being nurtured in a Cretan cave
by the Curetes of Ida, deceived Rhea
and slept with Philyra. The goddess found them
in bed together, and Cronus leaped up
in the form of a horse with a flowing mane.
Philyra, though, Ocean's daughter, left in shame
and came to the long Pelasgian ridges,
where after her union with the metamorphosed god
she gave birth to enormous Cheiron, half horse and half man.

Book Two

From there they sailed on past the Macrones   1240
and the extensive land of the Becheiri
and the haughty Sapeires, followed by the Byzeres,
constantly making headway with a gentle tailwind
until they entered a gulf from which the steep crags
of the Caucasus Mountains rose into the sky.
There Prometheus, limbs bound to the granite
by chafing bronze fetters, fed with his liver
an eagle that kept winging back to its prey.
They saw it whirring through the air at dusk
just below the clouds, its huge beating wings   1250
shaking the sail, not so much like a bird's wings
as the extended polished oars of a vessel.
Not long after they heard the grievous cry
of Prometheus as his liver was being ripped out.
The air pulsed with his cry until they saw the eagle
soaring back from the mountain on the same course.

That night, thanks to Argus's piloting, they reached
the wide Phasis River, and the sea's farthest rim.
They furled the sails, stowed them below
along with the yardarm, and lowered the mast   1260
until it lay flat. Then they rowed quickly
into the river's mighty stream, the water surging
around the ship's prow. On the left side there was
the Caucasus range and the Cytaean city of Aea,
and to starboard the plain of Ares and his sacred grove
where the serpent kept watch over the Fleece
hanging on the leafy branches of an oak. Jason himself
poured from a golden goblet libations of honey
into the river, and of pure wine to Earth
and to the gods of the country and the souls   1270
of heroes deceased, praying to them all
to lend gracious assistance and to welcome their ship
with favorable omens. Then Ancaeus had this to say:

"We have arrived at Colchis and the river Phasis.
Now we need to take counsel whether to approach Aeetes
with diplomacy, or if another course of action is called for."

He spoke, and Jason, acting on Argus's advice,
had them row into a shaded marsh and drop anchor.
It was not far, and they passed the night there,
anxiously awaiting the first rays of dawn.   1280

Book Three

Invocation of Erato

Come now, Erato, stand at my side, and tell me
how Jason brought the Fleece back to Iolcus
aided by Medea's love for him, for you share
Aphrodite's power, and charm lovesick
unwedded girls, and your very name means Love.

So the heroes waited in ambush amid the thick reeds,
unobserved by anyone except Hera and Athena.
These two, hiding from Zeus and the other immortals,
went into a room and started plotting together.
Hera went first, feeling out Athena: 10

"Now, daughter of Zeus, you be first to advise.
What must be done? Will you concoct some scheme
for them to spirit the Golden Fleece of Aeetes away
to Hellas, or to cajole him, coaxing him with soft words?
He is dreadfully pompous, to be sure. Still, it is right
to hazard all tasks with an unflinching heart."

Thus Hera, and Athena was quick to respond:

"Just as I too was thinking all this over,
Hera, you ask me outright. But I have yet
to work out a plan to help the heroes' courage,   20
although I have mulled over many designs."

At that, the two goddesses just stared at the floor,
lost in their own thoughts. Then Hera had an idea:

"Come, let us go to Cypris. Let's both accost her,
urge her to order her son, if he will obey, to target

the daughter of Aeetes, the sorceress, with his arrows,
and bewitch her with love for Jason. Her shrewd designs
might enable him to carry the Fleece back to Hellas."

This seemed like a good plan to Athena,
and speaking softly she said so to Hera: 30

"Hera, I was fathered never to face her boy's arrows,
and I know nothing of love potions. But if you like this plan,
I'll follow, of course. You must speak, though, when we meet her."

Hera and Athena persuade Aphrodite to help

With that they set out, and soon came to the palace
of Aphrodite, built by her husband, the lame blacksmith,
when he first brought her from Zeus to be his wedded wife.
Entering the courtyard they stood in the entryway of the room
where the goddess would make up a bed for Hephaestus,
who had himself gone early to his anvil and forge
in a huge cavern off on a floating island 40
where he wrought all sorts of marvelous things.
She was sitting alone on an inlaid chair facing the door,
both her white shoulders mantled by her long tresses,
which she was parting with a golden comb
as she prepared to do them up in braids. When she saw
the goddesses before her, she stopped combing,
invited them in, and seated them on couches.
Then she herself sat down, gathered up her uncombed locks,
and addressed them with wily words such as these:

"Dear friends, what purpose or need drives you here 50
after all this time? Why have you come? Your visits have not
been too frequent before, though you are first among goddesses."

To this Hera had a ready response:

"You scoff, but our hearts are stirred with worry. Already
Aeson's son is mooring his ship on the river Phasis,

Book Three

he and all his comrades seeking the Fleece. Their task
at hand, we are struck with dreadful fear for all of them,
chiefly Aeson's son. Him I will save to the last drop
of my strength, though he were to sail down to Hades
to free Ixion from his bronze fetters. I'll not have Pelias   60
laughingly dodge wretched fate—he who dishonored me
by haughtily scorning my sacrifices. What's more,
I had a great love for Jason before this, ever since
he met me at the mouth of the teeming Anaurus
on his return from the hunt, as I tested men's virtue.
All the mountains and lofty peaks were dusted with snow,
and torrents rolled down from them in a furious rushing roar.
He pitied me in my guise as a crone, and hoisting me
on his shoulders he carried me through the surging tide.
So he has honor from me, forever. But Pelias   70
will not pay the price for the outrage he committed,
unless you grant Jason a safe return home."

The Cyprian goddess was speechless at first,
awestruck that Hera was supplicating her,
and then responded with these gracious words:

"Solemn goddess, may there be no sorrier creature
than Cypris, if I spurn your request in word or in deed,
whatever these feeble arms of mine can strive to attain,
and may there be no thought of you paying me back."

Hera responded to this with all due prudence: 80

"We've not come needing might or strength of hands.
Just gently urge your son to charm Aeetes's daughter
with love for Aeson's son. If she is well disposed and
conspires with him, he'll win the Golden Fleece with ease,
I think, and return to Colchis. She's cunning by nature."

And Aphrodite, speaking to both of them:

"Hera and Athena, he will obey you more than he will
me. Brazen as he is, a hint of shame will haunt his eyes
at the sight of you. But he flouts and bickers with me,
going on and on. And, too, plagued by his impishness,   90
I grew livid, and meant to shatter his bow and arrows,
vile-sounding things, in plain sight, for he, enraged,
threatened that if I don't keep my hands off of him
while he curbs his temper, I will blame myself later."

The goddesses smiled at this and looked at each other.
But Aphrodite continued, deeply concerned:

"To others my troubles are fodder for jokes. It's not right
for me to share them with everyone; I know them
all too well myself. As it is, since this plan pleases
you both, I will try to soothe him, and he'll not disobey."   100

At this Hera took her slender hand and smiling gently said:

"Finish this task at once, Cytherea, just as you say.
And do not be angry or irked into quarreling
with your son. In due course he'll cease to worry you."

Hera said this, stood up, and went back with Athena.

Aphrodite bribes Eros to shoot Medea with his arrow

And Aphrodite went through the vales of Olympus
to find her son. She found him in the lush orchard of Zeus,
not alone but with Ganymede, whom Zeus, enamored
of the boy's beauty had brought to live among the immortals.
They were playing for golden dice, a favorite game for boys   110
living together, and greedy Eros already was clutching
a handful of them under his chest as he stood upright,
his cheeks blushing sweetly. The other boy sat crouching
with a frown on his face and only two dice left,
which he threw in succession, angered by Eros's loud laughter,

Book Three

losing them right away along with the others.
He went off empty-handed and did not notice
Aphrodite approaching. She stood facing her boy
and putting her hand on his lips said to him:

"What are you smiling about, you infernal miscreant?   120
Did you cheat him like this, and unjustly get the better
of him in his innocence? Come, and finish willingly
for me the task that I will tell you, and I'll give to you
the dazzlingly beautiful plaything of Zeus—
the toy his dear nurse Adrasteia made for him
in his wide-eyed infancy, in the Idaean cave—
a ball, well-rounded, a better novelty than any toy
you could get from the hands of Hephaestus.
Its sections are formed of gold, and around each of them
wind two circular strips of webbing. Its seams are hidden,   130
with a dark blue spiral running over all of them.
If you toss it up in your hands, it casts a blazing trail
through the air, like a star. I will give it to you.
But you must shoot Aeetes's daughter with your arrows
and bewitch her with love for Jason. Make no delay.
My gratitude would be less if I have to wait."

These were welcome words for the boy to hear.
He threw down all his toys and grabbing hold of her robe
on this side and that, clung to his goddess mother
and begged her to give him the gift at once.   140
She smiled at him, touched his cheeks, kissed him,
and then giving him a hug, replied with a smile:

"Now may your precious head and my own bear witness—
I will surely give you the gift and will not cheat you,
if you hit Aeetes's daughter with one of your arrows."

When she said this, he scooped up his dice, counted them up,
and threw them into his mother's resplendent lap.
Then gripping its golden baldric, he slung his quiver

onto his back from where it rested against a tree
and grabbed his curved bow, and made his way through   150
the palace's orchard and through the gates of Olympus
in the upper atmosphere. From that height there descends
a pathway from heaven, the twin poles rearing above
the steep mountain peaks, the pinnacles of Earth
where the rising sun's first ruddy rays gleam.
Beneath him now appeared the life-giving earth,
the cities of men, the sacred streams of rivers,
and then mountain peaks and the surrounding ocean
as he glided through the enormous atmosphere.

And now the heroes, lying low up the river,   160
met in council seated on the Argo's benches.
Jason himself was speaking among them
and they listened in silence sitting row upon row:

"Friends, I'll be candid and say what seems good to me
myself. Your part is to bring it fully to pass.
Our task is shared, and our freedom to speak is shared,
equally open to all. As for the man who shrouds his thought
and counsel in silence, let him know that he, and he alone,
robs this crew of its return. The rest of you wait with the weapons.
Hold your peace. I will go to Aeetes's palace, taking Phrixus's sons,   170
and two other companions besides. When face to face
I'll try him first with words, if perhaps, for friendship's sake,
he might agree to give the Golden Fleece, unforced
or not, and trusting to his power he spurns us in our quest.
In this way we'll first learn his baseness from himself.
Then we'll think on whether to engage in battle
or, shunning the war-cry, to turn to help from other counsel.
Let's not strip away what's his, using merely brute force,
without testing him first in a trial of words.
No, far better to go and flatter him first with speech.   180
What strength can hardly grasp, a word's light touch can grip.
A fitting phrase can smooth the way to fill a wanting need.
And he did once greet as friend the blameless Phrixus,

89

who fled from his stepmother, scheming woman,
and from his father, whose altar called for blood.
All men everywhere, even the most audacious,
respect Zeus, god of hospitality, and heed his law."

Jason's speech met with the heroes' approval,
and no one had any other suggestions.
He then recruited the sons of Phrixus   190
along with Telamon and Augeias, and himself
picked up Hermes's wand. Off they went
from the ship, leaving behind the reeds and water,
and up to a plain that is sometimes called Circe's.
Here there is a stretch of willows and osiers
from whose topmost branches are suspended corpses
bound there with cords. For to this day it is taboo
for the Colchians either to cremate the dead
or to bury them under a mound of earth. Instead,
they shroud them in untanned ox-hides and hang them   200
in trees far from the city. But they do bury women,
so earth and air have equal roles. That is their custom.

The Argonauts' embassy to Aeetes

As they went on, Hera did them a favor
by spreading a thick fog throughout the city
so that they could proceed to the palace of Aeetes
without being seen by mobs of Colchians.
When they did come up from the plain to the palace
Hera dispersed the mist. Standing at the entrance
they marveled at the courtyards, the wide gates, the columns
rising in ordered array around the palace's walls   210
and capped by stone coping resting on triglyphs of bronze.
They crossed the threshold in silence. Nearby was a garden
trellised with vines, its green foliage clustered with blooms.
Beneath them were four fountains, flowing continually,
carved out by Hephaestus, one gushing with milk,
another flowing with wine, and a third with fragrant oil.

The fourth fountain flowed with water that grew warm
when the Pleiades were setting, and then at their rising
poured out from the hollow rock as cold as ice-crystals.
Such were the wonders crafted by the god Hephaestus 220
in the palace of Cytaean Aeetes. He also wrought for him
bulls with feet of bronze and bronze mouths that exhaled
a terrifying flame. And out of a single piece
of inflexible adamant he forged a plow for Helios
to thank the god for taking him up in his chariot
when he was exhausted in the Phlegraean battle
between the gods and the giants. Nearby was a courtyard
with many close-fitting doors leading into bedrooms,
and all along its sides was a well-crafted gallery.
On both sides higher buildings stood at angles. 230
Lord Aeetes dwelled with his queen in the highest,
and in another Aeetes's son Apsyrtus, borne to him
by Asterodeia, a Caucasian nymph, before he married
Eidyia, youngest daughter of Oceanus and Tethys.
The Colchians gave him a nickname, Phaethon,
because he outshone all the other young men.
The other buildings were occupied by handmaids
and Chalciope and Medea, Aeetes's two daughters.
Medea happened to be going from room to room,
looking for her sister, who had been kept inside 240
by Hera that day. Medea was not usually
inside the palace but in Hecate's temple,
since she was herself the goddess's priestess.
When she saw the men she screamed. Chalciope heard her
along with her maids, who threw down their sewing.
They rushed out in a throng, and when Chalciope saw
her sons among the men she lifted up her hands in joy.
They greeted their mother in much the same way
and wrapped their arms around her. And, sobbing, she said:

"So, then, you were not meant to abandon me heartlessly 250
and roam far abroad, but destiny has turned you back.
What a wretch I am! What a deep yearning for Hellas

Book Three

you latched onto from some deadly madness, driven
by your father Phrixus's commands! As he died,
his orders pierced my heart with loathsome sorrows.
And why would you go to the city of Orchomenus,
whoever this Orchomenus is, for Athamas's wealth,
deserting your mother in her time of grief?"

Chalciope spoke, and then Aeetes, hearing her voice,
came in, and with him Eidyia, his queen, last of all. 260
And soon the whole court was filled with people.
Some servants were busy with a huge bull, while others
were chopping wood or heating up bath water,
none easing up on their toil in serving the king.

Eros's arrow strikes Medea

And Eros was there too, invisible in the grey mist,
sowing confusion,
              like a gadfly, which oxherds
call a breeze, buzzing among a herd of grazing cattle.

He strung his bow quickly beneath the porch's roof beam,
drawing from his quiver a stinging arrow
never shot before, and glided unseen over the threshold. 270
Looking around, he stood close to Jason, notched the arrow
in the center of the bowstring, and drawing it all the way back,
he let it fly at Medea, leaving her speechless, astounded.
The god then left the high-roofed hall, laughing out loud
as the shaft burned deep, enflaming Medea's heart.
She kept flashing glances at Jason, sheer anguish causing
her heart to beat faster, all remembrance fading away
as her soul dissolved into a pool of sweet pain.

As a poor woman piling dry twigs around a burning brand—
a woman who makes her living spinning wool 280
so that she might have a fire to keep her warm
when she awakens early—and the flame flares up

wondrously from the small brand and consumes
the whole pile of twigs:
                    so too Love the Destroyer
enveloped her heart and burned secretly there.
Her soft cheek's complexion fluctuated between
pallid and red in her spirit's confusion.

When the servants had laid out a banquet for them
and they had taken warm baths that left them refreshed,
they satisfied their souls with food and drink.   290
Aeetes then questioned his grandsons in words such as these:

"Sons of my daughter and of Phrixus, whom I've honored
above all strangers in my halls, how is it that you
have made your way back again to Aea? Did some crisis
interrupt your safe escape? You refused to listen
when I declared the endless length of the voyage.
I learned it the time I whirled around in the chariot
of Helios, my father. He was bringing my sister
Circe to the western country, and we came to the shore
of the Tyrrhenian mainland. Even now she still lives   300
there, far remote from the land of Colchis. But what joy
do words bring? Tell me plainly what adventures you've had,
and who these companions of yours are, and where
you disembarked from your hollow ship."

Those were his questions, and Argus, as the elder
of the brothers, and being anxious for Jason's mission,
speaking softly, replied in words such as these:

"Aeetes, raging squalls made short work of that ship
and tore it apart. Huddling on the timbers, we
ourselves were cast ashore by a wave on the island   310
of Enyalius under the dark shadows of night.
Some god saved us. Not even the birds of Ares
that had previously haunted the desert island—
not even those beasts did we find still upon it.
But these men, who had disembarked from their ship

the day before, had driven the birds off. Either Zeus,
resolved to pity us, delayed them there, or some fate did,
since they promptly lavished us with food and clothing
when they heard the distinguished name of Phrixus,
as well as your own, for they travel to your city. 320
If you wish to know their object, I'll not hide it from you.
It concerns this man. A certain king desperately longs
to drive him far from his homeland and property,
because he might eclipse all Aeolus's sons in strength,
and so he sends him here on a hopeless errand.
He maintains that the kin of Aeolus will never escape
the heart-aching wrath and rage of Zeus, ever relentless,
or the unbearable curse and sanction for Phrixus's flight
until the Fleece reaches Hellas. And Pallas Athena
built the ship, one that is nothing like the kind of ships found 330
among the Colchians—and we came by the most horrid
of those, for the brutal waves and winds ripped it to pieces.
But hers, held firm by its bolts, rides out the wildest of storms,
and its speed is equally swift, whether propelled by wind
or by the crew doggedly plying the oars in their hands.
On board he's gathered the finest heroes of all Achaea,
and has come to your city from ranging through many towns
and over the treacherous open sea, in hopes that you'll
give him the Fleece. Still, it will turn out as pleases you,
for he does not come planning to use force, but proposes 340
to pay you a price worthy of the gift. Hearing from me
of the Sauromatians' profound enmity toward you,
he intends to subdue them and bring them under your rule.
And if you are eager to know their names and lineage,
who these heroes are, I will tell you in full.
This man for whose sake the rest were rallied from Hellas
they call Jason, son of Aeson, Cretheus's grandson.
If he is in fact descended from Cretheus himself,
then he would be our relative on his father's side.
Cretheus and Athamas were both sons of Aeolus, 350
and Phrixus was son of Athamas, Aeolus's son.
Then this man, if you have heard of Helios's offspring,
it's Augeias you see. And this is Telamon, son

of renowned Aeacus. Zeus himself fathered Aeacus.
All the others, too, every one of his companions
in the voyage, are sons and grandsons of immortals."

That was the tale Argus told. And the king grew angry
as he listened, his heart swelling with rage.
He lashed out most of all at the sons of Chalciope,
thinking it was for their sake the strangers had come. 360
His eyes flashed with fury as he yelled at them:

"Begone! Out of my sight now, you worthless louts,
be off and away from this land, you and your treacheries,
before someone sees a fleece and Phrixus, to his regret.
Your band's hasty voyage to Hellas was not for the Fleece,
but you've come here to steal my scepter and sovereignty.
If you had not first eaten from my table, be sure that
I would have cut out your tongues, lopped off both your hands,
and sent you forth with nothing but your feet, so that
you would be stopped from making a second attempt, 370
and since you have even dared to attribute
such flagrant lies to the blessed gods!"

So Aeetes spoke in his wrath. And from the depths of his heart
Argus longed to defy him with a deadly rejoinder,
but Jason held him back, responding gently before him:

"Aeetes, please be lenient with this expedition.
Our coming to your city and palace is not as you think,
and our aim is not as you surmise. Who would choose
to risk crossing so vast a sea for a stranger's goods?
No, Fate and the cold-blooded command of a haughty king 380
urged me on. Show favor to us your suppliants,
and I will relay to all Hellas your glorious fame.
Even now we are ready and willing to repay you
with a swift compensation in war, whether it is
the Sauromatians or some other people you crave
to conquer and bring under your rule."

Book Three

Aeetes's challenge and Jason's response

Jason spoke gently, playing up to him. But the king
was brooding over whether to kill them then and there
or to put their strength to a test, which seemed the better course,
and so he responded to Aeson's son this way: 390

"Stranger, why should you tell your tale so thoroughly?
If you truly are of the gods' bloodline, or are otherwise
not inferior to me in your quest for strangers' goods,
I will give the Golden Fleece as yours to take, if you wish,
once you have been tested. I do not resent brave men,
as you yourselves claim this ruler in Hellas to be.
Your trial will be a contest of courage and strength,
one I have achieved with my own hands, though it is lethal.
Two bronze-footed bulls of mine graze on the plain of Ares,
their mouths breathing flames. I drive them under the yoke 400
across the rugged plowland of Ares, four acres wide.
I plow it up briskly, as far as the headland, and cast
in the furrows not seed that yields Demeter's grain,
but rather the teeth of a fearsome serpent, and they grow
into the form of armed soldiers. These I slay on the spot,
mowing them down with my spear as they rush at me
on all sides. In the morning I yoke the oxen, and at dusk
I draw my harvesting to a close. But as for you,
if you accomplish such wondrous feats as these, then
on the same day you will carry off this Fleece for your king. 410
Until then, I will not give it, nor should you expect it,
for it is a truly shameful turn of events
for a noble man to give way to a weaker one."

Hearing this, Jason stared at the ground and sat stock-still,
speechless, utterly helpless in this dire situation.
For a long time he thought things over, but couldn't find
the courage to take on this insurmountable task.
At last he responded with carefully chosen words:

"Aeetes, your appeal to justice leaves me little choice,
which is why I'll submit to your contest, though heinous, 420
even if I'm doomed to die. There's no force more bone-chilling
constraining the human race than fiendish Necessity,
which is what drove me here at another king's whim."

Thus Jason, utterly helpless to do otherwise.
And the king, still brooding, answered him grimly:

"Go now, join your crew, since you're aching for toil,
but if you shy away from placing the yoke on the oxen
or shrink from the murderous crop, then I will take matters
into my own hands and see to it that another man, too,
may shudder to approach a man who is his better." 430

He spoke curtly, and Jason rose from his seat,
followed at once by Augeias and Telamon.
Argus too fell in, but without his brothers,
whom he signaled to stay. And so they went out,
Jason as radiant as a god in his beauty and grace.
And Medea, pushing aside her bright veil,
stole glances at him, her heart smoldering
and her spirit creeping like a dream in his wake.
And so they left the palace troubled at heart.
Meanwhile, Chalciope, protecting herself 440
from Aeetes's wrath, had gone to her chamber
with her other two sons. Medea left also,
brooding upon all the cares the Loves awaken.
She could see before her eyes just what he looked like,
the clothes he was wearing, how he sat in his chair,
how he walked to the door, and in her fantasy
she thought there never had been such a man as he.
His voice, the honey-sweet words he uttered,
constantly rang in her ears. And she feared for him,
afraid that the oxen, or Aeetes himself 450
with his own hand would kill him, and she mourned him
as if he had already been killed, and in her paranoia

a round tear swelling from pity and grief ran down her cheek,
and weeping softly she said aloud to herself:

"Why does this distress seize wretched me in its clutches?
Whether he shall meet his death as the most magnificent
of all heroes or as the worst of them, let him go!
Though I truly wish that he had escaped unharmed—
yes, esteemed goddess, daughter of Perses, let this at least
be so, that he may elude death and return home! But if   460
Fate constrains him to be laid low by the bulls, let him first
know that I, for one, do not relish his tragic downfall."

And so the maiden's heart was tortured by love.

The Argonauts' discussion

Now when the others had left the city behind
by the same path by which they had come from the plain,
Argus addressed Jason in words such as these:

"Son of Aeson, although you'll detest my advice,
but to be candid, there's no dignity in giving up
on an effort, even in dire straits. You yourself
have heard me speak before of a certain girl, daughter   470
of Perses, skilled in potions and inspired by Hecate.
If we could persuade her, I think, there would be no more
reason to fear that you'll be vanquished in the contest.
But I'm filled with horrible dread at the thought
that my mother will not take on this task for me.
Still, I'll go back again and plead with her,
since a common destruction hangs over us all."

He spoke with good intentions, and Jason replied:

"My good friend, if you favor this plan, I won't object.
Hurry, go, stir your mother's pity with well-worded pleas.   480
Our hope is a feeble flicker indeed,
if we rely on women for our journey home."

As he finished speaking they reached the backwater.
Overjoyed at the sight of them, their comrades
pelted them with questions. Jason, though,
was sick with grief and had this to say:

"My friends, cruel Aeetes's heart is seething with rage
against us. There would be no point in telling details,
either for me or for you who are asking what happened.
But he said that two bronze-footed bulls graze on Ares's plain,   490
their mouths breathing flames. He ordered me to plow the field
with them, four acres of plowland, and said that he
would give me seed from a serpent's jaws, which would produce
Earthborn men with bronze armor, and I must slay them
the very same day. This is the charge, and yes—because I
had no better idea—I agreed to it outright."

After Jason said this, it seemed to all of them
that this was a contest that no one could win.
For a long time they looked at each other in silence,
overwhelmed with despair. But at last Peleus   500
had some encouraging words to share with the heroes:

"It's time to think about what we should do,
though I don't believe that we will benefit from brains
in counsel so much as the brawn of our hands. Now then,
heroic son of Aeson, if you have in mind yoking
Aeetes's bulls and are eager for the toil, you should
indeed keep your promise and make yourself ready.
But if your heart is not fully convinced of its own valor,
don't bother to hurry yourself or to sit idle and
look around for another man to act, because I   510
for my part am not about to hold back, since
the most grievous pain will only be death."

So spoke Peleus. Telamon's soul was stirred
and up he rose. Then Idas was the third to stand up,
followed by Tyndareus's twin sons, and with them

Book Three

Oeneus's son, who was counted among the strongest heroes
though his cheeks showed not even the fuzz of a beard,
so great was the courage that sustained his spirit.
The rest of the crew held their peace and hung back.
And now Argus had this to say for those longing to fight: 520

"My friends, surely fighting to death is our last resort.
But I think that help will come to you from my mother
at just the right time. So, then, although you crave action,
restrain yourselves and wait in the ship yet a bit longer,
as you did before. It's better to hold back, anyhow,
than to be reckless and choose an evil fate for yourselves.
There is a certain girl, raised in Aeetes's palace,
whom the goddess Hecate taught to be exceptional
in the cunning art of all drugs produced by land or
in the full-flowing waters. Wielding these she soothes   530
even tireless flames, abruptly halts roaring rivers
mid-flow, and reins in stars and the sacred moon's pathways.
We thought of her as we were walking here on the path
from the palace, wondering if my mother, her sister,
might be able to persuade her to help in the contest.
And if this plan meets your approval, too, I'll lose no time
and will go back to Aeetes's palace this very day
to try, and perhaps a god will aid in my attempt."

He finished, and the gods graciously granted a portent.
A trembling dove fleeing a hawk fell from the sky,   540
terrified, right into Jason's lap, and the hawk
impaled itself on the ship's stern-ornament.
Mopsus was quick to interpret this portent:

"For you, friends, this sign has come about, by the gods' will.
There is no better interpretation for it than this:
to go to the maiden with a sweeping petition,
employing all kinds of tactics. I think she'll pay heed,
if in fact Phineus was right when he declared
that our return rests on the goddess Cypris. This gentle bird

that escaped its death was hers. As my beating heart foresees 550
in accord with this avian omen, so may it be.
Hurry, my friends. Let us invoke Cytherea to help,
and not hesitate to comply with what Argus advised."

He spoke, and the warriors, remembering Phineus's advice,
all approved, except for Apharean Idas,
who leaped up and shouted in terrible anger:

"For shame! We must have sailed here with a band of women,
calling on Cypris to come to our rescue, giving up
on the mighty strength of Enyalius. What, you look
to doves and hawks, and you cower from contests? 560
Curse you! Drop all your cares for the exploits of war,
and take to seducing helpless girls with your heartfelt cries."

Eager words from Idas. Many of his comrades
murmured low, but no one responded, making him angry,
and down he sat. Jason roused them at once, speaking his mind:

"Let Argus start from the ship, since everyone agrees
on that. But as for us, we'll leave the river now and
openly fasten our hawsers to land. Surely by now
it's unseemly to stay hidden, cringing from cries of war."

Jason spoke and immediately sent Argus 570
off to the city. The rest of the crew,
following his orders, pulled up the anchors
and rowed the ship to shore, away from the backwater.

The Colchians in assembly

Meanwhile, Aeetes was holding an assembly
of the Colchians, away from his palace
in a place where they sat in the past to devise
sinister treachery against the Minyae.
And he made this threat: that as soon as the oxen
dismembered the man who had volunteered

for that burdensome mission, he would cut down
the oak grove above the forested hill
and incinerate both the ship and all her crew
so that their outrageous insolence and haughty plans
would all end in ruin. For he never would have welcomed
Phrixus, an Aeolid, as a guest in his palace,
Phrixus, a paragon of gentility and fear of the gods,
had not Zeus himself dispatched Hermes from heaven
to ensure that he met with a friendly host.
Much less would pirates coming to his land
remain unpunished for long, men who wanted only
to lay their hands on the goods of others, plot secretly,
and raise a ruckus raiding the steadings of herdsmen.
He also said that the sons of Phrixus
should pay to himself a penalty for returning
in the company of criminals in order to drive him
recklessly from his position of honor;
for he had heard once a baleful prophecy
from his father Helios that he must beware
of his own children's treacherous schemes.
And so he was dispatching them, as they desired,
to the land of the Achaeans, a lengthy journey.
He had no fear whatsoever that his daughters
would ever devise treachery of any kind,
nor that Apsyrtus would plan any such mischief.
The evil resided solely in Chalciope's children.
And in his rage he proclaimed dire consequences
for the strangers, threatening inescapable
violence to both the ship and its crew.

Argus, meanwhile, had gone to Aeetes's palace
to plead with his mother to enlist Medea's aid.
Chalciope already had the same idea,
but she had held back for fear that either Fate
would oppose her efforts and they would be in vain—
Medea being fearful of her father's lethal wrath—
or if Medea was persuaded by her prayers,
her own part in it would be obvious to all.

A sound sleep had relieved Medea of her love pangs
as she lay in her bed, but all of a sudden,
she was assaulted by the sort of anxious,
deceitful dreams that trouble those in grief. 620
She thought that the stranger had agreed to the contest
not to win the ram's Fleece, had not come to Aeetes's city
for that reason at all, but to lead her away
to his own home as his wedded wife. And she dreamed
that she herself had contended with the oxen
and completed the task with superlative ease,
but that her own parents refused to fulfill their promise,
contending it was not the maiden they had challenged
to yoke the oxen but the stranger himself;
and from that there arose further arguments 630
between her father and the contingent of strangers,
with both sides laying the final decision on her,
and that she suddenly rejected her parents and chose
the stranger, causing them immeasurable grief,
and that they cried out in anger, and with that cry
sleep released its hold on her. Trembling with fear
she stared at the walls of her room, struggled
to collect herself, and finally blurted out:

"Wretch that I am, how sorely grievous dreams have struck me
with terror! I'm afraid that this voyage of the heroes 640
may usher in some vast evil. My heart is fluttering
over the stranger. Let him woo an Achaean girl
far away among his own people, and let my worries
be limited to the concerns of maidenhood
and my parents' household. Still, I'll render my heart
utterly shameless, and no longer keep my distance.
I'll test my sister to see if she begs me to help
in the contest out of grief for her sons, which would
quell the misery that troubles my heart."

She said this to herself, rose, and opened 650
her bedroom's door, barefooted and wearing
only her nightgown. She wanted to go to her sister

Book Three

and crossed the threshold, but stayed a long time
at the entryway, held back by shame. She went back,
came out again, and turned back a second time,
her feet taking her this way and that. Every time
she tried to leave, shame held her in the room
and though restrained by shame, intrepid desire
kept urging her on. Three times she tried
and three times she held back. On the fourth time   660
she fell face-down on the bed tossing and turning.

A newly-wed bride lamenting her youthful husband,
to whom her brothers and parents have given her,
stays apart from her attendants out of shame and because
she can think only of him, whom some doom has destroyed
before they have enjoyed each other's charms,
and she silently weeps, her heart on fire as she looks
at her widowed bed and fears the women will mock her.

So too Medea in her lamentation. And then suddenly
one of her young maidservants took notice of her   670
and went straight to Chalciope, who sat with her sons,
considering how they could win over her sister.

Medea and Chalciope

When Chalciope heard the maidservant's tale
she thought it strange but, far from disregarding it,
rushed in alarm to the room where Medea
lay in her grief, having scratched open both of her cheeks.
Seeing her eyes blurred with tears, Chalciope said:

"Dear me, Medea, why this flood of tears? What's happened
to you? What awful sorrow has made its way into your heart?
Has a fateful disease sent by the gods ensnared your joints,   680
or have you heard of a mortal threat made by our father
against me and my sons? If only I'd never laid eyes
on my parents' home here or the city, but that I'd lived
at the ends of the earth, where no one has even heard of Colchis!"

Medea's cheeks flushed as Chalciope said this,
and though she longed to reply, her modesty
restrained her. At one moment a word was on
the tip of her tongue, at another it fluttered back
deep into her breast, only to strive to be uttered
by her lovely lips, but no sound issued forth until, at last,   690
pressed hard by the Loves, she said guilefully:

"Chalciope, my heart reels for your sons. I'm afraid
that our father will kill them at once, with the strangers.
Just now, while slumbering in a fleeting sleep, I had
such agonizing dreams—may a god make them meaningless,
and may you never realize poignant grief over your sons."

She was feeling out her sister to see if she would first
ask for help for her sons. And when she heard this
an unbearable grief swept over Chalciope's soul
for fear it might come true, and then she replied: 700

"I was mulling over all these same things myself, and sought
you out to ask if you'd plan with me and devise some help.
First swear by Earth and heaven that you will keep my words
in your heart and that you will work with me as an ally.
I beg you by the blessed gods, by you yourself, and
by our parents, not to stand by and watch as they
are woefully destroyed by an evil death, or else
may I perish with my precious sons and ever after
be to you a loathsome Fury of vengeance from Hades."

As soon as she said this she burst into tears,   710
and clasping her sister's knees lay her head on her breast.
They lamented piteously over each other,
and the sound of women weeping in anguish
sifted through the halls. And Medea said:

"Poor thing! What cure can I work out for you
in the circumstances you've described, hateful curses
and Furies? Would that I had the sure and certain power

Book Three

to rescue your sons! Be my witness the lofty oath
of the Colchians, the one you press me to swear by,
and great heaven and Earth beneath, the mother of the gods,   720
as much strength as lies within me, you'll want for nothing,
at least so far as your prayers can be answered."

She spoke, and Chalciope said this in reply:

"Then to help the stranger, who is longing for it himself,
could you take it upon yourself to contrive a trick
or some plan for winning the contest, for my sons' sake?
Argus has come to me from him pleading that I secure
your help. I left him to wait in the house while I came here."

When she heard this, Medea's heart pounded with joy.
She blushed, her eyes misting over as she said in reply: 730

"Chalciope, whatever appeals to you and your sons
and makes you glad, I will do. May I never see the light
of day, and may you no longer look on me still living,
if I put anything before your life or your sons' lives—
brothers to me, cherished defenders and comrades.
I affirm that I am both your sister and your daughter,
since you took me as an infant to your breast, just as
you did them. I always heard our mother speak of it
in times past. But come, keep my kindness a secret, so that
I can fulfill my promise without our parents knowing,   740
and at dawn I'll bring potions to Hecate's temple,
charms to cast a spell upon the bulls in the contest."

Chalciope then left and told her sons of the help
Medea had given her. And Medea, left alone now,
was again overcome by fear and a sense of shame
that she would thwart her father by devising such schemes.

Night then drove darkness over all the earth,
and sailors at sea looked from their vessels
toward the Great Bear and the stars of Orion,

and wayfarers and watchmen now yearned for sleep, 750
and deep slumber embraced the mother
whose children had died, nor could there be heard
the barking of dogs or the sound of men's voices,
but deep silence engulfed the darkening gloom.

Medea's anguish

But sweet sleep did not come to Medea,
whose love for Jason and its attendant cares
kept her awake. She dreaded the might of the bulls,
whose fury would all too likely consign him
to an unseemly fate in the field of Ares.
And her heart beat fast, quivering
                      as a sunbeam dances 760
on the wall of a house, reflected from water
just poured into a pail, flashing and dancing
this way and that on the eddies.
                          So too Medea's heart
in her breast. Tears of pity flowed from her eyes,
and she was constantly tortured by a smoldering fire
throughout her body, along the network of nerves
in the nape of her neck, where pain pierces keenest
whenever the tireless Loves take dead aim at the heart
with their agonizing arrows. Now she decides
to give him the charms that would cast a spell on the bulls, 770
now she decides not to, now that she would die herself,
now that she would neither die nor give him the charms,
but simply endure her destiny in silence.
Finally she sat down, still wavering, and said to herself:

"Poor me, am I doomed now to be tossed to and fro
in despair? My wits are at a loss wherever I turn,
nor is there any help for the agony. It burns on like this,
unrelenting. If only I'd been slain by Artemis's
rushing arrows before I laid eyes on him, before
Chalciope's sons reached the land of Achaea! A god 780

or some Fury led them back here from there to cause me pain,
bringing a sea of tears. Let him die in the contest,
if he's doomed to die in the field. After all, how could I
brew the drugs without my parents knowing? What story
can I tell? What trick, what cunning ruse will help? If I see
him without his companions, how will I greet him?
Unlucky me! I have no hope of rest from my torment,
even with him dead. Then there would be misery for me
when he had lost his life. Away with shame,
away with glory! Once he's been saved thanks to me,   790
then let him go wherever his heart takes him, unharmed.
But as for me, on the very day when he carries off
the contest, let me die, either hanging by the neck
from a roof beam or ingesting lethal poisons.
Even so, after my death, people will jeer at me
with insults, and the whole city will shout out the story
of my doom. It'll echo afar, and the Colchian
women, bearing my tale on their lips everywhere
they go, will rail against me with cheap derision.
'She cared so much for a foreigner that she died,' and   800
'she disgraced her home and her parents by yielding
to raging lust.' What shame won't be mine?
Oh, the weight of my madness! Surely I'd be far better
off to quit life this very night in my bedroom, dying
abruptly and escaping all sinister slander,
before I carry out these outrageous atrocities."

When she finished she took out a small chest
that contained many drugs, some for healing,
some for killing, and resting it on her knees,
she wept, soaking her bosom with tears that flowed,   810
that flowed in torrents, lamenting her own fate.
She wanted to choose a death-dealing drug
and place it in her mouth, and was already undoing
the bands of the chest, lost in her misery.
But suddenly her heart was seized with fear
of loathsome Hades, and she held her hand back,

speechless, visions of all of life's little pleasures
crowding around her, all the delightful things
the living enjoy, her joyous playmates,
and the sun became sweeter than ever 820
to look upon as her soul longed for all this.
She removed the chest from her lap, transformed
by Hera's prompting, and no longer wavered.
She now longed for the sun to rise quickly
so she could give him the promised drugs
and at long last meet him in person.
She often slid open the bolts on her door,
looking for the first hint of dawn, and welcomed
the early-born light when it finally appeared
and people began to move all over the city. 830

It was then that Argus asked his brothers to remain
to learn what they could about Medea's intentions
while he himself left to return to the ship.

Medea and Jason at Hecate's temple

As soon as Medea saw the first light of dawn
she bound up the golden hair that had been spread
all over her shoulders, washed her tear-stained face,
and brightened her skin with nectar-sweet ointment.
Then she put on a beautiful robe fitted with clasps,
and on her lovely head a veil that gleamed silver.
As she walked about the palace she was oblivious 840
to the divinely ordained woes thronging around her
and of all the others that were destined to follow.
Then she called to her maids, twelve in number,
who slept in the vestibule of her bedroom,
all as young as herself, all unmarried,
and ordered them to yoke the mules to the chariot
that would take her to Hecate's beautiful shrine.
While they were readying the chariot, Medea
took from its box an herb that men call

the magic herb of Prometheus. If a man 850
anointed his body with this, after first
appeasing the only begotten Maiden
with nocturnal sacrifice, he could not be wounded
by bronze weapons, nor by blazing fire,
and for that day he'd be invincible in might and main.
This herb first shot up when the ravenous eagle
on the Caucasus's rocky slopes let drip
the bloody ichor of tortured Prometheus.
Its flower, the color of Corycian crocus,
bloomed on twin stalks a cubit above ground, 860
but the root was more like fresh-cut flesh.
Its dark juice, which was like a mountain oak's sap,
she had collected in a Caspian seashell
to make the drug, after bathing seven times
in ever-flowing streams and calling seven times
on Brimo, Queen of the Dead, in the gloom of night,
wearing dusky clothes. The earth shook below
and bellowed when the Titanian root was cut,
and Prometheus himself, son of Iapetus, groaned,
his heart troubled and afflicted with pain. 870
Medea now brought out this root and tucked it
in the band she wore just beneath her ambrosial bosom.
Leaving the palace she climbed into the chariot
flanked by two maidservants. She herself took the reins,
and holding in her right hand the well-crafted whip
she drove through the city, and the handmaids,
holding onto the chariot, trotted alongside
on the broad road, their light robes bound up
above their white knees.
     After bathing in the warm water
of Parthenius or in the Amnisus River, Leto's daughter stands 880
in her golden chariot, rolling over the hills
with her fleet-footed deer for a rendezvous
with a steaming hot hecatomb. She comes attended
by nymphs, some from the Amnisus, others from glens
and the high mountain springs, and around her

Book Three

*the cowering beasts whine and fawn as the goddess
speeds along.*
        So too Medea and her entourage
sped through the city, and on both sides the people
made room for her, avoiding the royal maiden's eyes.
When she had left the city's paved streets behind   890
and driving through the plains was nearing the shrine,
she alighted with a will from the smooth-rolling car
and, surrounded by her maidens, said to them:

"Friends, I've made a great mistake, and that's for certain.
I did not realize that I should not go out
among the strangers who are roaming our countryside.
The whole city is thunderstruck, so none of the women
who used to congregate here each day has come out.
Still, since we have arrived, and no one else is nearby,
come, let us enjoy the comforts of song and dance until   900
our hearts are satisfied, and then pluck lovely flowers
from the soft grass. We will go back afterward,
at the same time as always. And you might return home
with many gifts today, if you indulge this wish of mine,
for Argus pleads with me to change my mind, and so does
Chalciope herself. But keep what you hear from me
silently locked away in your minds, so that word does
not reach my father's ears. It regards the stranger.
They urge me to accept his gifts and to save him
from the fatal contest. Yet I've agreed to their counsel,   910
and called him to come and meet me privately, in person,
so that we can divide among ourselves any gifts that he
might happen to bring with him, and give him our own present,
more noxious than his: an enchanted drug. Although you
must please stand at a distance from me when he comes."

The shrewd plan that Medea outlined pleased them all.
And Argus took Jason apart from his comrades
as soon as his brothers told him that Medea
had left at sunrise for Hecate's sacred shrine,

and he led him across the plain accompanied by Mopsus, 920
Ampycus's son, who could foretell the future
from the flight of birds and so was well able
to advise travelers setting out on a journey.

Never before had there been such a hero,
not even of those descended directly from Zeus,
as on that day Hera made Jason, both in his looks
and in how he spoke. Even his comrades
were amazed as they looked at him, radiating grace,
and the son of Ampycus rejoiced in their journey,
with foreknowledge already of every detail. 930

Beside the path across the plain, close to the shrine,
stood a poplar with a crown of innumerable leaves,
in which cawing crows would often roost. One of them,
clapping her wings high in the branches,
gave voice to the admonitions of Hera:

"Paltry seer this is! He has no sense to give any thought
to things that even children know—that no girl will utter
a single sweet or lovely word to a young man when
strangers are near. Away with you, you sorry excuse
for a seer, sorry excuse for a thinker! Neither 940
Cypris nor the tender Loves breathe kindly upon you."

Thus the scolding crow, and Mopsus, smiling to hear
the god-sent voice of the bird, said to his comrades:

"You, son of Aeson, go to the goddess's temple, where
you will find the girl. She will accept you and your requests
favorably, as prompted by Cypris, who will help you
in the contest, just as Phineus, Agenor's son, said.
But the two of us, Argus and I, will wait right here
until you return. You must go to her on your own
and plead your case, shrewdly winning her over." 950

Wise words of advice, and both gave their approval.
And though Medea kept singing, her mind never turned
to other thoughts, nor did any song she sang
entertain her for long. She was distracted
and couldn't keep her eyes resting upon
the throng of her handmaids, averting her gaze
to the paths in the distance instead. Her heart
would sink weakly deep into her bosom
whenever she thought she heard the sound
of footsteps, whenever the wind shifted.   960
But before very long, there he was, Jason,
before her yearning eyes, striding along,
head lifted high,
      like Sirius rising
up out of the ocean, bright and beautiful
to behold, but bringing indescribable harm
to the flocks,
      so too Jason, son of Aeson,
coming to her now, beautiful as starlight,
but the sight of him made her even more lovesick.
Her heart sank, the world went dark, she flushed
with crimson, she was unable to bend   970
her knees, her feet were rooted to the ground.
Her handmaids had all drifted away, so it was
just the two of them, standing face to face
without a word or a sound,
      like oaks or tall pines
standing silently beside each other on a mountain
when the wind is still, but when a breeze stirs them
they whisper ceaselessly.
      So also these two
would before long converse, breathed upon by Eros.
Jason, seeing that Medea was sorely bewildered,
spoke to her gently, with these soothing words: 980

"Why, maiden, are you so fearful of me when I'm alone?
I'm not like other men, vain braggarts that they are,
nor was I before, even when I lived in my own country.

Book Three

So, then, young lady, don't be too bashful before me,
either to ask whatever you'd like or to speak freely.
No, since we have met each other on friendly terms,
in a sacred place, where sinning is unlawful,
speak openly. Ask what you like, and don't deceive me
with appealing words. You did at the start promise
your own sister that you would give me ample potions   990
to suit my need. I implore you, by Hecate herself,
or by your parents, or by Zeus, whose protective hands lie
upon strangers and suppliants—and I come here as both
supplicant and stranger, bending my knee to beg for help
in my dire straits, for without both you and your sister
I will not win through the woeful contest. And in return
you'll win my thanks forever after for your help, which is
only right, and is proper for those who dwell
in another part of the world. I'll secure you a name
and glorious reputation, and the other heroes will   1000
likewise celebrate you after returning to Hellas,
as will the heroes' wives and mothers, who now,
I suppose, sit wailing on the shore. You could
scatter their painful sorrows to the wind.
Once upon a time the maiden daughter of Minos,
Ariadne, took compassion, and rescued Theseus
from grisly contests. Pasiphae, daughter of Helios,
gave birth to her. But when Minos's anger had eased, she
joined Theseus on the ship and left her homeland behind.
Even the immortal gods themselves loved her,   1010
and as a sign a crown of stars, which they call Ariadne's crown,
rolls along in the midst of the sky all night long,
among the constellations of the heavens. So too
you will have thanks from the gods, if you save
such an impressive band of chieftains. Surely, judging
from your lovely form, you excel in compassion."

In response to his compliments she lowered her eyes
with the sweetest of smiles. Uplifted by his praise,
her heart melted within her. She looked into his eyes,
and eager to pour out everything at once   1020

did not know what to say first, but without hesitation,
she pulled the charm from her sash. He took it gladly
into his hands. Exulting in his eagerness,
she would have drawn out the very soul from her breast,
such was the flickering of Love's flame around
Jason's golden head. He entranced her gleaming eyes,
and her heart melted away like dew around roses
in the warm morning light. And now they both
cast down their eyes in embarrassment, but soon
were throwing glances at each other, smiling   1030
with love-light beneath their radiant brows.
It was only then that the maiden addressed him:

"Now take my words to heart, that I may arrange help for you.
Once you've gone to my father and received from him
the lethal teeth from the serpents' jaws, ready for sowing,
then watch for the middle of the night, when it's split into two,
and bathe in the streams of a tireless river.
Go off alone, apart from the others, in a dark cloak,
and dig a circular trench. In it slay a sheep—a ewe,
that you must sacrifice whole—and heap it on a pyre   1040
positioned carefully over the pit itself. And then
appease Hecate, Perses's one and only child,
by pouring from a goblet a libation of honey,
the product taken from industrious bees' hive.
Once you've delicately sought the goddess's favor,
draw back from the pyre. Do not be tempted to turn back,
whether you hear the tread of footsteps or the howling
of hounds, otherwise you might undermine all the rituals
and deprive yourself of returning to your comrades
in good order. And at dawn, soak this drug, strip off your clothes,   1050
and anoint your body as you would with oil. The charm
holds unlimited courage and mighty strength,
and you would swear that it's not a match for men,
but for the immortal gods. Let your spear, shield, and sword
be sprinkled with it, as well, and then the Earthborn soldiers'
spear-points will not pierce you, nor the overpowering flame

that shoots from the deadly bulls. Yet you will not have these
qualities for long, but only for one day. All the same,
never shrink back from the contest. Besides, I will share
another piece of advice that you will find helpful. 1060
As soon as you have yoked the burly oxen and swiftly
plowed the whole stretch of the rugged field with the force
of your hands and your valor, and now the Earthborn are
starting to sprout up in the furrows when the serpent's teeth
have been sown in the dusky soil, if you glimpse scores
of them springing from the fallow land, toss a hefty stone
without them seeing you. Like ravenous dogs over food,
they will kill each other over it. You yourself hurry,
make straight for the fray. Following these instructions,
you will indeed carry the Fleece to Hellas, somewhere 1070
far away from Aea. Still, go wherever you like,
or wherever you please after you have left here."

Medea spoke, and then looked down at her feet,
her beautiful cheeks wet with tears out of sorrow
that he would soon travel far from her over the sea.
Then looking right at him she once again addressed him,
with mournful words now, and she took his right hand,
her eyes now clear of any sense of shame:

"Remember, if you do in fact ever reach home again,
the name Medea. And I likewise, though you are 1080
far away, will remember you. Be kind enough to tell
me this—where is your home? Where will you travel now,
crossing the sea in your ship? Will you sail close
to wealthy Orchomenus, perhaps, or near the island
of Aeaea? And tell me of this maiden you named,
whoever she is, the well-known daughter
of Pasiphae. She is a relative of my father."

Medea said this, and now Love the Destroyer,
hard upon the tears of the maiden, overcame
Jason as well, who now answered her: 1090

"Without a doubt, I believe that I, too, will never
forget you, neither by night nor by day, after I
have escaped death, if I do in fact escape unharmed
to the Achaean land and Aeetes does not confront
us with a worse contest than this. But if you'd like to learn
about my homeland, I will tell you. Indeed, my own heart
prompts me to speak. There is a land surrounded
by lofty mountains, all lavish with fine sheep and
exquisite pasture, where Prometheus, Iapetus's son,
fathered noble Deucalion, who first founded cities   1100
and built temples to the immortal gods, and first to rule
over mortal men. Neighbors call the land Haemonia.
Iolcus lies in it, my city, and many others are
situated there, as well, where they have not so much as
ever heard the name of the island of Aeaea.
Anyhow, a story goes that Minyas set out from there,
Minyas the son of Aeolus, and that long ago
he built the city Orchomenus on the Cadmeans'
borders. But why do I tell you all of this, tossing words
to the wind with my talk of our home and the far-famed   1110
Ariadne, daughter of Minos? That is her name,
her glorious name, the one they call the lovely maiden
about whom you asked me. If only, just as Minos
came to terms with Theseus for her sake, your father
would similarly extend his hand in friendship!"

Jason said this trying to soothe her with gentle words,
but her heart was grieved, and she responded with anger:

"In Hellas I suppose it's a fine thing to respect
agreements, but Aeetes does not conduct himself
among men in the way that you describe Minos,   1120
Pasiphae's husband, nor will I compare myself
to Ariadne, so don't speak of hospitality.
Simply do this: when you do reach Iolcus,
remember me, and I, even despite my parents,
will remember you, too. And may a rumor reach my ears
from afar or a bird come as messenger to report

when you've forgotten me, or may swift gusts sweep me off
and carry me over the sea from here to Iolcus myself,
so that I can reproach you face to face as I remind
you that you escaped due to my goodwill. May I then   1130
appear as an unexpected guest at your palace's hearth!"

She said this with tears streaming down her cheeks,
prompting Jason to make this response:

"Poor woman, let the windy gusts wander abroad empty,
and the same, too, for the messenger-bird. You speak nonsense.
If you come to that home of mine and the land of Hellas,
you'll find honor and reverence from men and women.
They will adore you in every way as a goddess,
since their sons returned home again thanks to your counsel,
and then their brothers, kinsmen, and strapping husbands   1140
were saved from disaster. And you will prepare our bed
in our bridal chamber. Nothing will come between our love,
not until the destiny of death enfolds us."

Jason said this, and her soul melted away,
but she still shuddered at the violence to follow.
Poor woman, she was not destined to refuse
a home in Hellas much longer. It was Hera's plan
that she would forsake her homeland,
and come to Iolcus as a curse to Pelias.

Her handmaids, looking on from a distance,   1150
were silently grieving. It was now time for Medea
to return home to her mother. But she had no thought
of returning, and would have gone on delighting
in Jason's beauty and his way with words,
had he not at last come to his senses, and said:

"It's time to leave before the sun sets and we lose
the daylight, or some outsider takes notice.
But we will come back here to meet again."

In this way the two of them felt out each other
with gentle words, and then went their separate ways. 1160
Jason, in a buoyant mood, hurried back to the ship
and his comrades there, Medea to her handmaids.
They all came to greet her, but she hardly noticed
as they gathered around, for her soul had soared
up to the clouds. Her feet found their own way
up onto the chariot. She took the reins in one hand
and the intricately crafted whip in the other
to drive the mules, and they sped on to the palace.
When she arrived, a distraught Chalciope
questioned her about her sons, but Medea, 1170
distracted by her swiftly changing train of thoughts,
neither heard her words nor was inclined to respond.
She sat on a low stool at the foot of her bed,
her cheek on her left hand and her eyes wet with tears,
brooding on the evil that she had concocted.

Preparations

When Jason had rejoined his men in the area
where he had left them, he set out in their company
to go back to the ship. When the heroes saw him,
they put their arms around him and asked him
about all that had happened. He recounted to them 1180
Medea's machinations and showed them
the charmed herb. Of all his comrades
Idas alone sat apart, swallowing his rage.
All the others celebrated, and when night fell
took their rest peacefully. When the new day dawned
they dispatched two men to go to Aeetes
to ask for the seeds: Telamon himself, dear to Ares,
and Aethalides, Hermes's illustrious son.
They did not journey in vain. When they arrived,
lordly Aeetes gave them the dire teeth 1190
of the Aonian dragon, guardian of Ares's spring,
that Cadmus killed in Ogygian Thebes

when he came there in his quest for Europa.
And he settled there, led by the heifer
that Apollo by prophetic utterance assigned him.
It was Tritonian Athena who tore out the teeth
from the dragon's jaws and bestowed them upon
both the dragon's slayer and Aeetes as well.
Cadmus then sowed them on the Aonian fields,
founding an Earthborn people from the survivors   1200
of the reaping that Ares did with his spear.
These teeth Aeetes readily delivered
to be borne back to the ship, for he couldn't imagine
that Jason would ever conclude the contest,
even if he succeeded in yoking the oxen.

The western sun was sinking below the dark earth
far beyond the utmost Ethiopian hills,
and Night was harnessing her steeds as the heroes
were preparing beds by the hawsers. But Jason,
as soon as the brilliant stars of Helice, the Great Bear,   1210
had set, and the air had all gone still under the sky,
went to a lonely spot, as if he were a furtive thief,
with some needed provisions he had prepared
earlier that day. And Argus came too, bringing
from the ship a ewe and some milk from the flock.
When the hero found an isolated place
in a clear meadow under the open sky,
he first bathed reverently in a sacred river
and put on a dark robe that Hypsipyle
had given him some time ago in Lemnos,   1220
a memorial of all their lovemaking. Then he dug
a pit a cubit deep, cut the ewe's throat
and placed the carcass on top of firewood
that he had heaped up, and then kindled the logs,
pouring libations to Hecate Brimo
and calling on her for help in the contests.
When he had called on her, he drew back.
And the dread goddess heard him from deep below

and came to Jason's sacrifice. Horrific reptiles
writhed around her in the oak trees, illumined   1230
by the gleam of innumerable torches,
and the hounds of hell howled all around her.
All the meadows trembled under the tread
of the goddess, and the nymphs haunting the river
and the marshes shrieked, as did all who danced
around the meadow of Amarantian Phasis.
Jason was in the grip of fear, but even so
did not falter until he returned to his comrades
when dawn shed her light above the snowy Caucasus.

Meanwhile, Aeetes was strapping on the stiff corselet   1240
Ares had given him after he killed Phlegraean Mimas
with his own two hands. Then he placed on his head
a golden helmet with four crests, gleaming like
the orb of the sun when it first rises from Ocean.
And he brandished his shield wrought of many hides,
and his formidable spear, whose shock none of the heroes
could have withstood now that they had left behind Heracles,
who alone could have stood up against it in battle.
The king's well-built chariot, drawn by swift steeds,
was held nearby by Phaethon. Aeetes mounted,   1250
and holding the reins in his hands drove from the city
down the broad highway to the site of the contest,
and with him rushed forth a vast multitude.

As Poseidon mounts his chariot and rides to the contest
in Isthmia, or Taenarus, or to Lerna's water,
or to the grove of Hyantian Onchestus,
and then drives his steeds as far as Calaureia,
the Haemonian rock or forested Geraestus,

so too Aeetes, the Colchian king.

Meanwhile, Jason, as Medea had instructed,   1260
soaked the magic herb in water and used it
to sprinkle his shield, his stout spear, and his sword.

His comrades tested his weapons with all their might,
but failed to put even a dent in that spear,
which remained intact in their hands as strong as ever.
This infuriated Idas, Aphareus's son,
who with his great sword hacked at the spear's shaft,
and the sword blade leaped back as if from an anvil,
prompting the heroes to shout with optimistic joy.
Jason then sprinkled himself, and a terrifying strength   1270
pervaded his body, indescribable, dauntless,
and intensifying the power of both his hands.

A stallion eager for battle neighs and pounds the ground
with his hooves, lifting his head high with ears pricked up.

So too Jason, exulting in the strength of his limbs.
And he would jump about, high in the air,
juggling his bronze shield and ash-wood spear,

like lightning flashing in the gloomy winter sky
that keeps shooting out of cloudbanks
poised to pour down their blackest rainstorm.   1280

The Argonauts could not wait any longer.
Off they sped to the plain of Ares and began
seating themselves in rows of benches
on the opposite side of the city, about as far
as the turning point in a chariot race
lies from the start in funeral games for a dead king.
There they found Aeetes and the Colchians,
the latter stationed on the Caucasian heights,
the king by the banks of the winding river.

Jason and the contest

Jason, as soon as his men had secured the hawsers,   1290
leaped from the ship, and armed with spear and shield
made his way to the contest, taking with him
the gleaming bronze helmet filled with sharp teeth,

his sword slung around his shoulders, resembling
Ares in some ways and in some ways Apollo
of the golden sword. Looking over the field
he saw the bulls' bronze yoke and next to it
the adamantine plow. Coming closer
he planted his spear butt-first into the ground
and taking off his helmet propped it against the spear.   1300
Then he went ahead with only his shield
and examined the countless footprints of the bulls,
both of whom now charged out from their smoky
underground lair exhaling tongues of flame.
The watching heroes were terrified at the sight,
but Jason, taking a wide stance, stood as fast
as a rocky reef withstanding waves in a storm-blast.
He held his shield before him and both of the bulls,
charged right into him, horns lowered and bellowing,
but did not budge him a bit.
                              Imagine a blacksmith   1310
working the bellows and sending a blast of hot air
through the holes of a furnace, kindling
a raging flame, and then when the blast dies down
the fire shoots up with a roar.
                                 So too the bulls roared,
breathing fire from their mouths, and the ravenous heat
surrounded him and hit him like lightning,
but Medea's charmed herb protected the warrior,
who then gripped the horn of the bull on his right
with one hand, dragged it to the yoke and forced it
down to its knees, suddenly striking the bronze foot   1320
with his own. In much the same way he wrestled
the other bull down with one blow as it charged him.
Then he threw his broad shield onto the ground
and pinned them down where they had fallen on their knees,
threading his way swiftly through the exhaled flames.
Aeetes was astounded at the hero's might.
Meanwhile, Tyndareus's sons, as arranged beforehand,
brought him the yoke from where it lay on the ground

so he could bind it tightly onto the bulls' necks.
Then lifting up the bronze pole between them, 1330
he fastened it to the yoke by its golden tip.
The twin heroes then started back toward the ship.
But Jason picked up his golden shield again,
slung it onto his back, picked up the helmet
filled with sharp teeth, and using his spear
like a plowman with a Pelasgian goad
pricked the bulls' flanks while he firmly guided
the well-fitted handle of the adamantine plow.

At first the bulls raged, breathing furious flames,
their breath roaring like hurricane winds 1340
that prompt sailors to haul in their largest sails.
But after a while, prompted by the spear, they moved on,
and behind them the unplowed prairie was cloven
by the might of the bulls and the stalwart plowman.
The huge clods of earth groaned along the furrows
as they were torn up, each as heavy as a man could lift,
and Jason's feet pressed them down firmly
as he followed the plow, sowing the teeth as he went,
flinging them far and turning his head back
out of fear that the lethal crop of Earthborn men 1350
would rise up and attack him first. And the bulls
kept trudging onward with their bronze hooves.

When the third part of the day was still left,
and weary workers yearn for the sweet hour
of unyoking to hurry, the whole field was plowed
by the weariless plowman, four acres though it was,
and he unhitched the plow from the oxen
and shooed them away to the open country.
Then he returned to the ship while he saw the furrows
free of the Earthborn men. His men crowded around him, 1360
cheering and shouting. He used his helmet
to draw water from the river, and he quenched his thirst.
Then he flexed his knees until they felt supple,

and filled his great heart with courage, raging
like a boar when it sharpens its teeth against hunters,
foam dripping to the ground from its fuming mouth.

And now the Earthborn men were sprouting up
all over the field, and the precinct of the War God
bristled with shields, double-edged spears,
and glittering helmets. The radiance flashed through the air 1370
all the way up to Olympus, and,
     as when a huge snowfall
has blanketed the earth, and the wind has cleared away
the murky clouds from the sky, and all of heaven's stars
shine through the dark night,
     so too those warriors shone
as they sprang up from the earth. Jason remembered
Medea's stratagem then, and he picked up from the field
a huge round boulder that could have served as a weapon
for Ares Enyalius. Four strong young heroes
could not have raised it even a bit from the ground.
Jason held it in his hands and then rushing forward 1380
hurled it far into their midst, and then crouched unseen
behind his shield, trusting what would happen.
The Colchians shouted, a shout as loud as the roar
of the sea breaking on shoals, and Aeetes was speechless,
astounded at the soaring flight of the boulder.
And the Earthborn men leaped upon each other
like racing hounds and, yelling loudly, began
to slaughter each other, falling on Earth their mother
beneath their own spears like oak trees or pines
beaten down by a windstorm, and
     as a shooting star 1390
streams across the sky, leaving a shining furrow behind it,
a portent to men who see it gleaming across
the dusky heavens,
     so too Jason charging against
the Earthborn men, and brandishing his sword
he began mowing them down, slicing many

on the belly and side, some that had half risen
from the ground, others only as far as their shoulders,
some standing upright, others rushing into battle.

Just as when a feud arises over boundary lines,
and a farmer, fearing his field will be ravaged, 1400
picks up a sharp sickle and quickly cuts down
the unripe crops without waiting for the sunlight
to parch them,
        so too Jason cut down the crop
of the Earthborn men, and the furrows were filled
with blood, just as a spring's channels with water.
Some fell face-down, teeth biting the rough clods,
some on their backs, and others on their hands
or their sides, as grotesque as sea monsters.
Others, hit before lifting their feet from the ground,
doubled over from the waist and remained like that, 1410
their damp heads hanging limply.
                    As when Zeus
has rained ceaselessly, and newly planted shoots
droop to the ground, cut off by the gardeners,
and the owner of the farm, who planted them,
is sick at heart,
        so too the bitter grief of Aeetes,
who went with the Colchians back to the city,
pondering how he might retaliate quickly.
The day was done, and Jason's contest concluded.

Book Four

Invocation of the Muse; Medea flees

    Speak now, divine Muse, and in your own voice recount
the laborious schemes the Colchian maiden now wove.
My own soul quavers with speechless bemusement
as I try to decide whether she left the Colchians
out of sheer panic or love-stricken grief.

Aeetes spent the whole night in council
with his bravest captains, devising vengeful plans
to pay back the Greek heroes. The odious contest
had aroused wrath in his heart, nor did he believe
that all this happened without his daughters' knowledge.   10

Hera now infused fear into Medea's heart,
and she started to tremble like a nimble fawn
terrified by the baying of hounds in the woods,
for she had suddenly, and correctly, surmised
that her aiding Jason was no longer a secret,
and she would soon be faced with calamity.
She feared too her handmaids' complicit guilt.
Her eyes burned, and her ears rang terribly.
She would clutch at her throat, pull out her hair
by the roots, and groan in woeful desperation.   20
She would have swallowed poison then and there
and by her death canceled the plans of Hera
if the goddess had not driven the bewildered woman
to take flight with Phrontis and Argus,
the two sons of Phrixus. This decision calmed her.
She poured the drugs from her bosom back into the casket.
Then she kissed her bed and the room's folding doors,
stroked the walls, and tore out a long tress of her hair
to leave in the room for her mother, in memory
of her maidenhood. Then she sobbed out this lament: 30

Book Four

"I go leaving this flowing lock of hair in my place,
my mother. I wish you a fond farewell, though I go
far away. Farewell, Chalciope, and my whole home.
Oh, if only the sea had dashed you to pieces
before you reached the land of Colchis, stranger!"

As she said this she wept a flood of tears.
And then,
    *as a woman just enslaved takes her leave
from a wealthy house, never having experienced
hard labor, unused to misery and terrified
by what she will have to endure at the hands*   40
of a harsh mistress,
                  just so did this lovely maiden
rush out of her home. The bolts of the doors slid open
suddenly at the magical strains of her chanting.
She walked quickly with bare feet along the narrow paths,
her left hand holding her robe over her forehead
to veil her beautiful face, and her right hand
lifting up the hem of her chiton. She walked quickly
along the dark path alongside the great city's towers.
Fearful as she was, none of the watchmen saw her
speeding along as she headed for the temple.   50
She knew the way well, having come there often,
as a sorceress would, looking for corpses
and noxious herbs, yet her heart fluttered with fear.
And then Selene, the moon, Titanian goddess,
saw her and addressed her, heart to heart:

"Then I'm not the only one to make off
to the Latmian cave, or the only one to burn
with love for handsome Endymion who slept there.
So very often I have hidden away at the thought
of my love, driven by your crafty spells, so that you   60
could work your magic in the dark of night undisturbed,
fixing the charms that bring you pleasure. But now
you yourself have been fated to a similar madness,

Book Four

and an irksome god has given you Jason
as a heart-wrenching woe. Well, go, for all that,
and as clever as you are, harden yourself
to bear a burden teeming with groans."

The moon goddess said that, and Medea's feet
bore her swiftly along. She was glad to reach
the river's high bank, and to see on the other side   70
the gleam of a fire. The heroes had kindled it
and kept it burning all night in celebration
of the contest's outcome. Then through the night's gloom,
in a clear voice from across the stream, she called on
Phrontis, Phrixus's youngest son, and he recognized,
along with his brothers and Jason, Medea's voice,
and when they were sure of it, they were filled with wonder.
Three times she called, and at the company's insistence
three times, Phrontis returned her call. Meanwhile, the heroes
were hard at the oars trying to find her. They had not yet   80
tied up at the opposite bank when Jason leaped
from the upper deck, followed by Phrontis and Argus,
down to the ground. And Medea, clasping their knees, said:

"Save me, the accursed wretch, my friends—and yourselves, too—
from Aeetes. It's all come out, with no help to be seen.
Hurry, before he mounts his swift chariot, let's escape
by ship. I will give you the Golden Fleece by lulling
to sleep the serpent that serves as its constant guardian.
As for you, stranger, in the sight of your shipmates,
swear by the gods as your witnesses that you will keep   90
your promises to me, and once I've sailed far from here,
do not leave me friendless, a target of scorn and shame."

Medea spoke in anguish, but Jason's heart pounded
with joy, and as she fell at his knees, he lifted her up,
embraced her, and spoke these comforting words:

"Poor soul! Olympian Zeus himself be my witness,
and Hera, too, goddess of marriage, Zeus's own bride,

I will surely settle you in my home as my lawfully
wedded wife upon our return to the land of Hellas."

As he spoke, Jason clasped her right hand in his 100
and ordered the ship to be rowed to the sacred grove,
which was close by, so that they could carry off the Fleece
before Aeetes knew it. No sooner said than done
for this eager crew. They took Medea on board
and pushed off from shore, the oars crashing noisily
through the surf. Medea was taken aback at this
and desperately held out her hands to the shore,
but Jason calmed her down with some cheerful words.

Jason and Medea seize the Fleece and the Argo departs

It was now the hour when hunters, trusting their hounds,
keep their eyes open, staying awake at the end of the night, 110
before dawn's white beams erase both the track and the scent
of their quarry. It was then that Jason and Medea
stepped from the ship onto a grassy spot
called the Ram's Bed. This is where the animal
first rested, bearing on his back Athamas's Minyan son.
And close by, grimed with soot, stood the altar
that the Aeolid Phrixus dedicated to Zeus Phyxios
when he sacrificed the golden prodigy
as ordered by Hermes, who had benevolently
met him on the way. It was to this spot that Argus 120
directed the crew to put Medea and Jason ashore.

The two of them went down the path to the sacred grove,
looking for the great oak on which was hung the Fleece,
blushing red like a cloud in the fiery beams
of the rising sun. But right in front of the Fleece
was a serpent, who with his keen, unsleeping eyes
saw them coming and, stretching out his long neck,
hissed horribly, a hiss that resounded all around
the riverbanks and echoed throughout the boundless grove.
That hiss was heard throughout the Colchian land, 130

far from Titanian Aea, near the mouth of the Lycus,
the river that splits off from the roaring Araxes
and blends his sacred stream with the Phasis,
their waters flowing together into the Caucasian Sea.
Young mothers were startled awake, and anxiously
threw their arms around their newborn babies,
who fussed at that hiss.
                  And as above a pile
of smoldering firewood, eddies of smoke and soot
roll up one after another, rising aloft from below
in swirling wreaths,
                  so too did that monster   140
keep rolling his coils covered with hard, dry scales.
Medea came before his eyes as he was writhing,
and in dulcet tones summoned Sleep, the highest of gods,
to come to her aid, and she beseeched the queen
of the underworld, the night-wanderer, to come to her aid.
Jason followed nervously, but by now the serpent,
charmed by her chanting, was relaxing his long spine,
his numerous coils lengthening like a murky wave
silently rolling over a sluggish sea, but even so
he lifted his gruesome head, ready to snap his jaws   150
around them both. But Medea, dipping a fresh sprig
of juniper into her witchy broth of untempered drugs
while she uttered incantations, sprinkled them
on the serpents' eyes, lulling the monster to sleep.
His jaw sank down on the spot, and his countless coils
stretched out deep into the trees of the forest.

Jason immediately snatched the Golden Fleece
from the oak, as Medea directed, but she stood there
smearing the drug on the monster's head, until
Jason himself had her return to the ship,   160
and she left the dusky shade of Ares's grove.

A maiden catches on her fine-spun cloak
the light of the full moon as it rises above

*the high roof of her chamber, and her heart is glad
as she observes the beautiful glow.*
                              So too Jason
lifting up the massive Fleece in his hands,
and his cheeks and brows flushed with a flame-red glow
reflected from the shimmering mass of wool.
It was about as big as the hide of a yearling stag,
that hunters call a brocket, the Fleece golden above,   170
heavy, and thickly flocked. As the hero strode along,
the sheen was reflected up from the ground.
He wore it over his left shoulder, and it reached
down to his feet, but every now and then
he gathered it up in his hands, terribly afraid
some god or man might try to take it away.

Dawn was spreading her light over the world
when they reached the crew of heroes, all of whom
marveled at the magnificent Fleece, gleaming
like lightning from Zeus. They were all eager   180
to touch it, but Jason restrained them,
and threw over it a newly woven mantle.
Then he seated Medea in the stern and said to them all:

"No more delays in returning to our homeland now,
friends. Our task, the reason we dared this taxing voyage
full of blood and tears, has been deftly handled thanks to Medea.
With her consent, I will take her home to be my wife.
You, however, since she is the noble protector
of all Achaea and of you yourselves, are obliged
to protect her. Without a doubt, I am sure, Aeetes   190
will come with his forces to block our way from the river
to the open sea. So every other man of you
sit to ply the oars, while the other half guard our return
by holding your ox-hide shields in front as a screen,
ready to deflect enemy missiles. At this moment
we hold our children, cherished homeland, and aged parents
in our hands. In our venture, all of Hellas is at stake,
coming away with either disgrace or glorious fame."

When Jason finished speaking he put on his armor,
and the crew cheered wildly. Then he drew his sword
from its sheath, cut through the stern-hawsers,
and took his stand, already armed, close to Medea
and near Ancaeus, the pilot. The crew rowed hard,
desperate to drive the ship clear out of the river.

By now Medea's love affair and all she had done
had become known to Aeetes and all the Colchians,
who now thronged to the assembly in arms.

*As innumerable as the waves stirred up by the wind
on a stormy sea, or as the leaves that fall
to the ground in a forest of innumerable trees—
who could count them?—in the month when leaves fall,*

so too these frenzied men pouring along the riverbanks.
Aeetes in his well-crafted chariot outshone them all,
his horses, a gift from Helios, swift as the wind,
his left hand holding his curved shield aloft,
in his right hand a blazing pine-torch, his spear standing
close to his side. Apsyrtus held the steeds' reins.
But the Argo was already plowing through the sea,
propelled by the oarsmen and the river's strong current.
The king lifted his hands in agony and called upon
Helios and Zeus to witness their evil. And he issued
terrible threats against all his subjects, swearing
that if they failed to lay their hands on the maiden,
whether on land or on the high seas, and bring her back,
so that he might satisfy his soul by taking vengeance
for all those wrongs, they would pay with their own lives
for not attending to all his outrageous vengeance.

Aeetes said as much, and on that very same day
the Colchians launched their ships, loaded the tackle,
and sailed out to sea. You wouldn't say that this armada
was a fleet of ships, but more like a countless flight
of swarming birds clamoring over the ocean.

Book Four

Voyage to Paphlagonia and up the Ister River

The wind picked up, as the goddess Hera had planned,
so that Medea might reach Pelasgian shores
as quickly as possible to afflict the house of Pelias.
And when the third day dawned they tied their stern cables
to the Paphlagonian shore at the mouth of the Halys,
this at the prompting of Medea so that they might
propitiate Hecate by offering her sacrifice.
May no one ever know what the maiden prepared   240
for this sacrifice, and may my soul not urge me
to reveal it in song. Awe seals my lips, but the altar
that the heroes built on the beach to the goddess remains
and may still be seen by men in these latter days.

Then Jason and the rest of the heroes remembered
how Phineus had said that their route from Aea
would be different, but what he meant was not clear to them.
Then Argus spoke, and they were eager to listen:

"Orchomenus was our destination, the route
that truthful seer Phineus, whom you met earlier,   250
divinely prescribed to you. There is another way,
you see, declared by the priests of the immortal gods born
from Tritonian Thebes. Not all of the constellations
existed in their heavenly rounds yet, nor was there yet
a sacred race of Danaans for word of it to reach
the curious. There were only Apidanean
Arcadians, Arcadians who, the story goes, lived
even before the moon came to be, and ate acorns
in the mountains. The Pelasgian land was not ruled
by Deucalion's renowned sons back then, in the days when   260
Eerie, lavish in grain, was still the name for Egypt,
mother of the robust ancients, and the richly flowing
river was still Triton, watering all of Eerie.
Rain from Zeus never wets the ground, but the fields, soaked
by the flooding streams, yield generous crops. From there,

so they say, a certain man traveled through all of Europe
and Asia, relying on his troops' might, strength, and courage.
He founded countless cities as he went along.
Some may still be inhabited, while others are not.
Many a generation has come and gone since then. 270
Aea, at least, has firmly stood the test of time,
along with the descendants of the men whom
that king settled there as Aea's inhabitants.
In fact, they preserve their ancestors' writings, pillars
inscribed with all the roads and the boundaries
of both sea and land for wayfarers in the region.
And there is a river, Ocean's most northern branch,
wide and very deep, easy for a merchant's barge to cross.
Ister, they call it, and they've traced out its farthest points.
For quite a while it cuts through boundless fields 280
as a single stream, since the springs at its source far
beyond the blasts of the north wind roil and roar
in the remote reaches of the Rhipaean Mountains.
But when it enters the Thracians and Scythians' borders,
then it splits into two. It runs part of its water east
into the Black Sea and the opposite part, it sends
through a deep gulf that juts out from the Trinacian Sea—
the sea that borders on your realm, if the Achelous
really does flow forth from your land."

Argus said this, and the goddess sent a good omen 290
that caused all who saw it—a trail of light in the sky—
to shout with approval that this was the right course.
So they gladly left behind there the son of Lycus
and soon set sail for the Paphlagonian Mountains.
They did not round Carambis, though, for the wind
and the light of heaven only lasted until
they reached the mighty stream of the Ister.

Meanwhile, some of the Colchians, in a futile search,
sailed from Pontus and through the Cyanean Rocks,
but the rest, led by Apsyrtus, went to the river, 300

and then veered into the mouth, which is called Comely,
and outstripped the heroes by traversing a neck of land
into the farthest stretch of the Ionian Sea.
For there is an island called Peuce that the Ister surrounds,
three-cornered, its base stretching along the coastline,
with a sharp angle pointing at the Ister,
which then flows out in two separate branches.
One branch they call the mouth of Narex,
and the other, at the lower end, the mouth of Comely.
It was through this one that Apsyrtus and his Colchians   310
rushed through full speed ahead. But the heroes
went a long way upward toward the island's tip,
where shepherds left their flocks in the meadows
in fear of the ships, thinking they were monsters
coming out of the sea. For they had never before
seen seagoing vessels, nor had the Scythians
living among Thracians, nor the Sigynni,
nor the Graucenii, nor even the Sindi,
who now inhabit Laurium's vast desert.
But the Colchians—after skirting Mount Angurum,   320
and the cliff of Cauliacus far from that mountain,
around which the Ister, splitting into two streams,
falls into the sea on this side and that—sailed into
the Cronian Sea, cutting off all means of escape.
The heroes came down the river behind them
and soon reached the two Brygean islands of Artemis.
In one of them there was a sacred temple,
but they landed on the other, avoiding Apsyrtus's forces,
for the Colchians had avoided these, along with many
that stood in the river, doing so out of reverence   330
for the daughter of Zeus. But all the other islands
were occupied by the Colchians, barring the way,
as too on the other islands close by, as far as
the Salagon River and the Nestian land.

The Minyae, vastly outnumbered, would have
surely been defeated in a grim encounter.
But to avoid such a battle, they had made a covenant

among themselves. As for the Golden Fleece,
since Aeetes himself had already promised
that if they prevailed in the contest it was justly theirs, 340
it did not matter if it was obtained by guile
or even in the king's despite. But as for Medea,
because of whom the strife began, she should be left
as a ward of Artemis, secreted in the temple,
until one of the kings who arbitrated disputes
should give his judgment as to whether
she must be returned to her father's house
or follow the Argonauts to the land of Hellas.

When Medea had taken all this in,
her heart fluttered with anguish. She took Jason 350
off to one side, far from the others,
and face to face, sobbing, said to him:

"Son of Aeson, what conspiracy are you all plotting?
Have your triumphs gone to your head, erasing your
memory? Do you have any regard for what you said when
you were trapped by necessity? Where went your oaths to Zeus,
suppliants' god, where went your honey-sweet promises?
Because of them, against all decency and fixed
on shameless purpose, I forsook my country, the glories
of my home, my parents themselves, all I held near and dear. 360
Far abroad, all alone, I'm borne overseas
with the doleful kingfishers as my companions—
because of your troubles, simply so I could help you win
the contests with the oxen and Earthborn men, safe and sound.
And lastly, the Fleece. When the truth had come out, you won
that by my folly, too, while I showered tragic disgrace
upon women. So I proclaim that as your daughter, wife,
and sister, I travel with you to the land of Hellas.
In every way, then, stand by to protect me.
Don't leave me too far away when you go visiting kings. 370
Fight for me, plain and simple. Shore up justice
and divine law. We both consented to it. Otherwise,
this instant take your sword and slash my neck right through,

so that I may reap a reward that fits my mad lust.
Cruel wretch! If this king whom you both trust
with your dreadful pact decrees that I go to my brother,
how will I face my father? With a grand reputation?
What punishment or harsh penalty will I not suffer
in torment for the terrible deeds that I have done?
And will you gain the homecoming that is dear to your heart? 380
May Zeus's wife, queen of all, your glorious boast, never
bring that to pass! And may you remember me someday,
ravaged by cares. May the Fleece vanish into the netherworld
of Erebus, like a dream, carried off on the breeze.
May Furies of my vengeance chase you from my country at once.
How much anguish I've suffered due to your callousness!
Moral law prevents my curses from falling to the ground
unfulfilled, since you've broken a mighty oath, you brute!
But you can be sure that all of you will not blithely sit
and mock me for long on the strength of your treaties." 390

Thus Medea, seething with wrath. She longed
to set fire to the ship and hack it to pieces
and to fall herself into the conflagration.
And Jason, more than a little afraid, answered:

"Stop! You're like a woman possessed. None of this
pleases me, either. But we're seeking to put off the battle,
such a thick cloud of foes blazes around us because of you.
The whole population yearns to help Apsyrtus, to take
you home again to your father, as if we'd kidnapped you.
We would all die a loathsome death ourselves, if we met them 400
in hand-to-hand combat, and that pain will be ghastlier
still for you, if we die and leave you to be their prey.
This agreement is only a ruse for us to lure him
to his death. Nor will the locals engage us
in battle over you to win the Colchians' favor
once they are deprived of their leader, your defender
and brother. And I will not retreat from the Colchians
in outright war, not if they hinder my voyage back home."

He was trying to calm her down, but her response was deadly:

"Now mark my words. Steeped in heinous deeds, I've no choice   410
but to devise a scheme here, too, since I was misled
by my folly, and I carried out wicked intrigues,
all by divine will. In the fray, you stave off the spears
of the Colchians, while I lure him into your hands.
Show him a warm welcome, with splendid gifts, if I can
somehow manage to persuade the heralds when they leave
to bring him back alone to speak with me privately.
Then, if you agree with the deed—I won't resent it—
kill him, and go to battle with the Colchians."

So the two of them agreed, weaving a guileful web   420
for Apsyrtus. They assembled many gifts
suitable to present to guests and among them,
a sacred, crimson robe of Hypsipyle. The Graces
had woven it with their own hands for Dionysus
on the island of Dia, and he later gave it to Thoas,
his son, who in turn left it for Hypsipyle,
and she presented it, along with many other gifts,
to Jason, for him to wear. You could never satisfy
your desire to touch it or even to gaze at it.
And a divine fragrance wafted up from the fabric   430
ever since the king of Nysa lay down upon it,
drunk with wine and nectar, as he embraced
the lovely breast of the daughter of Minos
after Theseus abandoned her on the island of Dia
when she had followed him from Cretan Cnossus.

Jason and Medea betray and kill Apsyrtus

After Medea now had convinced the heralds
to persuade her brother to come as soon as she reached
the goddess's temple, as agreed, in the darkness of night,
so she could devise with him a stratagem for her to take
the Golden Fleece, which, she claimed, the sons of Phrixus   440

Book Four

had forced upon her for the stranger to abscond with,
and return it to Aeetes's palace—with beguiling words
such as these she scattered in the air her bewitching charms,
which could have, even at a distance, drawn down
savage beasts from a high mountain top.

Ah, pitiless Love, humankind's greatest curse,
you are the source of deadly strife, lamentation
and groans, and you are grief's stormy birth-mother.
Arise, Divinity, and take up arms against
the sons of our foes as you did when you filled 450
Medea's heart with ill-fated madness. Tell us how,
by what evil doom, she murdered Apsyrtus
when he came to meet her, for we must sing that next.

After the heroes had left her on Artemis's island,
according to plan, both sides came ashore separately.
Jason went to lie in ambush, waiting for Apsyrtus
and later for his comrades. Lured by dire promises,
Apsyrtus sailed quickly over the sea-swell
and in the gloom of night disembarked on the island
and went up alone to negotiate with his sister, 460
like a child trying to wade through a wintry torrent
that not even strong men could cross, to determine
if she had some plan to beguile the strangers.
When the two of them had agreed on every particular,
Jason bounded out from his ambush,
naked sword in hand. Medea quickly covered
her averted eyes with a veil so as not to see
the blood of her brother when he was cut down.
Eyeing him, Jason struck him down like a butcher
dispatching a powerful, strong-horned bull 470
next to the temple of Artemis built by the Brygi,
who dwelled on the mainland across the strait.
He fell to his knees in the vestibule there,
and as he breathed his last, he clutched with both hands
at the blood as it welled up out of his wound

and dyed his sister's veil red as she shrank away.
And with hardly a glance, the pitiless Fury
witnessed the deadly attack. Then the heroic Jason
hacked off all of the dead man's limbs and licked up
some blood and spat it out three times, as one should do   480
to atone for a treacherous murder. Then he hid
the clammy corpse in the ground, where to this day
Apsyrtus's bones still lie in the Apsyrtians' land.

As soon as the heroes saw the blazing torch
that Medea held up to signal an attack,
they pulled the Argo up to the Colchian ship
and slaughtered every last man,
                    as kites slay
*whole flocks of wood-pigeons, or as a lion,
having leaped into a sheepfold wreaks havoc
among them.*
            Not one of them survived the attack   490
of the heroes, who snuffed them out like a flame.
Jason joined them toward the end, eager to assist
where no help was needed, though he was still welcome.
They then sat to consider the rest of their voyage.
Medea joined them as they deliberated,
but it was Peleus who was first to speak:

"I urge you to embark right now, while it is still night,
and row your way along the passage that faces the one
the enemy blocks, for at dawn, when they see the
situation, I expect there will be not a single argument   500
that will persuade them to press on in the chase.
Like people bereft of their king, they would bicker
and break into factions. Later, on our return voyage
after the people have dispersed, our path will be easy."

He spoke, and the young heroes were persuaded
by Aeacus's son. They boarded ship quickly
and labored at the oars without stopping
until they reached the sacred isle of Electra,
the loftiest of all, near the Eridanus River.

Book Four

When the Colchians learned that their prince was dead, 510
they were fervent to pursue the Argo and its crew
all the way across the Cronian Sea. But Hera
restrained them with such terrible lightning
that at last they hated the thought of returning
to their homes in the Cytaean land, cringing
at the thought of Aeetes's fury. And so they landed,
and set up homes throughout the region.
Some trod on those very islands where the heroes
had stayed, and still inhabit the region,
called by a name recalling Apsyrtus. 520
Others built a fortified city by the dark and deep
Illyrian River, where can be found the tomb of Cadmus
and Harmonia, in the Enchelean heartland.
Others live in mountains called the Thunderers
from the time when the thunder of Zeus, son of Cronus,
stopped them from crossing to the island nearby.

Through the Eridanus and Rhone Rivers to Italy

Now the heroes, when their return seemed safe,
sailed on, and tied up their ship in the Hylleans' country.
For at this point the islands clogged up the river,
making the route hazardous for sailors there. 530
And, not as before, did the Hylleans harass them,
but of their own accord helped with the passage,
for which they won a massive tripod of Phoebus Apollo,
who had given to Jason a pair of tripods
to take along on the journey that faced him.
This was when Aeson's son went to sacred Pytho
to inquire about the voyage he was now making,
and learned it was fated that wherever these tripods
were established, that place would never be ravaged
by enemies. And so even today this tripod is hidden 540
in that land, near the pleasant city of Hyllus,
far underground, never to be seen by mortals.
But they did not find King Hyllus alive there,

Hyllus, whom beautiful Melite bore
to Heracles in the land of the Phaeacians.
The hero had come to the home of Nausithous
and to Macris, Dionysus's nurse, to purify himself
after he murdered his children. It was there he seduced
Melite, a water-nymph, daughter of the river Aegeus,
and gave birth to Hyllus, who, when he grew up,   550
chose not to live on that island under the rule
of King Nausithous, and recruiting a host of Phaeacians,
traveled to the Cronian Sea, his journey aided
by Nausithous himself. After he had settled there
the Mentores killed him as he protected his oxen.

Tell me now, goddesses, how it came to be
that beyond this sea, close to Ausonia
and the Ligystian Isles, called also the Stoechades,
tradition has it that the Argonauts sailed?
What force drove the heroes to travel so far?   560
What were the winds that filled their ships' sails?

When Apsyrtus had been brutally overthrown,
Zeus himself, lord of Olympus, seethed with wrath
at what the heroes had done, and so he ordained
that they must be cleansed of their awful blood-guilt
under the auspices of Aeaean Circe
and suffer countless troubles before reaching home.
None of the heroes knew this, and on they sped
away from Hyllea and all of the islands
that once were inhabited by the Colchians,   570
the Liburnian Isles, Issa, Dysceladus,
and lovely Pityeia. Then they came to Corcyra,
where Poseidon settled Asopus's daughter,
fair-haired Corcyra, far from Phlius, the island
from which he had carried her off out of lust.
When sailors view its dark woods from the sea,
they call it Black Corcyra. Then they passed Melite,
thoroughly enjoying the gentle breeze,
and then steep Cerossus, and far off Nymphaea,

Book Four

  where Calypso, daughter of Atlas, dwelled.   580
  And they thought they saw the misty mountains
  of Ceraunia. It was then that Hera mused upon
  Zeus's wrathful counsels concerning them,
  and so she contrived an end to their voyage,
  stirring up storm-winds before them, driving them
  back to the rocky island of Electra.
  And then, suddenly, they heard speaking to them
  with a human voice, the beam of the Argo,
  made of Dodonian oak, laid by Athena herself
  into the keel. They were seized with terror   590
  as they heard the voice, telling them of the grievous
  wrath of Zeus, proclaiming they would never escape
  the endless seaways or the terrible storms
  until Circe herself absolved them of the guilt
  of murdering Apsyrtus. The voice also commanded
  Castor and Polydeuces to pray to the immortals
  to grant them a path through the Ausonian Sea
  that led to Circe, daughter of Helios and Perse.

  That was the Argo's cry through the gloom.
  And the sons of Tyndareus rose, lifted their hands   600
  to the immortals, and prayed these godsends,
  but the other Minyan heroes were dejected.
  The Argo sailed swiftly ahead and entered
  the Eridanus's stream bed, where Phaethon,
  his chest struck by lightning, fell half-consumed
  from Helios's chariot and into that water's abyss,
  which still belches steam from that smoldering wound.
  And no bird can spread its wings over that water
  without fluttering down into that conflagration.
  And surrounding the lake Helios's maiden daughters,   610
  encased in tall poplars, wail wretchedly, their eyes
  shedding to the ground bright drops of amber.
  The sun dries these upon the sand, but whenever
  the lake's dark water overflows, they roll en masse
  into the Eridanus with the rising tide.
  But the Celts tell a different story, that these tears are shed

by the son of Leto, Apollo, borne along on the eddies,
the tears he poured out when he came to the sacred race
of the Hyperboreans, leaving heaven's radiance
when his father scolded him, angry about his son 620
whom divine Coronis bore in sunny Lacereia
at the mouth of the Amyrus. So the story goes.
As for the heroes, they had no appetite
for food or drink, and no joy in their hearts,
struggling all day with the nauseating stench
that the Eridanus exuded from Phaethon still burning,
and at night hearing the daughters of Helios
shrilly wailing, and as they lamented,
their tears floated on the water like droplets of oil.

From there they entered the deep channel of the Rhodanus, 630
which flows into the Eridanus, and at their confluence,
the mingling waters roar. That river rises
at the ends of the earth, where stand the portals of Night,
bursts forth on one side upon the beach of Ocean,
at another empties into the Ionian Sea,
and at a third flows through seven mouths
into the boundless bay of the Sardinian Sea.
Sailing down the Rhodanus they entered stormy lakes
spread throughout the enormous Celtic mainland,
where they almost met an inglorious end. 640
The branch of the river they were floating on
led to a gulf of Ocean that in their ignorance,
they were about to enter and would have never
returned from safely. But Hera, leaping from Olympus,
pealed forth a cry from the Hercynian rock,
shaking the whole crew with fear, so terrifying
was the din that resounded through the sky.
They reversed their course, thanks to the goddess,
and saw the path that was in the right direction.

A long time later, by Hera's devising, they arrived 650
at the beach of the surging sea, passing unscathed

through countless tribes of Celts and Ligyans,
for the goddess had enveloped them in a dreadful mist
day after day as their journey continued.
And so, sailing through the midmost mouth of the delta,
they arrived safely at the Stoechades Islands,
where altars and sacred rites in their honor
are still celebrated today, not only in their honor,
for Zeus included ships of future sailors as well.
Leaving the Stoechades they reached Aethalia Isle, 660
wiping away the sweat from their labor with pebbles,
and skin-colored pebbles are still strewn on that beach.
Their quoits are there too, and their wondrous armor,
and the Argoan Harbor still bears their name.

Purification by Circe

Sailing quickly from there they spotted Ausonia's
Tyrrhenian shores and arrived at Aeaea's
famous harbor, where they tied up their ship.
Here they found Circe. The goddess was washing her hair
in the salty sea-spray, for she had just awakened
from a terrible nightmare. In her dream her own chambers 670
and all her palace's walls were running with blood,
and flames were consuming all of the magical herbs
she used to bewitch whatever strangers arrived,
and she was quenching the flames with murderous blood
scooped up in her hands, somewhat calming her deadly fear.
So she rose at dawn and was washing her hair and clothes.
And creatures, not like wild beasts, but not humans either,
with an assortment of limbs, were thronging about,
as sheep in a fold follow the shepherd.
Earth herself had once engendered such species, 680
composed of various limbs, from the primordial slime
when she had not yet solidified beneath a rainless sky
nor been relieved of moisture by the scorching sun,
and before Time combined these forms and gave them order.
Such were unformed monsters that followed her now.

Book Four

The heroes were seized with amazement, and gazing
at the features and face of Circe, they surmised
that this woman was the sister of King Aeetes.

When she had banished her fearful nocturnal vision,
she started to walk backward, casting a spell with her hand   690
to make the heroes follow her. But at Jason's command
the crew stayed in place, and he drew along with him
the Colchian maiden. The two walked together
until they reached Circe's hall. Amazed at their coming,
she invited them to sit on polished chairs, but they,
as suppliants should, without a word sat down by the hearth.
Medea buried her face in her hands, but Jason
thrust into the ground the great hilted sword
with which he had killed Aeetes's son. None of them
lifted their eyes to meet her gaze. Circe immediately   700
recognized a suppliant's lot and the guilt of murder.
And so, in obedience to Zeus, god of suppliants,
who, though wrathful, mightily assists slayers of men,
she began to offer a sacrifice that absolves from guilt
even cold-blooded suppliants when they approach the altar.
Atoning first for the still unexpiated murder,
she held above their heads the offspring of a sow
whose teats still swelled from the fruit of the womb,
and, cutting her neck, sprinkled their hands with the blood.
Then she made appeasement with other liquid offerings,   710
summoning cathartic Zeus, the redeemer
of murder-stained suppliants. Her attendants,
naiad nymphs, removed all the defilements
out of the palace, while Circe, still by the hearth,
kept burning atonement cakes without any wine,
all the while praying to restrain the Furies
from their terrible wrath, and that Zeus himself
be propitious and gentle to both of them,
whether with hands stained by the blood of a stranger,
or as kin polluted with the blood of a kinsman,   720
coming before him to pray for his grace.

Book Four

When she had finished all these tasks, she got them up
from the floor and had them sit on the polished chairs,
and sat down herself, face to face with them.
Then she asked them outright what was the purpose
of their voyage, where they had been before coming
to her land and her palace, and why they were sitting
as suppliants at her hearth. The truth was that
her hideous dreams had reappeared as she pondered.
And she wanted to hear the voice of the maiden,   730
whom she knew was her kinswoman as soon as she lifted
her eyes from the ground, for the descendants of Helios
were easy to discern from the golden radiance
that flashed forth from their eyes. And so Medea,
the daughter of gloomy Aeetes, speaking gently
in the Colchian tongue, answered all her questions,
both about the quest and the heroes' journey,
and the difficult contests in which they labored.
She also told them how she had gone astray
through the counsels of her sorrowful sister,   740
and how she had fled with the sons of Phrixus
far from the tyranny of her horrible father.
She quailed at telling her about Apsyrtus's murder,
but did not fool Circe, who nevertheless
took pity upon the weeping maiden, and said:

"Poor wretch, you've surely contrived a return marked by evil
and disgrace. I think that you will not escape Aeetes's
violent wrath for long. Soon he will even storm districts
that belong to Hellas to avenge his son's murder,
because the deeds you have done are beyond bearing.   750
Still, since you are my suppliant and my own flesh and blood,
I will design no further ruin for you, coming here
as you have. But off with you, leave my halls with your stranger,
whoever this man of mystery is, the one you have chosen
in spite of your father. Do not plead for protection
at my hearth. I, for one, will condone neither
your plotting nor your contemptible flight."

When Circe said this, immeasurable anguish
came upon Medea. She cast her robe over her eyes
and poured forth her grief until the hero 760
took her by the hand and led her out of the hall,
shaking with fear. And so they left Circe's home.

The Sirens, Scylla, Charybdis, and the Wandering Rocks

All of this came to the attention of Hera,
whom Iris alerted when she saw them leaving the hall,
for Hera had asked her to watch for the time
when they returned to the ship. Now she addressed her again:

"Dear Iris, if ever you've fulfilled my commands, do so now.
Come, hurry on your swift wings, and tell Thetis to rise
from the sea and come here. I have overwhelming need
of her. Then go to the beaches where Hephaestus's 770
bronze anvils are struck by sturdy hammers, and tell him
to hush his fiery bellows' blasts until the Argo
passes them by. Next go to Aeolus, as well,
Aeolus, who lords over the winds born in the sky,
and explain my purpose to him, so that he'll bring
all heaven's gusts to a standstill, letting no breeze
ripple the sea. Only let a fair west wind blow
until they reach Alcinous's Phaeacian island."

As soon as Hera finished, Iris leaped down from Olympus
and soared with wings outspread. Then, plunging down 780
into the Aegean Sea, she came to the dwelling of Nereus.
She met Thetis there first, and as prompted by Hera,
told her the whole story and roused her
to go to the goddess. Then she came to Hephaestus
and quickly had him cease from banging his hammers,
and the sooty bellows soon stopped blasting out air.
Thirdly, she came to Aeolus, scion of Hippotas,
and when she had delivered her message to him also,
she rested her knees. Then Thetis, leaving Nereus

Book Four

and her sisters, came from the sea to Olympus 790
and to Hera, who sat her down and said this to her:

"Hear now, divine Thetis, what I'm eager to tell you.
You know how much honor I have at heart for the hero,
Aeson's son, and for the others who help in his struggle,
how I saved them as they passed through the Clashing Rocks
where flaming tempests roar around the craggy reefs.
But now a voyage awaits them beyond the great cliff
of Scylla and Charybdis's dreadful eruptions.
I've raised you since you were an infant, and I love you
above all others who dwell in the sea because you 800
refused to share Zeus's bed, though he desired it.
He is always absorbed in such behavior,
dallying with either immortal or mortal women.
For all that, you respected me and had a fearful heart,
and shunned him, and so he then swore a mighty oath
that you would never be called wife of an immortal god.
Still, he did not stop watching you, unwilling as you were,
until esteemed Themis told him everything—how you were
destined to bear a son stronger than his father.
That is why he gave you up, despite his longing, 810
ridden with fear that someone might prove his match
and rule the immortals. He was guarding his own power.
But I gave you the finest man on earth for your husband,
so that you could enjoy a heartwarming marriage
and bear children, and I invited all the gods to join
the feast together. With my own hands I held high your
bridal torch, all because of that tender-hearted respect
you held for me. But come, I will tell you a sure truth.
When your son Achilles reaches Hades's Elysian plain,
now the nursling charge of Naiads in the centaur Cheiron's den 820
and still craving your milk, he is fated to be husband
to Medea, Aeetes's daughter. Help her, then, as your
daughter-in-law, acting as her mother-in-law, and help
Peleus himself. Why is your anger so ironclad?
He was foolish, true. Even gods are subject to folly.

Book Four

There is no question, I'm sure, that at my commands
Hephaestus will stop stoking his raging fire
and Hippotas's son Aeolus will restrain his swift winds
mid-flight, except for a tranquil west wind, until they
put in at the Phaeacians' port. It's for you to devise   830
their carefree journey home. Rocks and ruthless waves pose
the only fear, which you can divert with your sisters' help.
Mind you don't let them fall helplessly into Charybdis,
so that she sucks them down and sweeps them all away,
or let them sail close to Scylla's odious lair—murderous
Ausonian Scylla, whom night-roving Hecate,
known as Cratais, the Mighty One, bore to Phorcus—
otherwise she might swoop upon them with her awful jaws
and wreak havoc on prized heroes. But steer the ship
to the place where there will be an escape   840
from destruction, however narrow it may be."

Thus Hera, and Thetis made this reply:

"If the raging fire's fury and the frenzied storm-winds
will in fact cease, then yes, I will confidently pledge
to save the ship, though the waves assail her, as long as
the west wind blows sweet and clear. But it's time to take
my own long journey, of untold distance, to search out
my sisters who will help me, and then to the spot where
the ship's hawsers are fastened, so that at daybreak
the crew may turn their thoughts to the journey home."   850

Having said this, Thetis sped down from the sky
and vanished into the eddies of the deep blue sea
and summoned to her aid the rest of the Nereids,
who heard her call and gathered together.
Thetis informed them of Hera's request
and quickly dispatched them to the Ausonian Sea.
And she herself,
   swifter than the blink of an eye
or the rays of the sun when it clears the horizon

Book Four

from a distant land,
                sped through the sea
until she reached Tyrrhenia's Aeaean beachhead,   860
where she found the heroes alongside the ship
passing the time with quoits and shooting arrows.
She came up and just touched the hand of Peleus,
who was her husband. No one else could see her clearly;
she appeared only to him and had this to say:

"No more lingering on the Tyrrhenian shores now.
At dawn loosen the swift ship's hawsers, obeying Hera,
who helps you. On her orders Nereus's daughters are all
coming together to conduct your ship safely
through the Wandering Rocks. Fate makes this your path.   870
But do not point out my form to anyone when you see
me coming with the group. Keep your thoughts to yourself,
or else you might make me even angrier than before,
when you acted rashly and provoked my ire."

With that, she vanished back into the briny depths.
Peleus was deeply wounded, for he hadn't seen her
ever since she left her bed and bridal chamber, angry
on account of their baby, Achilles, whose mortal flesh
she ensconced in fire by night and anointed
his tender body every day with ambrosia   880
to make him immortal, and so render his body
immune from loathsome old age. But Peleus
leaped out of bed when he saw his dear son
gasping for breath in the fire, and in his folly
uttered a terrible cry, to which Thetis responded
by snatching up the child, throwing him screaming
onto the floor, swooshing out of the hall
like a dream, and leaping into the sea in her anger,
never to return. Hence Peleus's astonishment now.
Nevertheless, he announced to his comrades   890
all that Thetis commanded. They immediately
broke off from their contests, had their supper,
and took their accustomed rest on the ground.

When light-bringing Dawn touched the sky's rim
and the west wind freshened, they boarded ship,
gladly pulled up the anchors and rigged the tackling,
spreading the sail above and stretching it taut
with sheets from the yardarm. And a fresh breeze
wafted the ship on. They soon spotted an island,
Anthemoessa, where the clear-toned Sirens, 900
daughters of Achelous, used to beguile sailors
with their sweet songs and then destroy them.
One of the Muses, lovely Terpsichore,
bore them to Achelous, and they once tended
Persephone, Demeter's noble, unwed daughter,
and sang to her in chorus, cheek to cheek,
each of them back then part bird and part maiden.
Ever on watch from their high perch in that harbor,
they deprived many sailors from their sweet return home,
wearing them away with wearying desire, 910
and now suddenly sent forth from their lips to the heroes
their delicate voices. The crew would have cast the hawsers
out onto the shore, had not Thracian Orpheus,
plucking the strings of his Bistonian lyre,
sounded the notes of a rippling melody,
making all their ears ring with the rhythm
as he swept the strings tumultuously,
and the lyre drowned out the voice of the Sirens.
So the west wind and the resounding waves
rushing from behind bore the ship onward, 920
as the Sirens kept voicing their ceaseless song.
But even so, only Butes, Teleon's son,
leaped up from his bench and into the sea,
his soul melted by the clarion voice of the Sirens.
The wretched man swam through the dark sea-surge
up onto the beach, where the Sirens surely
would have robbed the wretch of his day of return,
but the Cyprian goddess in pity snatched him away
while he was still in the eddies, a gracious rescue,
to live out his life on Cape Lilybaeum's height. 930

Book Four

The heroes, sick at heart, left the Sirens behind,
but still worse marine hazards, perilous for ships,
awaited them where seas meet in the Straits of Messina.

On one side could be seen the smooth rock of Scylla,
on the other Charybdis ceaselessly erupted.
Elsewhere the Wandering Rocks were crashing
beneath the mighty sea-surge, where earlier
a burning flame spurted from the top of the crags,
above the rock glowing with fire in the smoky air
through which you could not see the sunlight.   940
At that time, although Hephaestus had ceased from his toils,
a warm vapor was still rising up from the sea.
The daughters of Nereus convened on both sides,
while Thetis at the stern had her hand on the rudder
to guide them through the Wandering Rocks.
                                *As when
in fair weather herds of dolphins come to the surface
and cavort in circles around a ship, now seen in front,
now behind, and again at the side, and the sailors
are filled with delight,*
                          so too the Nereids
darted upward and circled all around the Argo   950
while Thetis guided its course from behind.
And when they were about to touch the Wandering Rocks,
the Nereids lifted the hems of their robes
over their snow-white knees, and on top of the rocks,
right where the waves broke, they scurried along
on this side and that, apart from each other.
Then, when the current hit her, the Argo was lifted
by waves that mounted up over the rocks,
touching the sky at one time like a towering crag,
and then subsiding to the floor of the sea, the waves   960
flooding over them. And now the Nereids,
                                     *like girls
on a beach rolling their dresses up to their waists
and out of the way, play with a ball, throwing it*

Book Four

> *back and forth high into the air, not letting it ever*
> *fall to the ground,*

tossed the ship back and forth
over the waves as it sped away from the rocks,
the seawater spouting and foaming around them.
And no less than Hephaestus, standing at the summit
of a smooth cliff-face, his muscled shoulder resting
on the handle of his hammer, surveyed the scene, 970
as did Hera as she stood above the gleaming sky,
and she threw her arms around Pallas Athena,
so frightened she was at what she saw below.
The Nereids struggled for a length of time
no less than that of a long springtime day,
heaving the ship between the echoing rocks,
until finally the heroes had the wind at their backs
and, sailing swiftly ahead, passed the meadow
in Thrinacia where the cattle of Helios grazed.
There the nymphs dove underwater like seagulls, 980
having fulfilled the orders of Zeus's wife Hera.
And just then the sound of sheep bleating
and the lowing of cattle came through the mist.
Phaethousa, the youngest daughter of Helios,
was tending the sheep, a silver crook in her hands,
and Lampetia, holding a golden orichalcum shaft,
followed behind, herding the cattle,
which the heroes saw grazing by a riverbed,
beyond the plain and a marshy meadow.
None of the cattle were black; all were white as milk 990
and magnificent with their horns of gold.
They cruised by in daylight, and when night came on
they were glad to be cutting through open water again
until early born dawn was lighting their course.

Alcinous, Arete, and the Phaeacians

Just in front of the Ionian gulf lies a fertile island
in the Ceraunian Sea, with a harbor on both sides,

Book Four

beneath whose soil lies the sickle—forgive me, Muses,
I don't tell the old tale willingly—that Cronus used
to callously castrate his father; although others call it
Demeter's Sickle, for the goddess once lived there   1000
and taught the Titans to reap ears of wheat,
all for the love of Macris, and so it is called Sickle Island,
the sacred nurse of the Phaeacians,
making the Phaeacians the blood of Ouranus by birth.
There the Argo arrived, intact despite many trials,
wafted by the breezes from the Thrinacian Sea.
Alcinous and his people were glad to welcome them
with a hospitable sacrifice, and you might think
it was over their own sons they made merry.
The heroes themselves strode gladly through the crowd,   1010
as if they had landed in central Haemonia,
but they would soon be armed and raising the battle cry,
for a huge army of Colchians now appeared on the scene,
after having sailed through the mouth of the Pontus
and the Cyanean Rocks in pursuit of the heroes.
What they wanted now was to carry off Medea
to her father's house or, if denied, to raise the war-cry
with utmost brutality, both then and upon
Aeetes's arrival. But lord Alcinous restrained
their lust for war, longing to allay the rancor   1020
between both sides and avoid the clash of battle.
And Medea pleaded with the comrades of Jason,
and touching the knees of Arete, Alcinous's wife, she said:

"I beg you, queen, for your mercy. Do not hand me over
to the Colchians for them to take me to my father,
if you too truly belong to the mortal race. Our minds
rush headlong into ruin simply through minor offenses,
just as happened when all my wits abandoned me—
though not because of lust. Be witness, sacred light
of Helios, be witness, rites of night-roving   1030
Hecate, Perses's daughter; I did not freely choose
to set out from home with strangers. No, terrible fear

induced me to fixate on this escape once I had gone
astray and there was no other recourse. My sash
of virginity still remains, as in my father's house,
undefiled and untouched. Pity me, lady! Soften
your husband's heart. May the immortals grant you a full life,
splendor, children, and the glory of an unsacked city."

That was her plea to Arete, and shedding tears,
she addressed all of the heroes in turn: 1040

"For your sakes, men of matchless valor, I am distraught,
and for your struggles, and for my part in your struggles.
It was I who helped you yoke the bulls and reap
the lethal harvest of the Earthborn men, and thanks to me
you will soon return to Haemonia with the Golden Fleece.
Here I am, I who lost my parents, who lost my home,
who lost all of the happiness in my life.
As for you, I enabled you to live in your country
and homes once more, and you will yet relish the sweet sight
of your parents, even though a heavy-handed god has 1050
certainly snatched away my pleasures, and I wander
accursed, with strangers. Fear your treaties and oaths,
fear the avenging Fury of suppliants and the gods'
retribution, if I fall into Aeetes's hands
and am butchered, a victim of outrageous brutality.
I am thrust on you alone, without shrines or turreted
tower or any other shelter to defend me.
Implacable, heartless rogues! You feel not an ounce
of shame in your hearts as you see me helplessly
stretching out my hands to the knees of a foreign queen. 1060
Yet in your eagerness to win the Fleece, you'd have
gone spear to spear with all the Colchians, and pompous
Aeetes himself! But now, you've forgotten your courage,
when these forces are alone and cut off from the others."

So she pleaded with them, and whomever she bowed to
and pleaded with, that man tried to hearten her

Book Four

and quench her anguish. And they all shook their spears
and unsheathed their swords, swearing they would never
hold back from aiding her were she to be judged unfairly.
They were all weary, and night fell upon them,   1070
night that puts men's work to rest and the earth asleep.
But to Medea no sleep brought rest, her heart throbbing
with anguish.
       As a poor woman turns her spindle
all through the night, her orphan children moaning around her,
for she is a widow, and her cheeks are wet with tears
when she thinks of her dreary life,
                             so too Medea's cheeks,
and her heart was in agony, pierced with sharp pain.

Inside the palace, Alcinous and Arete,
his revered wife, lay in bed, devising
all through the night plans to help Medea.   1080
Arete turned to her beloved husband and said:

"Come, my dear, let's save the poor girl from the Colchians
as a favor for the Minyae. Argos and the men
of Haemonian Thessaly are close to our island.
Aeetes, however, lives nowhere nearby.
We do not know Aeetes at all; we only hear
of him, while this girl broke my heart with her pleas.
She's suffered so dreadfully. My lord, do not deliver her
to the Colchians to be taken home to her father.
She acted foolishly at first when she gave Jason   1090
the drugs to charm the oxen. Next she tried to right one wrong
with another, as we often do when we go astray,
and she fled from her overbearing father's wrath.
But I hear that ever since then, Jason has been bound
by mighty oaths that he will make her his wedded wife
in his halls. So then, dear, don't deliberately turn
Aeson's son into a perjurer, nor let a father
in a fit of rage unleash torment on his daughter.
Fathers are all too jealous of their own children, you know.

Book Four

Think of Nycteus's plots against lovely Antiope,　　　　　　　　1100
pregnant with twin sons of Zeus; think of how miserably
Danae, too, suffered at sea with her son, adrift
by her father's wickedness! And just recently,
not far away, the wanton king Echetus stabbed his own
daughter's eyeballs with bronze pins, and she is wasting away
with sad fate in a dark granary, grinding grains of bronze."

That was her plea, and Alcinous, his heart softened
by his wife's words, answered her this way:

"Arete, I could take up arms and drive out the Colchians
as a favor to the heroes, for the sake of the girl.　　　　　　　　1110
But I'm afraid to take Zeus's righteous justice lightly,
and to slight Aeetes, as you suggest, is no small thing.
There is no one more kingly than Aeetes. If he wished,
remote as he is, he could bring war against Hellas.
I think it proper, then, to render the judgment
which all men will find best. I'll not conceal it from you.
If she is a virgin, my decree is that they take her
back to her father, but if she shares a husband's bed,
I will not separate her from her spouse, and if she has
a child in her womb, I'll not give it to enemies."　　　　　　　　1120

Alcinous said this and at once fell asleep.
Arete took his wise words to heart,
rose from her bed, and went through the palace.
Her maidservants eagerly assembled around her,
but she quietly summoned her herald and prudently
gave him a message to deliver to Jason,
urging the hero to wed Medea and to abstain
from imploring Alcinous, who, she said,
will decree to the Colchians that if she is still a virgin,
he will deliver her to be taken to her father's house,　　　　　　　1130
but if she shares her bed with a husband,
he would not sever her from her wedded love.

Book Four

Marriage of Jason and Medea

    Arete spoke to the herald, whose feet quickly bore him
out of the hall to inform Jason of Arete's plan
and likewise the intention of god-fearing Alcinous.
He found the heroes keeping watch in full armor
in the haven of Hyllus just outside the city
and delivered the entire message, at which
they all rejoiced, for it was indeed most welcome.

    They immediately mingled a bowl of libations   1140
for the blessed ones, as is right, and reverently led
sheep to sacrifice at the altar. Then they prepared
for that very night a bridal bed for the maiden
in the sacred cave, once the home of Macris,
daughter of Aristaeus, who understood bees
and honey and plump olives, the fruits of labor.
And it was Macris who first held in her bosom
the Nysaean son of Zeus in Abantian Euboea,
moistening his parched lips with honey when Hermes
carried him out of the flames. When Hera saw this,   1150
she expelled her from the entire island in anger,
and Macris came to dwell in the distant,
sacred cave of the Phaeacians, and made them wealthy.

    And now the heroes laid out a great couch, spreading upon it
the lustrous Golden Fleece, so that the marriage
would be honored and become the subject of song.
And the nymphs gathered for them variegated flowers
carrying them into the cave in their white bosoms,
the golden tufts of the Fleece gleaming around them
and kindling in their eyes a poignant desire.   1160
Yet for all their longing, a sense of awe restrained
each of them from laying her hand upon it.
Some were called daughters of the Aegeus River,
others haunted the crests of Mount Meliteia,
and others were woodland-nymphs from the plains.

Hera herself, wife of Zeus, had sent all of them
to honor Jason. Even now that cave is known as
Medea's sacred cave, where they spread the fine-spun,
fragrant linen and brought these two together.
And the heroes wielded their spears for battle 1170
in case enemies should stage a surprise attack,
but their heads were wreathed with leafy sprigs,
and all in harmony with Orpheus's clear-toned lyre
sang the marriage hymn at the bridal chamber's entrance.
Jason had not planned to consummate his marriage
in the house of Alcinous, but in his father's hall
when he had come home to Iolcus, as was the will
of Medea herself; but necessity forced them
to wed when they did. No, we forlorn mortals
might walk sure-footed the road of delight 1180
but bitter sorrow always keeps pace with our joy.
And so these two, although their souls were melting
with sweet love, were still fearfully uncertain
whether Alcinous's sentence would be fulfilled.

And now Dawn, returning with her immortal rays,
dissolved the black night throughout sky's dome,
and the island beaches roared with laughter,
as did all the paths in the distant, dew-drenched plains,
and there was a din in the streets. The people
were about throughout the city, as were the Colchians 1190
in the distant bounds of the isle of Macris.
Alcinous immediately went, as agreed, to see them
to announce his decision concerning Medea.
He held in his hand a golden staff, the staff of justice
he used when meting out righteous decisions
throughout the city. And with him, in martial order,
and arrayed in uniform, marched the Phaeacian chieftains.
Women crowded forth from the towers to see the heroes,
as did the country folk when they heard the news,
for Hera had sent forth reliable dispatches. 1200
One citizen led out the choicest ram in his flock,
another a heifer that had never felt a yoke,

Book Four

others set out jars of wine for mixing,
and the smoke of sacrifices curled up far and wide.
And women bore fine linen, as women will,
the fruit of the loom, along with gifts of gold,
and adornments such as are given to newly-wed brides.
And they all marveled when they laid eyes upon
the beautiful physiques of the gallant heroes,
among whom Orpheus, keeping time with his sandal   1210
tapping the ground, sang to the tune of his resounding lyre.
And all the nymphs, when he recalled the marriage,
raised the lovely bridal chant, and at times sang alone
as they circled in the dance, in your honor, Hera,
for it was you who planted in Arete's heart
the notion to proclaim Alcinous's wise decision.
And as soon as he had announced it, and the final rites
of the marriage has been proclaimed, he saw to it
that it would remain so. He was untouched by any fear
of Aeetes's wrath, and he kept his oaths unbroken.   1220
When the Colchians understood their pleas were in vain
and they were ordered either to obey Alcinous
or keep their ships away from his lands and harbors,
they began to dread their own king's wrathful response,
and beseeched Alcinous to receive them as allies;
and they lived a long time with the Phaeacians
until, as the years went by, the Bacchiadae,
a people from Corinth, settled among them
and the Colchians relocated to an adjoining island.
From there they would eventually migrate   1230
to the Ceraunian hills of the Abantes
and to the Nestaeans and Oricum, but all this
would not take place until long centuries had passed.
The altars Medea built on the site sacred to Apollo,
god of shepherds, still receive annual sacrifices
in honor of both the Fates and the nymphs.

When the Minyae departed, Alcinous gave them
many gifts of friendship, as did Arete.
And she gave Medea twelve Phaeacian handmaids

out of the palace to be her companions. 1240
Seven days later, at dawn, they departed
from Drepane on a fresh breeze from Zeus
and sped along with the wind in their sail,
but it was not fated for the heroes to land on Achaea
until they had labored in the depths of Libya.

Storm-driven to Syrtis

They soon left behind the gulf called Ambracia,
and, sails spread wide, the land of the Curetes,
and then the narrow islands of the Echinades,
and they had just sighted the land of Pelops
when a prodigious blast of the north wind seized them 1250
and for nine days and nine nights swept them toward
the Libyan Sea, until they came deep into Syrtis,
from which ships never return once they have entered.
In every part of that gulf, there lurk shoals
and masses of seaweed floating up from the depths,
a noiseless light foam washing over them,
and sandbars stretching in every direction
out to the dim horizon, and nothing that creeps or flies.
And as one might expect, the flood tide that ebbs out to sea
only to surge back with a roar, flooding the beach, 1260
thrust them suddenly onto the shore, with only
a little of the keel remaining in the water.
The crew leaped out of the ship and were dismayed
as they looked at the fog and the vast level land
stretching into the distance. No oasis, no path,
no huts for herdsmen in sight, only a deadly calm.
One depressed hero asked of another:

"What country is this? Where have the stormy winds driven
us? If only we'd bravely spurned deadly fear and sped
straight through the rocks, along the same route we came! 1270
It would have been better to die trying some great exploit,
even if we were overstepping Zeus's mandate.
But what should we do now, detained here

by winds for even a short time? What a desolate
shore, what an enormous terrain looms before us!"

So one of them spoke, and Ancaeus, the helmsman,
despairing of their plight, with a heavy heart answered:

"We are surely doomed to a gruesome death.
There's no escaping catastrophe. We're meant to suffer
terribly, fallen on this wasteland, even if inland   1280
breezes do blow this way. When I gaze into the distance,
I see shallow pools all around. Rippling water runs
steadily over the gray sand. This sacred ship would have been
long since smashed to bits far offshore,
if the tide itself had not swept her from the sea to the coast.
But now the tide is rushing back to the sea
and only dregs of the brine are swirling about,
just a shallow wash over the surface of the land.
That being so, I think that all our hope of cruising out,
and of reaching home, is now cut off. Let someone else   1290
show his skill. Anyone who aspires to save us is free
to sit at the helm. But the fact is that Zeus does not wish
to grant us a homecoming, despite all our toils."

He shed tears as he spoke, and all of them
with any knowledge of sailing agreed.
Their hearts were numb, and their cheeks sallow.

As men roam like ghosts all over a city
awaiting the outcome of pestilence or war,
or hurricane winds that demolish the labor
of field-oxen, or when imagined specters   1300
are dripping with sweat and blood, and bellowing
is heard in temples, or when at noon the sun
draws night into the sky and stars shine in the mist,

so too the heroes wandered the endless strand,
feeling their way along. And then evening darkened,
and they embraced each other piteously

saying their final farewells with tears in their eyes,
so they might each in solitude fall on the sand
and die. They went this way and that to choose
a resting place, wrapping their heads in their cloaks,   1310
and lay down fasting all that night and through the next day,
awaiting a piteous death. The maidens, though, huddled
apart from them and lamented with Medea.

As when unfledged birds abandoned by their mother
after they have fallen from a rocky cleft
will chirp shrilly, or when along the Pactolus's banks
swans lift their voices in song, and the riverbanks
and dewy meadows resound with their echoes,

so too these maidens, their golden hair in the dust,
wailed their piteous laments all the night long.   1320
These bravest of heroes all would have left this life,
nameless, unknown, but as they sank away in despair,
the heroine nymphs, guardian deities of Libya,
took pity on them. These were the very nymphs
who found Athena after she leaped in full armor
from Zeus's head and bathed the newborn goddess
in the waters of Lake Tritonis. They came at high noon,
when the sun's fiercest rays were scorching the land.
Standing by Jason, they gently drew the cloak
away from his head. The hero cast his eyes down   1330
out of respect for the goddesses, and as he lay in a daze
they spoke to him directly with gentle words:

"Hapless soul, why are you laid so low with impotence?
We know your quest for the Golden Fleece. We know your toils
one by one, all the valiant deeds you've achieved by land
and all those by sea in the course of your roaming voyage.
We are this land's sole goddesses, human-voiced
heroines, Libya's defenders and daughters.
Come then, up! No more of this grieving and mourning of yours.
Rouse your companions. As soon as Amphitrite   1340

unyokes her husband Poseidon's well-wheeled chariot
for you, then you must compensate your mother
for the sufferings she endured when she carried you
in her womb for such a long time, and by so doing,
you may yet return to most holy Achaea."

So they spoke, and disappeared when they finished.
Jason sat on the ground, looked about him, and cried:

"Be gracious, noble desert-ranging goddesses,
though I don't quite grasp your meaning about our return.
I'll surely call my comrades together and tell them.   1350
Perhaps together we can search out some inkling
of how to escape, since many heads are better than one."

Having said this, Jason jumped to his feet
and shouted to his comrades, caked with dust

like a lion roaring through a forest
in search of his mate, and in the distant mountains,
the very dells tremble at his thundering voice,
and the field-oxen and herdsmen cower in fear,

although to his comrades, Jason's voice was nothing
to be feared, but the voice of a friend, to whom   1360
they now came, heads lowered. He had them sit down
by the ship, the women too, and said to them all:

"Listen, friends. As I lay grieving, three goddesses
clad in goat-skins all the way from their necks down
and around their backs and waists, like girls,
stood very close by, above my head. They uncovered me
by drawing back my cloak with their nimble hands,
and urged me to wake up and to go and rouse you,
and pay lavish recompense to our mother
for the sufferings she endured when she carried us   1370
in her womb for so long, and do this as soon as

Book Four

 Amphitrite unyokes Poseidon's chariot.
But I have no idea what to make of this prophecy.
At any rate, they said they were heroines,
Libya's defenders and daughters. And everything
that we ourselves have endured by land, everything
by sea, they claimed to know it all, in detail. Then
I had no more view of them in their place, but some mist
or cloud came between us and veiled them from my sight."

 They all marveled at what Jason was saying,   1380
and then a wondrous portent appeared to the Minyae.
An enormous horse, his golden mane rippling
about his neck, leaped from the sea onto dry land,
shook off a lot of spume, and ran like the wind.
Peleus was delighted and said to his comrades:

 "I fancy that Poseidon's chariot has just now been
unyoked by his dear wife's hands, and I infer that
our mother is none other than the ship herself.
She suffers painful travails from carrying us
perpetually in her womb. But we'll employ unflinching   1390
strength and unyielding shoulders to lift her up high
in the interior of this sand-packed land, advancing
where the swift horse sped along its hoofs, since
he will not plunge beneath the dry ground, and his tracks
should point us to a bay farther in from the sea."

 Everyone approved of Peleus's plan.

Overland journey to Lake Tritonis and the Hesperides

 Now this is the tale told by the Muses,
and I sing in obedience to the Pierides,
passing on the true report I have heard,
which is that you, by far the mightiest   1400
sons of kings, by main force and valor
there on the desert sands of Libya
lifted the great ship with all its cargo

Book Four

onto your shoulders and carried it there
for a full twelve days and nights.
But who could tell of all the grievous pain
the heroes endured in that labor? Surely
they were of the blood of the immortals,
such a staggering task they shouldered,
constrained by harsh Necessity.　　　　　　　　　　　　　　　　1410
How far forward they bore her gladly
to the waters of the Tritonian lake,
wading in and setting her down from their shoulders!

Then they ran like rabid hounds in search of a spring,
for besides all the bodily pain they suffered,
they had a parching thirst. Their search led them
to the sacred plain where Ladon, the local serpent
who until recently guarded the golden apples
now laid in Atlas's garden, and the local nymphs,
the Hesperides, were busy chanting their lovely song.　　　　　　1420
It happened that Heracles had just shot Ladon,
and he lay on the ground by an apple tree, only
the tip of his tail still wagging, otherwise lifeless
from his head on down; and where his arrows,
steeped in the bitter gall of the Lernaean hydra,
had spilled his blood, dead flies lay withered
in the festering wounds. And nearby the Hesperides,
their white arms stretched over their tawny heads,
chanted their shrill laments, but at the heroes'
sudden approach, they became dust and dirt　　　　　　　　　　1430
on the very spot where they stood. Orpheus observed
the divine portent and prayed to them on behalf of all:

"O goddesses lovely and kind, be gracious, queens,
whether you are numbered among the heavenly goddesses
or those beneath the earth, or are called solitary
nymphs—come, O nymphs, sacred offspring of Ocean,
manifest yourselves openly to us who long for you,
show us some stream of water from a rock, some holy flow
from the land, something so we can quench our relentlessly

burning thirst. And if we ever do sail home again 1440
to the land of Achaea, then to you, first
among goddesses, we will offer countless gifts,
libations, and banquets with gladdened hearts."

Thus Orpheus, earnestly beseeching the nymphs,
who pitied the heroes from their place in the earth,
and, wondrously, first caused grass to spring up,
and then tall shoots above the grass, and soon
flourishing saplings standing upright and tall.
Hespere became a poplar and Eretheis an elm,
and Aegle the sacred trunk of a willow. 1450
And from inside the trees, they looked the same
as they did before, an astonishing miracle,
and Aegle spoke gently in response to their longing:

"To be sure, a truly tremendous help has come here
for you in your struggles—the utterly shameless wretch
who stole away our guardian serpent's life, plucked
the goddesses' solid gold apples, then went on his way,
leaving in his wake loathsome grief for us, for yesterday
came a man positively lethal in his violence
and imposing stature, eyes flashing under his fierce brow. 1460
Ruthless brute! He was clad in a massive lion's hide,
raw, untanned, and he carried a sturdy olive branch
and a bow, which he used to shoot arrows and kill this beast.
Well, that man came here, and, like any wayfarer
crossing the region by foot, was parched with thirst. He darted
throughout this place in his search for water, little chance
that he had of seeing it anywhere. Near Lake Tritonis,
however, stands this certain rock, and either by his own
design or by divine inspiration, he kicked
beneath its base with his foot, and the water gushed out, 1470
a gurgling flood. Then, leaning both hands and his chest
on the ground, he gulped a seemingly endless draught
from the split rock, until, bowed low like an animal
at pasture, he satisfied his colossal belly."

Book Four

As soon as she finished they sprinted joyfully
to where Aegle had pointed out the spring to them,
and as
     earth-burrowing ants swarm around a narrow fissure,
or when flies alighting on a drop of sweet honey
cluster around it with insatiable appetite,
          so too the Minyae
huddled together around the spring from the rock,   1480
and one of them cried out with wet lips to the others:

"How uncanny! Even from afar, Heracles has saved
his comrades, wracked with thirst. If only we could somehow
find him walking along as we pass through the mainland!"

So he spoke, and those who were ready to try this
responded by going this way in their search.
The night winds had erased whatever footprints
had been in the sand. The two sons of Boreas
trusted to their wings and took flight, while Euphemus
relied on his swift feet, and Lynceus on his eyesight.   1490
And with them darted off Canthus, the fifth,
motivated by Fate and his own courageous desire
to learn from Heracles where he had left Polyphemus,
determined to question the hero on every particular
concerning his comrade. But Polyphemus,
after founding a glorious city in Mysia,
had traveled far overland in search of the Argo,
and eventually reached the land of the Chalybes,
who live near the sea, and it was there that his fate
finally overtook him. A monument to the hero   1500
stands under a poplar there, facing the sea.
On that day, though, Lynceus thought he saw Heracles,
all alone in the distance,
         as a man sees, or thinks he sees,
on the first day of the month, the new moon
in a bank of mist.
         And when he returned to his comrades
he told them that no one who went in search of him

would overtake Heracles. The others also returned,
as did the twin sons of Boreas after their futile flight.

The deaths of Canthus and Mopsus

But you, Canthus, were seized by Death in Libya,
when you happened upon a flock of sheep in a pasture   1510
and were met by the shepherd as you were leading away
some of his sheep to your needy comrades, and he
killed you with a stone that he cast. This man, Caphaurus,
was no weakling, but the grandson of Lycoreian Phoebus
and the chaste Acacallis, whom Minos, her father,
drove from her home to dwell in Libya
when she was pregnant by Phoebus, to whom she bore
a beautiful son, whom they call both Amphithemis
and Garamas. Amphithemis took to wife
a Tritonian nymph, who bore to him Nasamon   1520
and strong Caphaurus, who killed Canthus that day
in defense of his sheep, but did not escape the Minyae's
avenging hands when they learned what he had done.
When they found Canthus they buried the corpse
with much mourning and took the sheep with them.

And on the very same day Fate seized Mopsus also,
son of Ampycus, whose prophesying did not save him
from bitter doom, for there is no escaping death.
There lay in the sand, avoiding noontime heat,
a dire serpent, too sluggish to initiate an attack   1530
and not inclined to strike anything that would shrink back,
but once it injects its black venom into any living being,
its path to Hades is not even a cubit long,
not even if Paeeon, god of healing—if I may so speak—
would treat him when its teeth have merely grazed the skin.
For when Perseus Eurymedon, as his mother called him,
was bearing to the king the newly severed head
of the Gorgon Medusa, every drop of black blood
that fell to the earth produced a brood of these serpents.

Book Four

Mopsus happened to step on the end of its spine 1540
with the sole of his left foot, and it writhed around
in pain and bit him on the shin, tearing the skin
away from the muscle. Medea and her handmaids
ran off in terror. Mopsus bravely endured the pain,
which was not too severe, but already a numbness
was spreading beneath his skin and a dense mist
began to cover his eyes. And soon his heavy limbs
collapsed to the ground and his body grew cold.
His comrades, including Jason, gathered around,
shocked and amazed at the impending doom. 1550
And even when he died, his body could not lie
exposed to the sun for even a short while, for the poison
began to rot his flesh from within, and his hair withered
and fell from his skin. They hurried to dig a deep grave
with bronze pickaxes, and they tore out their hair,
both the heroes and the women, loudly lamenting
the dead man's pitiable suffering. When they had performed
due burial rites, they marched three times around the grave
in full armor and heaped up a great mound of earth.

When they had boarded ship, a south wind blowing 1560
over the sea, they began searching for a passage
out of the Tritonian lake, wandering aimlessly
without any plan,
   like a serpent writhing along
a crooked trail when he is scorched by the sun,
turning his head from side to side as he hisses
furiously, his eyes glowing like embers, until finally
he creeps into his rocky lair.
     So too the Argo,
searching for a channel to get out of the lake,
an outlet for ships. For a long time they wandered,
and then Orpheus ordered them to bring out Apollo's 1570
massive tripod and offer it to the local deities
to help smooth the way for their voyage home.
So they disembarked and set Apollo's gift on the shore.

Book Four

Triton's hospitality and help

And before them stood, in the form of a young man,
the powerful sea-god Triton. Lifting a clod from the earth
he offered it to them as a guest-gift, saying:

"Take it, friends. I have here nothing marvelous
to give as a host's gift to those who come as suppliants.
But if you're at all seeking paths through this sea,
as men often need journeying through foreign parts,   1580
I'll tell you. My father Poseidon trained me thoroughly
in the knowledge of this sea. And I rule over the shore—
if, that is, though far removed, you have heard word
of Eurypylus, born in Libya, where wild beasts live."

When he said this, Euphemus stretched out his hands
to receive the clod, and said to him in reply:

"If by any chance you know of Apis and the sea
of Minos, hero, give honest answers to our questions,
for we haven't come here willingly. No, we were driven
to this land's borders by heavy squalls and carried our ship   1590
high in the air through the mainland to this lake's waters,
bearing the heavy weight, and we truly don't know
where a ship's route to the land of Pelops might be."

When he said this, Triton stretched out his arm
and pointed to the lake's deep mouth and the sea, saying:

"There's the outlet to the sea, where the depths are strikingly
stagnant and dark. On each side ripple glassy white breakers.
The narrow path between the breakers is the way out.
That misty sea stretches to Pelops's divine land,
beyond Crete. Be sure to hold to the right when you move   1600
from the lake into the swell of the sea, though,
hugging the coastline as long as it trends northward.
But when the coast curves in the other direction,

Book Four

      then you have smooth sailing ahead, if you aim
straight ahead from where the cape juts out.
Go with light hearts! And don't grumble about the toil."

That was his kindly advice. And the crew went aboard
without delay, determined to row clear out of the lake.
As they sped on, Triton hoisted the massive tripod
and entered the lake, but none of them noticed   1610
how he vanished with the tripod while being so close.
But their hearts were happy that one of the immortals
had been kind to them. And they persuaded Jason
to sacrifice to the god the best of the sheep
and recite words of good omen. He quickly
chose the victim and, lifting it high, slaughtered it
over the stern, and uttered this prayer to the god:

"O god who showed yourself on this lake's borders,
whether you are Triton, marvel of the sea, or whether
the sea-born daughters call you Phorcys or Nereus,   1620
be gracious, and grant joyous success to our journey home."

As he spoke these words, he cut the victim's throat
over the water and threw it from the stern. And the god
rose from the depths in his true form,
                                    and as a man
trains a thoroughbred to compete on a race course
and runs alongside him grasping his shaggy mane
while the horse runs in sync with his master,
rearing his proud neck high, and the foam-flecked bit
chimes as he champs it,
                      so too the god, seizing the keel
of the Argo, and guiding her out and onto the open sea.   1630
His body, from the crown of his head and down
through his torso, bore a stunning resemblance
to that of the blessed ones, but from the waist on down,
a tail like a sea monster's stretched on and on,
forking to this side and that, and he slapped the top

Book Four

of the waves with its spines, which parted below
into curving fins, like a new moon's horns.
The god guided the Argo until he propelled her
into the open sea, and then quickly plunged down
into the vast abyss, and the heroes shouted,   1640
seeing the awesome portent with their own eyes.
The Harbor of Argo is there to be found,
along with altars to Poseidon and Triton,
for the heroes spent the rest of that day there.

But at dawn, they spread their sails and sped on
with the west wind at their backs, and the desert land
on their right. The next morning, they sighted
the jutting headland and the sea bending around it
into a bay. The west wind suddenly dropped,
and a breeze from the south blew through the clear sky,   1650
their hearts rejoicing at the sound it made.
But when the sun went down, and the star appeared
that makes the shepherd gather his fold
and brings rest to the weary plowmen, then the wind
died down in the dark of night. So they furled
their sails, lowered the mast, and strenuously plied
their polished oars all night long, through the next day,
and again when the next night darkened. Farther on,
the rugged island Carpathus awaited them,
and from there they crossed over to Crete,   1660
which rises from the sea above other islands.

Medea vanquishes Talos of Crete

There bronze Talos, breaking off rocks from the cliff-face,
prevented them from tying up at the shore
when they arrived at the docks in Dicte's haven.
He was the sole remainder of the race of bronze,
men sprung from ash trees, sons of the gods,
and Zeus gave him to Europa to be guardian of Crete,
striding around the island three times a day
on his feet of bronze. His entire body was bronze

Book Four

and he was invulnerable, except that under 1670
one ankle's sinew lay a blood-red vein
covered only with the thinnest layer of skin,
which would prove to be the critical difference
between life and death. And so the heroes,
although worn out with rowing, quickly backed the ship
away from the shore, utterly dismayed.
They would have been in a desperate situation,
kept far from Crete, tormented by thirst and pain,
had Medea not said to them as they turned away:

"Listen to me. I think that I can single-handedly 1680
defeat this man for you, whoever he is, even if
his whole body is solid bronze, unless he also
has an infinite lifespan. Simply be willing to hold
the ship here, beyond the range of his rocks,
until he concedes the victory to me."

Medea said this, and they rowed the ship out of range
of his missiles, resting on the oars, waiting to see
what unanticipated plan she would put into action.
Folding her purple robe over both her cheeks
she mounted onto the deck. Jason took her hand 1690
and guided her along the rowing benches.
Then she started to chant spells, invoking
the Death-heads, devourers of life, the hounds of Hades
who hover in the air and swoop down on the living.
Kneeling as a suppliant, she summoned them
three times with spells, three times with prayers,
and, training her mind and her gaze on evil,
she bewitched the eyes of Talos, the bronze he-man,
her teeth gnashing hostilely as she projected
diabolical phantoms in her frenzied rage. 1700

Father Zeus, amazement wells up in my mind
when I see that dire destruction befalls us
not only from bodily wounds and disease,
but can afflict us even from a distance! So too Talos,

Book Four

despite his bronze structure, yielded the victory
to the power of Medea the sorceress. It happened
that as he was heaving boulders to keep them at bay
he grazed his ankle on the sharp edge of a stone,
and the ichor gushed out like molten lead.
After that happened he did not stand for long   1710
high on the jutting cliff, but
               like a towering pine
high in the mountains that woodsmen have left half-hewn
with their axes when they went home from the forest—
at first it just shivers in the wind that night, but then
it finally snaps off at the stump and crashes down
to the ground,
           so too Talos stood for a while
on his weariless feet, swaying back and forth, until,
with no strength left, he crashed to the ground.

That night the heroes spent in Crete, but at dawn
they constructed a shrine to Minoan Athena,   1720
drew water, and boarded ship, so that they could
row past Salmone's height as soon as possible.

Apollo's light (St. Elmo's Fire)

But as soon as they were running on the great Cretan Sea
night began to terrify them, the night that they call
the Shroud of Gloom. Starlight cannot penetrate
that deadly night, nor even moonbeams. Black chaos
descended from the sky, or some other darkness
rose from the depths. The heroes could not tell at all
whether they drifted on the water or in Hades itself,
but simply entrusted their voyage home to the sea   1730
with no idea where it was taking them.
Jason lifted his hands and cried out to Apollo,
invoking the god to save them, tears streaming down
in his great distress, promising to bring
countless offerings to Pytho, to Amyclae,
and to Ortygia. And then, hearing his prayer,

177

Book Four

      O son of Leto, you darted down from the sky
      to the Melantian Rocks, which lie there in the sea,
      and standing upon one of the twin peaks lifted high
      your golden bow in your right hand, and the weapon   1740
      flashed a dazzling light in every direction,
      revealing to their sight one of the Sporades,
      a small island near to the tiny isle of Hippuris,
      where they cast anchor and slept through the night.
      Dawn came early, and when it was light they constructed
      a magnificent shrine for Phoebus in a shady forest,
      and a shady altar as well, invoking Phoebus as Gleamer,
      because of the far-seen gleam. And they named the island
      Anaphe, Revelation Isle, because Apollo
      had revealed it to them in their bewilderment.   1750
      And they sacrificed all that men could offer
      on such a desolate shore. So when Medea's
      Phaeacian handmaids saw them pouring water
      in place of wine for libations on the burning logs,
      they couldn't hold back their laughter, having seen
      elaborate sacrifices of oxen in Alcinous's palace.
      The heroes were delighted with this jesting
      and came back at the women with humorous taunts,
      and so the merry exchange of teasing continued.
      And that is the origin of women scoffing at men   1760
      whenever sacrifice on that island is offered
      to Apollo, the gleaming god, patron of Anaphe.

Euphemus's dream

      When they had cast off from there in fair weather,
      Euphemus remembered a dream he had that night,
      reverencing Hermes, the glorious son of Maia.
      In his dream he was holding a clod of earth,
      given to him by a god, close to his breast,
      and that it was being suckled by streams of white milk,
      and that from it, small as it was, there grew a woman,
      a virgin, and that he, overwhelmed with desire,   1770
      made love to her, and during that union

he pitied her, as though she were a maiden
whom he was nursing with his own milk;
but she comforted him with sweet, gentle words:

"I am Triton's child, my friend, your children's nurse—
not your daughter, since Triton and Libya are
my parents. Entrust me to the daughters of Nereus,
to live in the sea near Anaphe. I will later
return to the light of day, ready for your descendants."

He stored in his heart the memory of this   1780
and reported it to Jason who pondered for a while
Apollo's prophecy and then responded:

"My good friend, make no mistake, Fate has ordained
an illustrious honor for you. Once you've thrown the clod
into the sea, the gods will turn it into an island
where your children's young children will make their home,
for Triton presented this to you as a host's gift
from the Libyan mainland. It was he, and none other
of the immortals, who gave it to you when he met you."

Euphemus did not render Jason's response idle.   1790
Instead, cheered by the prophecy, he cast the clod
into the depths, and an island rose up from there,
Calliste, sacred nurse of the sons of Euphemus,
who in the past had lived in Sintian Lemnos,
and were driven from there by the Tyrrhenians
and ventured to Sparta, where they were suppliants.
Then, leaving Sparta, they were brought by Theras,
Autesion's son to Calliste, an island whose name
he changed to Thera, after his own. But all this
took place long after the time of Euphemus.   1800

Return to Pagasae

From there they steadily left in their wake
long stretches of sea. Camping on the beach of Aegina,

Book Four

    they took to a friendly competition to determine
who could draw water and bring it back to ship
fastest of all, a contest motivated both by their thirst
and their need to take advantage of a favoring wind.
And even to this day Myrmidon youths compete in races
carrying on their shoulders jars brimming with water.

    Be gracious, race of blessed heroes! And may these verses
be sweeter to chant year after year among men.   1810
For now, I have come to the glorious conclusion
of all your labors, for no further adventure
befell you as you came home to Aegina,
no storm-winds opposed you as you quietly skirted
the Cecropian land and Aulis inside Euboea
and the Locrians' Opuntian cities, and with joy
you disembarked on the beach of Pagasae.

END

Glossary

Abantes: A people founded by Abas, originally of Thrace; living on the island of Euboea

Abas: Son of Poseidon and Arethusa; founder of the Abantes; father of Canethus; grandfather of the Argonaut Canthus

Abas: Son of Lynceus and Hypermnestra; king of Argos

Abas: Son of Melampus and Iphianeira; foster father of the Argonaut Idmon; Argive seer

Acacallis: Daughter of Minos; sister of Ariadne; by Apollo, mother of Amphithemis

Acastus: Argonaut; son of Pelias; later king of Iolcus

Achaean: A name for inhabitants of Achaea; sometimes used collectively for Greeks

Achelous: Son of Oceanus and Tethys; a shape-changing river-god; father of the Sirens

Acheron: Son of Helios and Gaia; transformed into the river of the underworld; to enter the underworld, souls are ferried across the Acheron by Charon

Achilles: Son of Peleus and Thetis; leader of the Myrmidons and champion of the Greeks during the Trojan War; nearly made immortal and ageless by his mother, but fated to die before the fall of Troy; killed by the arrow of Paris

Actius: A name for Apollo, as god of the shore

Actor: Son of Myrmidon; father of the Argonaut Menoetius; king of Phthia

Actor: Father of Sthenelus

Admetus: Argonaut; husband of Alcestis; nephew of Aeson; king of Pherae, in Thessaly

Adrasteia: Cretan nymph who cared for the infant Zeus when he was hidden in the Dictaean cave

Aeacus: Son of Zeus; father of Phocus and the Argonauts Telamon and Peleus; king of Aegina

Aeetes: Son of Helios and Perse; brother of Circe, Perses, and Pasiphae; father of Medea, Chalciope, and Apsyrtus; king of Colchis; given the Golden Fleece by Phrixus, his later son-in-law

Aegaeon: Monstrous son of Ouranus and Gaia; one of the Hecatoncheires (hundred-handed), along with his brothers Cottus and Gyges (each brother was a giant with one hundred arms and fifty heads); supported the Titans against the Olympians in the Titanomachy; also called Briareus

Aegeus: A river-god; father of Melite, and grandfather of Hyllus

Glossary

Aegle: One of the Hesperides; transformed into a willow tree

Aenete: Daughter of Eusoros; wife of Aeneus; mother of Cyzicus

Aeneus: Son of Apollo; father of Cyzicus, and husband of Aenete; founder of the city of Aenus, in Thrace

Aeolid: A son or descendant of Aeolus

Aeolus: Son of Hellen; father of Cretheus, Athamas, and Minyas; king of Aeolia; sometimes conflated with Aeolus, keeper of the winds

Aeolus: Son of Hippotas; keeper of the winds; king of Aeolia

Aeson: Son of Cretheus and Tyro; father of Jason; legitimate king of Iolcus, in Thessaly

Aethalides: Herald of the Argonauts; son of Hermes and Eupolemeia; gifted with perfect memory

Agamestor: A local hero worshiped by the Boeotians (from Tanagra) and Nisaeans (from Megara) after they founded the Pontic city of Heraclea

Agenor: Son of Poseidon and Libya; father of the seer Phineus; king of Tyre

Alcimede: Daughter of Clymene and granddaughter of Minyas; wife of Aeson; mother of Jason

Alcinous: Son of Nausithous; husband of Arete; king of the Phaeacians, living on Drepane

Alcon: Son of Erechtheus; father of the Argonaut Phalerus; king of Athens

Aleus: Son of Apheidas; father of the Argonauts Amphidamas and Cepheus; grandfather of the Argonaut Ancaeus; king of Arcadia

Aloadae: The giants Otus and Ephialtes, known for their insolence against the Olympians; sons of Poseidon and Aloeus's wife Iphimedia; founded many human cities; kidnapped Ares; later tried to stack Olympus and other mountains in order to reach the heavens and overthrow the Olympian gods; killed by Apollo or tricked by Artemis into killing each other

Aloeus: Son of Poseidon and Canace; foster father of the giants Otus and Ephialtes (Aloadae)

Amazons: Race of fierce female warriors descended from Ares and Harmonia; renowned for physical strength and skills; ruled by queens and self-segregated from men; divided into the three tribes of Themiscyreians, Lycastians, and Chadesians

Amphidamas: Argonaut from Tegea; son of Aleus and Cleobule; brother of Cepheus

Amphion: Son of Zeus and Antiope; twin brother of Zethus; co-ruler of Thebes; associated with its founding myths; musician whose lyre charmed the stones into fitting themselves together to construct the city walls

Glossary

Amphithemis: Son of Apollo and Acacallis; by a Tritonian nymph, father of Nasamon and Caphaurus; also called Garamas

Amphitrite: Daughter of Nereus and Doris; wife of Poseidon; queen of the sea and mother of Triton

Ampycus: Son of Elatus; father of the Argonaut Mopsus; seer

Amycus: Son of Poseidon and the nymph Melie; king of the Bebrycians

Ancaeus: Argonaut from Tegea; son of Lycurgus

Ancaeus: Argonaut and helmsman from Parthenia; son of Poseidon and Astypaleia; king of Samos

Anchiale: Nymph of Crete; mother of Titias and Cyllenus; gave birth to the Idaean Dactyls in the Dictaean cave

Antianeira: Mother of the Argonauts Eurytus and Echion; Amazon queen succeeding Penthesilea; also called Laothoe

Antiope: Daughter of Nycteus, from Thebes; by Zeus, mother of twins Amphion and Zethus; fled from her father Nycteus but was returned to Thebes and forced to abandon her newborn twins; later reunited with her grown sons, who then conquered Thebes

Antiope: Amazon queen and daughter of Ares

Aphareus: Son of Gorgophone and Perieres; husband of Arene; father of the Argonauts Lynceus and Idas; king of Messenia; founder of the city Arene

Apheidas: Son of Arcas; father of Aleus; grandfather of the Argonauts Amphidamas and Cepheus; king of Tegea

Aphrodite: Divine daughter either of Zeus and Dione, or of Ouranus, sprung from his castrated genitals in the sea; wife of Hephaestus; associated with love, passion, lust, sexuality, and doves; also called Cypris and Cytherea

Apidaneans: The oldest Arcadians, said to have existed before the moon

Apollo: Divine son of Zeus and Leto; twin brother of Artemis; associated with archery, prophecy and his oracle at Delphi, and the arts; also called Phoebus, Actius, Embasius, Ecbasius, the Archer, Lycoreian, Paeeon, and Gleamer

Apsyrtus: Son of Aeetes and Asterodeia; brother of Medea and Chalciope; nephew of Circe; also called Absyrtus, and by the Colchians, Phaethon

Arcturus: The brightest star in the northern hemisphere; located in the constellation Boötes

Areius: Argonaut; son of Bias and Pero; brother of Talaus

Ares: Divine son of Zeus and Hera; associated with war, aggression, violence, and courage; also called Enyalius

Arestor: Father of the Argonaut Argus

Glossary

Arete: Daughter of Rhexenor, descended from Poseidon; niece and wife of Alcinous; queen of the Phaeacians, living on Drepane

Aretus: A Bebrycian warrior; trusted subject of King Amycus; killed by Clytius

Argestes: The northwest wind

Argo: A ship built by Argus with Athena's help, using timbers from Mount Pelion and a beam from Dodona; the vessel of Jason and the Argonauts on their quest for the Golden Fleece

Argonauts: Heroic crew of the Argo; also called the Minyae

Argus: Argonaut and, with Athena's aid, builder of the eponymous Argo; son of Arestor

Argus: Son of Phrixus and Chalciope; grandson of Aeetes; brother of Cytissorus, Phrontis, and Melas; shipwrecked on a voyage to Orchomenus and later accompanied the Argonauts to Colchis

Ariadne: Daughter of Minos and Pasiphae, of Crete; helped Theseus escape from the Minotaur in the labyrinth, but was deserted by him on the island of Naxos; rescued by Dionysus to become the god's wife

Aristaeus: Son of Apollo and Cyrene; cult hero associated with bee-keeping, cheese-making, husbandry, and hunting

Artaceus: A warrior of the Doliones; killed by Meleagrus

Artemis: Divine daughter of Zeus and Leto; twin sister of Apollo; associated with the moon, the hunt, wild animals, wilderness, childbirth, and virginity

Asopus: A river-god associated with multiple rivers, particularly in the Peloponnese and Boeotia; father of Sinope and Corcyra (Sinope was abducted by Zeus and later by Apollo; Corcyra was abducted from Phlius by Poseidon)

Asterion: Argonaut from Peiresiae; son of Cometes and Antigona

Asterius: Argonaut from Pellene; son of Hyperasius; brother of Amphion

Asterodeia: Daughter of Oceanus and Tethys; Caucasian nymph; by Aeetes, mother of Apsyrtus

Astypaleia: Daughter of Phoenix and Perimede; Phoenician princess; by Poseidon, mother of the Argonaut Ancaeus

Atalanta: Female warrior from Arcadia; dedicated to Artemis from childhood

Athamas: Son of Aeolus and Enarete; king of Orchomenus; husband (first) of Nephele, by whom he fathered the twins Phrixus and Helle; his second wife, Ino, plotted against the twins, leading to their escape on the golden ram; incurred Hera's wrath for fostering Dionysus, Zeus's son by Semele; driven mad by Hera and killed his son Learchus; exiled to Thessaly, where he married Themisto

Athena: Divine daughter of Zeus, born from his head; helped Argus build the Argo; associated with wisdom, crafts, courage, and warfare; also called Pallas, Tritonian, Itonian, and Jasonian (for her support for Jason)

Glossary

Atlas: Titan son of Iapetus; for his role in the Titans' battle against the Olympian gods, sentenced to spend eternity holding up the heavens

Augeias: Argonaut and grandson of Helios; king of Elis; known for his immense herd of cattle; associated with Heracles's labor of cleaning out the stables

Autesion: Son of Tisameus; father of Theras; king of Thebes, but later migrated to the Peloponnese and joined the Dorians in obedience to a divine oracle

Autolycus: Son of Deimachus; brother of Deileon and Phlogius; joined Heracles on his quest to the Amazons but wandered astray; met the Argonauts, whom he and his brothers accompanied to Colchis

Bacchants: Female followers of the god Dionysus; roved the woods in mad ecstasy, dancing, wearing fawn skins and ivy wreaths, and eating raw meat; also called Maenads

Bacchiadae: A ruling family of Corinth; claimed to be descendants of Heracles through the ancient king Bacchis; after being exiled, helped establish Syracuse, Corcyra, and a royal Etruscan dynasty in Tarquinia

Basileus: A warrior of the Doliones; killed by Telamon

Bebrycians: A tribe living in Bithynia; led by Amycus

Bias: Father of the Argonauts Areius, Talaus, and Leodocus; brother of Anaxagoras and the seer Melampus; one of the three kings of Argos

Boreas: The north wind; by Oreithyia, father of the Argonauts Zetes and Calais; father of Cleopatra

Brimo: A name for a goddess connected with the underworld and its terrors; conflated with Hecate or, in some texts, with Persephone

Butes: Argonaut; son of Teleon and Zeuxippe; rescued from the Sirens by Aphrodite; left on Cape Lilybaeum

Cadmeans: The Thebans; descendants of Cadmus

Cadmus: Son of Agenor and Telephassa, from Phoenicia; husband of Harmonia; founder of Thebes in Boeotia; originally sent to find his sister Europa, who was abducted by Zeus; divinely led to the site for Thebes; associated with bringing the Phoenician alphabet to Greece, slaying the sacred dragon that guarded Ares's Ismenian spring, and sowing the dragon's teeth; after warriors called Spartoi sprouted from the teeth, he tossed a rock among them and killed them while they were attacking each other; remaining Spartoi became inhabitants of Thebes; along with Harmonia, transformed into snakes

Caeneus: Lapith father of Coronus, from Thessaly; born female Caenis; transformed into an invincible male by Poseidon; overcome in battle with Centaurs

Calais: Wing-footed Argonaut; son of Boreas and Oreithyia; grandson of Erechtheus; brother of Zetes and Cleopatra

Glossary

Callichorus: River named after choruses and orgies established there by Dionysus

Calliope: Daughter of Zeus and Mnemosyne, the goddess of memory; one of the nine Muses; patroness of epic poetry and eloquence

Calydon: A city in Aetolia; home of the Curetes; after the Argo's voyage, site of the Calydonian Boar hunt, when Artemis was angered by King Oeneus and sent a boar to destroy the fields; many former Argonauts and renowned heroes joined in the hunt

Calypso: Daughter of Atlas and Pleione; living on the island Nymphaea

Canethus: Son of Abas; father of the Argonaut Canthus

Canthus: Argonaut; son of Canethus; killed by the shepherd Caphaurus

Caphaurus: Son of Amphithemis and a nymph; grandson of Apollo and Acacallis; brother of Nasamon; a shepherd in Libya

Castor: Argonaut; son of Tyndareus and Leda; twin brother of Polydeuces; along with Polydeuces, one of the Dioscuri; associated with horsemanship, chariots, and sailors; by his immortal brother's request, honored with Polydeuces in the constellation Gemini

Cecropia: The area of the Acropolis of Athens; named after King Cecrops of Attica

Celts: Various peoples living in central and western Europe

Centaurs: Creatures with the lower bodies of horses and upper bodies of humans; often described as descendants of Centaurus, who was born from Ixion and Nephele, a cloud made in the likeness of Hera and formed by Zeus to expose Ixion's evil lust

Cepheus: Argonaut from Tegea; son of Aleus and Cleobule; brother of Amphidamas

Chadesians: One of the three tribes of the Amazons; associated with warfare using javelins

Chalciope: Daughter of Aeetes; sister of Medea and Apsyrtus; niece of Circe; wife of Phrixus; mother of Argus, Cytissorus, Phrontis, and Melas

Chalybes: Tribe of Scythians making their living from iron ore

Charybdis: Monstrous daughter of Poseidon and Gaia; transformed by Zeus into a deadly whirlpool in the sea opposite Scylla

Cheiron: Son of Cronus and Philyra; renowned Centaur associated with wisdom and medicine; raised and educated Jason; also called Chiron

Circe: Divine daughter of Helios and Perse; aunt of Medea, Chalciope, and Aspyrtus; living on the island Aeaea; sorceress known for her magic herbs; temporarily transformed men from Odysseus's crew into pigs in the *Odyssey*; later hosted Odysseus and his crew, instructing him to visit Hades for information from the prophet Teiresias

Glossary

Clashing Rocks: Two rocks in the Bosphorus Strait clashing together at a ship's approach; also called the Symplegades and Cyanean Rocks

Cleite: Daughter of Merops; queen of the Doliones and newly-wed wife of Cyzicus; her name, meaning "illustrious," was given to the Cleite Spring

Cleopatra: Daughter of Boreas and Oreithyia of Athens; wife of Phineus the seer

Clymene: Daughter of Minyas; mother of Alcimede, from Orchomenus

Clytius: Argonaut, from Oechalia; son of Eurytus; brother of Iphitus

Clytoneus: Son of Naubolus, from Argos; father of the Argonaut Nauplius

Cometes: Father of the Argonaut Asterion, from Peiresiae

Corcyra: Daughter of Asopus and Metope; abducted by Poseidon, who loved her and brought her to the island later named Corcyra; mother of Phaeax, ancestor of the Phaeacians

Coronis: Daughter of Lapith king Phlegyas and Cleophema; by Apollo, mother of the healer Asclepius; had an affair with a mortal man, Ischys; killed by Artemis for the insult to Apollo, who rescued the unborn child Asclepius from the flames of her funeral pyre and gave the infant to be raised by Cheiron; transformed into the constellation Corvus

Coronus: Argonaut; son of Caeneus; king of Lapiths; later killed in warfare by Heracles

Cratais: A name for Hecate, meaning "mighty one"

Cretheus: Son of Aeolus and brother of Athamas; husband of Tyro; father of Aeson; grandfather of Jason; king and founder of Iolcus

Cronus: Titan son of Ouranus and Gaia; brother of Oceanus, Tethys, and Rhea; husband of Rhea; with Gaia's help, castrated and overthrew Ouranus; fearing a prophecy that he would be overthrown, swallowed his own children, including Demeter, Hera, Poseidon, and Hades; tricked by Rhea, swallowed a stone instead of the infant Zeus, who was hidden in the Dictaean cave of Crete; when grown, Zeus freed his siblings and overthrew Cronus and the Titans in the battle called the Titanomachy

Ctimenus: Father of the Argonaut Eurydamas, from Thessaly

Curetes: Divine guardians appointed by Rhea to watch over the infant Zeus when he was hidden in the Dictaean cave

Cyanean Rocks: A name for the Clashing Rocks

Cyclopes: One-eyed, giant sons of Ouranus and Gaia; forged Zeus's thunderbolts

Cyllenus: Son of Anchiale; brother of Titias; a metal-working Idaean Dactyl of Crete, associated with worship of Rhea

Cypris: A name for Aphrodite

Glossary

Cyrene: Daughter of Lapith king Hypseus and Chlidanope; a princess of Thessaly and later queen of the city of Cyrene; huntress admired by Apollo for wrestling with a lion to save her father's sheep; by Apollo, mother of Aristaeus and Idmon; transformed into a nymph

Cytherea: A name for Aphrodite

Cytissorus: Son of Phrixus and Chalciope; grandson of Aeetes; brother of Argus, Phrontis, and Melas; shipwrecked on a voyage to Orchomenus; later accompanied the Argonauts to Colchis

Cyzicus: Son of Aeneus and Aenete; king of the Doliones; founder of the city Cyzicus

Danaans: Referring collectively to the Greeks

Danae: Daughter of Acrisius, from Argos; warned by an oracle that her future grandson would kill him, Acrisius imprisoned her; Zeus loved her and slipped through the roof as golden rain, impregnating her with Perseus; furious, Acrisius cast Danae and the infant Perseus adrift in a wooden chest; divinely preserved, they came to the island of Seriphos and were saved by Dictys, brother of Polydectes

Danaus: Grandfather of the Argonaut Nauplius; king of Libya

Dascylus: Son of Tantalus; father of Lycus and Priolas; king of Mysia who entertained Heracles

Dascylus: Son of Lycus the Mysian; grandson of the Dascylus, who entertained Heracles; sent to accompany the Argonauts

Death-heads: A name for the Fates, hounds of Hades

Deileon: Son of Deimachus; brother of Autolycus and Phlogius; joined Heracles on his quest to the Amazons but wandered astray; met the Argonauts, whom he and his brothers accompanied to Colchis

Deimachus: Father of Deileon, Autolycus, and Phlogius, three comrades of Heracles in his labor to retrieve Hippolyte's belt from the Amazons; king of Tricca

Delos: Island birthplace of Apollo and Artemis; site of Apollo's main shrine and oracle

Delphyne: Monstrous female serpent born to Gaia; slain by Apollo at Delphi

Demeter: Divine daughter of Cronus and Rhea; sister of Zeus, Hera, Poseidon, and Hades; mother of Persephone; taught the Titans how to harvest wheat; associated with grain, crops, fertility, harvest, and the Eleusinian Mysteries

Deucalion: Son of Prometheus; husband of Pyrrha; angered by Lycaon's sacrilege and other human evils, Zeus sent a worldwide flood; Deucalion and Pyrrha survived the flood in a floating chest; received an oracle to throw their mother's bones over their shoulders; interpreting their mother as Gaia, tossed rocks over their shoulders; the rocks became humans to repopulate Earth

Glossary

Dionysus: Divine son of Zeus and the Theban princess Semele; born in Thebes; traveled through India; held dances along the river Callichorus, which was named after the choruses he established there; associated with wine, grapes, vegetation, ecstatic dance, religious frenzy and madness, Mount Nysa, and ancient theater; father of the Argonaut Phlias; also called Bacchus and Nysaean

Dipsacus: Son of the river-god Phyllis and a meadow-nymph

Dodona: Site of an oracle of Zeus, in Epirus; the oldest Greek oracle

Doliones: A people living on the southern coast of the Propontis; led by King Cyzicus and protected by Poseidon

Dolops: Son of Hermes; buried in Magnesia

Drepane: The island of the Phaeacians, in the Ionian Sea; literally, "sickle," associated with the castration of Ouranus and with Demeter

Dryopians: A people originally from Dryopis; driven away by Heracles

Earthborn Giants: violent six-armed men living in the Propontis

Echetus: Son of Euchenor and Phlogea; king of Epirus; known for his extreme cruelty; blinded his daughter Metope and imprisoned her, forcing her to grind grains of bronze

Echion: Argonaut; son of Hermes and Antianeira, from Alope; brother of Eurytus

Eerie: An early name for Egypt, meaning "with early morning" or "at daybreak"; associated with the rising sun

Eidyia: Daughter of Oceanus and Tethys; wife of Aeetes; queen of Colchis; mother of Medea, Chalciope, and Apsyrtus

Eilatus: Lapith father of Polyphemus; from Larisa

Eileithyia: Goddess of childbirth and midwives

Elare: Daughter of Orchomenus; loved by Zeus, who put her beneath the earth to hide her from Hera; by Zeus, mother of the giant Tityos

Electra: Daughter of Atlas and Pleione; lived on Samothrace; one of the seven Pleiades, who were transformed into stars by Zeus

Electryon: Son of Perseus and Andromeda; king of Tiryns and Mycenae; lost many sons in an attack by the Teleboans, who also raided his cattle; accidentally killed by his nephew Amphitryon

Elysian: A plain or fields in Hades; a place of paradise and happiness reserved for heroes and noble mortals

Embasius: A name for Apollo, as god of embarcation

Endymion: Son of Aethlius, from Aeolia; possibly founder or king of Elis; sometimes called a shepherd or astronomer; known for his beauty; loved by Selene, who watched him as he slept in the Latmian cave and asked Zeus that Endymion remain a handsome youth forever; cast into eternal sleep

Glossary

Enyalius: A name for Ares

Erato: Daughter of Zeus and Mnemosyne, the goddess of memory; one of the nine Muses; patroness of lyric and erotic poetry

Erechtheus: Father of Oreithyia; grandfather of the Argonauts Zetes and Calais; founding king of Athens

Eretheis: One of the Hesperides; transformed into an elm tree

Erginus: Argonaut and helmsman; son of Poseidon; from Miletus

Eribotes: Argonaut; son of Teleon; known for his medical skills

Erinys: One of the goddesses of retribution sprung from blood that fell to the ground from Ouranus's castrated genitals; lived in the underworld; invoked to pursue those who had sworn false oaths or committed crimes; also called Furies and (in plural) Erinyes

Eros: Divine son of Aphrodite; mischievous and young; carried a bow and arrows with the ability to make any victim fall in love; associated with love, sexuality, and infatuation; also called Love

Erytus: Argonaut; son of Hermes and Antianeira, from Alope; brother of Echion

Etesian winds: Annual summer winds which blow across the Aegean Sea

Euphemus: Water-walking Argonaut and helmsman, from Taenarus; son of Poseidon and Europa; associated with the founding of Cyrene and colonization of Libya

Eupolemaia: Daughter of Myrmidon; princess of Phthia; mother of the Argonaut Aethalides

Europa: Daughter of the giant Tityos; mother of the Argonaut Euphemus

Europa: Daughter of Agenor and Telephassa; sister of Cadmus; loved by Zeus, who abducted her by transforming into a bull among her father's herds; when she climbed aboard the bull, he swam into the sea and to Crete; mother of Minos, by Zeus

Eurydamas: Argonaut from Ctimene, in Thessaly; son of Ctimenus and Demonassa

Eurynome: Daughter of Oceanus and Tethys; early Titan queen and wife of Ophion; ruled on Olympus until thrown down by Rhea

Eurypylus: Son of Poseidon and Celaeno; husband of Sterope; king of Libya; Triton took his form to welcome the Argonauts

Eurystheus: Grandson of Perseus; king of Mycenae and Tiryns; caused Heracles to undergo the twelve labors

Eurytion: Argonaut; son of Irus and Demonassa; king of Phthia

Eurytus: Father of the Argonauts Clytius and Iphitus; king of Oechalia, in Thessaly

Furies: A name for the Erinyes

Glossary

Fury: One of the Furies or Erinyes

Gaia: Primordial goddess Earth; mother and wife of Ouranus; mother of the Titans, Cyclopes, giants, mountains, and sea

Ganymede: Son of Tros, founder of Troy; known for his beauty; kidnapped by Zeus to serve as his cupbearer; granted immortality and eternal youth; also called Ganymedes

Garamas: A name for Amphithemis; son of Apollo and father of Caphaurus

Genethlius: A name for Poseidon, meaning "kin(dred)" or "generative"

Gephyrus: A warrior of the Doliones; killed by Peleus

Glaucus: Sea-god and prophet; originally a mortal fisherman; transformed into a sea-bound immortal after eating a magical herb

Gorgon: Referring to one Gorgon or to the three Gorgon sisters

Gorgons: Daughters of Phorcys and Ceto; sisters of the Graeae, who appeared as old women sharing one eye and one tooth; described as having live poisonous snakes for hair and terrifying faces that turned onlookers to stone; traditionally, the sisters are Stheno, Euryale, and their mortal sister Medusa, killed by Perseus

Graces: Divine daughters of Zeus; three or more minor goddesses, traditionally including Aglaea, Euphrosyne, and Thalia; associated with charm, fertility, beauty, creativity, and goodwill

Great Bear (Ursa Major): Constellation visible all year in the northern hemisphere, with two stars pointing toward the northern pole star Polaris; also called Helice; includes the asterism the Big Dipper

Hades: The underworld, domain of the god Hades; where the souls of the dead go in the afterlife

Hades: Divine son of Cronus and Rhea; brother of Zeus, Hera, Poseidon, and Demeter; ruled the underworld, which was known by his name; husband of Persephone, whom he took from the living world in an agreement with Zeus; tricked her into eating in the underworld, thus keeping her from returning fully to the upper world; associated with the dead, the realm of the underworld, and his three-headed guard dog Cerberus

Haemonia: A name for Thessaly

Hagnias: Father of the Argonaut Tiphys

Halys: River-god who desired Sinope and promised to grant her fondest wish; when she requested her virginity, he was forced to keep his word

Harmonia: Nymph of the Acmonian woods; wife of Ares; mother of the Amazons

Harpies: Monstrous birds with the faces of human women, living in a cave lair on Crete; tormented Phineus and snatched his food until chased away by the Argonauts Calais and Zetes

Glossary

Hecate: Divine daughter of Perses and Asteria; mother of Scylla; associated with witchcraft, the moon, magic and sorcery, ghosts, and crossroads; also called Cratais and the Maiden

Helice: Constellation of the Great Bear

Helios: Divine son of Titans Hyperion and Theia; by Perse, father of Aeetes, Circe, Perses, and Pasiphae; father of foolish Phaethon and the Heliades, who were transformed into poplar trees shedding amber tears to mourn Phaethon; said to drive his four-horse chariot across the sky every day; associated with the sun

Hellas: A collective name for Greece

Helle: Daughter of Athamas and the goddess Nephele; twin sister of Phrixus; the twins' hateful stepmother, Ino, arranged a false oracle demanding their deaths in sacrifice; they escaped on a golden ram sent by Nephele, but Helle fell from the ram mid-flight and drowned in what came to be called the Hellespont (Sea of Helle)

Hephaestus: Divine son of Hera; husband of Aphrodite; made lame after he was thrown down from Olympus by Zeus, in anger; or thrown from Olympus by Hera, who resented his lameness at birth; rescued by Thetis or by the Sintians of Lemnos; associated with blacksmiths, metalworking, craftsmanship, and fire

Hera: Divine daughter of Cronus and Rhea; sister of Zeus, Poseidon, Hades, and Demeter; wife of Zeus; queen of the Olympian gods; favored Jason for kindness he showed her when she visited Greece in disguise; associated with women, marriage, and childbirth; also called Imbrasion for the Imbrasus River beside her shrine on Samos

Heracles: Argonaut; son of Zeus and Alcmene; foster son of Amphitryon; hated by Hera; accomplished twelve labors in forced service to Eurystheus; labors included killing the Nemean lion, killing the nine-headed Lernaean Hydra, capturing the golden-antlered Ceryneian hind, capturing the Erymanthian boar, cleaning Augeias's stables, defeating the Stymphalian birds, capturing the Cretan bull, stealing Diomedes's man-eating mares, acquiring Hippolyte's belt, acquiring Geryon's cattle, stealing golden apples from the Hesperides, and capturing Hades's guard-dog Cerberus

Hermes: Divine son of Zeus and Maia; messenger of the gods; escorts the dead to Hades; associated with trickery, commerce, flocks, heralds, and the caduceus, his staff or wand

Hespere: One of the Hesperides; transformed into a poplar tree

Hesperides: Daughters of Atlas or possibly of Nyx, the night; nymphs of the evening and the west; inhabited and guarded the garden of the golden apples; transformed into different trees in their encounter with the Argonauts; including Aegle, Eretheis, and Hespere

Glossary

Hippodameia: Daughter of Oenomaus; defeated by Pelops in the life-or-death challenge of a chariot race; queen of Pisa and wife of Pelops

Hippolyte: Daughter of Ares and Otrere; queen of the Themscyreian Amazons; wore Ares's belt until Heracles was sent to retrieve it as one of his labors

Hippotas: Son of Mimas; father of Aeolus, keeper of the winds

Hyacinthus: A warrior of the Doliones; killed by Clytius

Hyantian: Referring to the Hyantes, descendants of Atlas's son Hyas; lived in Boeotia until they were driven out by Cadmus

Hydra: Monstrous child of Typhon and Echidna; venomous creature with many heads and poisonous blood; lived near Lake Lerna; whenever a head was cut off, two heads grew in its place; killed by Heracles and his nephew Iolaus in Heracles's second labor

Hylas: Argonaut; son of Theiodamas; favorite companion and servant of Heracles

Hyllus: Son of Heracles and Melite; king of Hyllus

Hyperboreans: A mythical people said to live in a sunny, warm region of the far north, beyond the cold north wind; devotees of Apollo

Hypsipyle: Daughter of Thoas; queen of Lemnos; when the Lemnian women killed their husbands, Hypsipyle saved Thoas

Iapetus: Titan son of Ouranus and Gaia; brother of Cronus; father of Atlas and Prometheus; condemned to Tartarus with Cronus

Ida: The highest mountain on Crete; site of Zeus's birthplace, the Idaean cave

Idaean cave: Birthplace of Zeus, on Crete

Idaean Dactyls: Mythical metalworkers of Crete associated with the worship of Rhea

Idas: Argonaut; son of Aphareus and Arene; brother of Lynceus, from Messenia

Idmon: Argonaut and Argive seer; son of Apollo and Asteria; foster son of Abas

Ino: Daughter of Cadmus and Harmonia; second wife of Athamas and queen of Boeotia; mother of Learchus and Melicertes; unsuccessfully plotted against Phrixus and Helle by causing famine and arranging a false oracle to demand their deaths; fostered her nephew Dionysus, incurring Hera's wrath; when Hera drove Athamas mad, and he killed Learchus, Ino fell into the sea with Melicertes; deified as goddess Leucothea and Melicertes, as god Palaemon; thwarted Themisto's attempt to kill her other children so that Themisto's children died instead

Iphias: Priestess of Artemis, in the city of Iolcus

Iphiclus: Argonaut from Phylace; son of Phylacus and Clymene; uncle of Jason; healed of infertility by Melampus

Glossary

Iphiclus: Argonaut; son of Thestius; uncle of the Argonaut Meleagrus
Iphinoe: Hypsipyle's herald
Iphitus: Argonaut; son of Eurytus, from Oechalia; brother of Clytius
Iphitus: Argonaut; son of Naubolus; grandson of Ornytus; king of Phocis; former host of Jason in Pytho, the site of Apollo's oracle
Iris: Divine daughter of Thaumas and Electra; winged messenger of the Olympian gods; associated with the rainbow, caduceus, and a pitcher for serving the deities
Irus: Son of Actor; father of the Argonaut Eurytion
Isthmia: A city and sanctuary of Poseidon, on the Isthmus of Corinth; original site of the Isthmian Games, established by King Sisyphus of Corinth as funeral games for Melicertes
Itomeneus: A warrior of the Doliones; killed by Meleagrus
Itonian: A name for Athena
Itymoneus: A warrior of the Bebrycians; killed by Polydeuces
Ixion: King of Lapiths, in Thessaly; driven mad and shunned after killing his father-in-law; pitied by Zeus, but lusted after Hera; exiled from Olympus and struck by Zeus's thunderbolt; eternally punished by being chained to a fiery, revolving wheel
Jason: Leader of the Argonauts; son of Aeson and Alcimede; raised and educated by Cheiron; a favorite of Hera, whom he carried through the flooding Anaurus when she visited Greece in disguise; sent by Pelias on the voyage of the Argo in quest of the Golden Fleece
Ladon: Serpent guardian of the golden apples in the Garden of the Hesperides, in Libya; killed by Heracles in his eleventh labor, in the quest for the golden apples
Lampetia: Daughter of Helios and Neaera; tended her father's cattle on Thrinacia
Laocoon: Argonaut, from Calydon; son of Porthaon and a maidservant; brother of Oeneus
Lapiths: A people living in Thessaly; related to the Centaurs; known for their victory in the Centauromachy, a famous battle against the drunken Centaurs at the wedding of King Pirithous
Leodocus: Argonaut; son of Bias and Pero; brother of Areius and Talaus; also called Laodocus
Lernus: Foster father of the Argonaut Palaemonius, from Olenus in Aetolia
Leto: Daughter of Titans Coeus and Phoebe; by Zeus, goddess mother of twins Apollo and Artemis
Ligyans: A people living in Liguria, in northwestern Italy
Love: A name for Eros

Glossary

Loves: Winged gods associated with love, passion, sexuality, Aphrodite, and Eros

Lycaon: King of Arcadia and founder of the city Lycosura; butchered his own son and served him to Zeus as a test; transformed into a wolf by Zeus as punishment

Lycastians: One of the three tribes of the Amazons

Lycoreus: A Bebrycian man; trusted subject of King Amycus

Lycurgus: Father of the Argonaut Ancaeus; brother of the Argonauts Amphidamas and Cepheus, from Tegea

Lycus: Son of Dascylus; king of the Mariandyni

Lynceus: Lookout for the Argonauts; son of Aphareus and Arene; brother of Idas, from Messenia

Macris: Daughter of Aristaeus and Autonoe; nurse of Dionysus, in Euboea; later fled to Drepane

Maia: Oldest daughter of Atlas and Pleione; by Zeus, mother of Hermes; one of the seven Pleiades, who were transformed into stars by Zeus

Mariandyni: A tribe living in northeastern Bithynia; led by King Amycus

Medea: Daughter of Aeetes and Eidyia; sister of Aspyrtus and Chalciope; niece of Circe; wife of Jason; sorceress and priestess of Hecate

Medusa: Daughter of Phrocys and Ceto; one of the Gorgons, known for turning anyone who saw her face into stone; killed by Perseus, who ultimately took her head to Athena to be placed on Zeus's shield; drops of blood from her head generated serpents

Megabrontes: A warrior of the Doliones; killed by Heracles

Megalossaces: A warrior of the Doliones; killed by Castor and Polydeuces

Melampus: Son of Amythaon and Eidomene; seer and healer; helped his brother Bias win Pero as wife by serving Phylacus for a year and obtaining Phylacus's cattle, thus fulfilling a task demanded by Pero's father Neleus; healed Phylacus's son Iphiclus of infertility and received the cattle in return; adherent of Dionysus's cult in Argos, where he moved from Pylos

Melanippe: Amazon daughter of Ares; sister of Hippolyte, Antiope, and Penthesilea; captured by Heracles in his labor for Hippolyte's belt, which was traded to him as Melanippe's ransom

Melantian: Rocks in the Aegean Sea

Melas: Son of Phrixus and Chalciope; grandson of Aeetes; brother of Argus, Cytissorus, and Phrontis; shipwrecked on a voyage to Orchomenus and later accompanied the Argonauts to Colchis

Meleagrus: Argonaut, from Calydon; son of Oeneus and Althaea; killed the Calydonian Boar; fated to die when a particular log was consumed by fire; his mother, in angry vengeance after he killed her brothers, burned the log and caused his death; also called Meleager

Glossary

Melie: Nymph of Bithynia; by Poseidon, mother of King Amycus
Melite: Daughter of Aegeaus; a water-nymph; by Heracles, mother of Hyllus
Menetes: Father of Antianeira; grandfather of Echion and Eurytus
Menoetius: Argonaut, from Opus; son of Actor; father of Achilles's friend Patroclus
Mentores: A people living in the region of Illyria; killed Heracles's son Hyllus
Merops: Father of Cleite; king of Percote
Mimas: A warrior of the Bebrycians; killed by Polydeuces
Mimas: Giant son of Gaia; killed by Ares in the Gigantomachy
Minos: Son of Zeus and Europa; king of Crete; husband of Pasiphae; father of Ariadne and Acacallis; forced King Aegeus of Athens to send seven boys and seven girls annually (or in other accounts, every seven years or nine years) to be fed to the Minotaur in the labyrinth; after death became a judge of the dead in Hades
Minotaur: Beastly son of Pasiphae and a bull sent by Poseidon; creature with a bull's head and human body; lived in the maze-like labyrinth built by the craftsman Daedalus; fed fourteen Athenian youths every year (or in other accounts, every seven years or nine years) until killed by Theseus
Minyae: A name for the Argonauts, so named because Jason's mother Alcimede was a descendant of Minyas; also called Minyans
Minyas: Son of Aeolus; ancestor of the Minyans; founder of Orchomenus, in Boeotia
Mopsus: Argonaut; Lapith seer and augur from Titaresia, in Thessaly; son of Ampycus and a nymph; killed by a poisonous snake generated from Medusa's blood hitting the ground
Mossynes: The wooden towers and dwelling places of the Mossynoeci
Mossynoeci: A people living in the Pontus; named for their wooden towers (mossynes) used as their homes; noted for their unusual laws and customs
Muses: Divine daughters of Zeus and Mnemosyne, the goddess of memory; associated with the inspiration of the arts and sciences; traditionally, the nine Muses are Calliope, Clio, Erato, Euterpe, Melpomene, Polymnia, Terpsichore, Thalia, and Ourania
Myrmidon: Son of Zeus; ancestor of the Myrmidons from Thessaly
Myrtilus: Oenomaus's charioteer; persuaded by Pelops to sabotage the chariot, leading to Oenomaus's death and Pelops's victory
Naiad: Referring to a water-nymph
Nasamon: Son of Amphithemis and a nymph; brother of Caphaurus
Naubolus: Son of Lernus, from Argos; father of Clytoneus; grandfather of the Argonaut Nauplius

Glossary

Naubolus: Son of Ornytus; father of the Argonaut Iphitus; king of Phocis

Nauplius: Argonaut and expert sailor; son of Clytonaeus and Amymone; grandson of Danaus

Nausithous: Son of Poseidon and Periboia; king of the Phaeacians

Neleus: Son of Poseidon and Tyro; king of Pylos and brother of Pelias; father of Pero, Nestor, and many others, including his oldest son, the Argonaut Periclymenus

Nereids: Daughters of Nereus and Doris; sea-nymphs

Nereus: Son of Gaia and Pontus; sea-god called the "Old Man of the Sea"; shape-shifter and prophet; by Doris, father of one son and fifty daughters, including Thetis

Nestaeans: A people living in the region of Illyria

Nycteus: By Polyxo, father of Antiope; after killing King Phlegyas in Euboea, fled to Thebes; king of Thebes

Nymphaea: An island in the Adriatic Sea; home of Calypso

Nysa: Place where Dionysus was raised by nymphs

Nysaean: A name for Dionysus, raised in Nysa

Oceanus: Titan son of Ouranus and Gaia; brother of Tethys, Cronus, and Rhea; husband of Tethys; father of the Oceanids and river-gods; also called Ocean

Oeagrus: Father of Orpheus; king of Thrace

Oeneus: Father of the Argonaut Meleagrus; brother of the Argonaut Laocoon; king of Calydon in Aetolia

Oenoe: Naiad nymph of the island Oenoe; by Thoas, mother of Sicinus

Oenomaus: Father of Hippodameia; king of Pisa; after receiving a prophecy that his son-in-law would kill him, challenged his daughter's suitors to a chariot race, those who lost were doomed to be executed; Myrtilus sabotaged Oenomaus's chariot, leading to the king's death and Pelops's victory

Ogyges: husband of Thebe; king of Boeotia

Oileus: Argonaut; father of Ajax the Lesser (lesser of the two Ajaxes at Troy) and Medon; king of Locris

Olympus: Highest mountain in Greece and home of the Olympian gods

Ophion: Husband of Eurynome; early Titan king of Olympus; thrown down by Cronus

Opuntian: Referring to the region of eastern Locris

Orchomenus: Son of Lycaon, of Arcadia; founder of the city Orchomenus; with his father and brothers, tried to trick Zeus into eating human flesh when the god visited in disguise; killed by Zeus's lightning bolts

Oreides: A warrior of the Bebrycians

Glossary

Oreithyia: Daughter of Erectheus; wife of Boreas; mother of Zetes, Calais, and Cleopatra; mountain-nymph

Orion: Constellation, named after the mythological hunter Orion

Ornytus: Son of Phocus; father of Naubolus; grandfather of the Argonaut Iphitus

Ornytus: A Bebrycian man; trusted subject of King Amycus

Orpheus: Argonaut; musician, prophet, and bard; son of Oeagrus and Calliope; born in Pimpleia, in Pieria; founder of the Orphic mysteries; charmed nature with his lyre-playing; one of the few heroes to enter Hades and return, although he could not recover his wife Eurydice; ruled in Bistonian Thrace; killed by the Thracian women

Ortygia: A name for Delos

Otrere: Wife of Ares; Amazons' first queen and founder; associated with building the Temple of Artemis in Ephesus

Paeeon: A name for Apollo, as the god of healing

Palaemonius: Argonaut; son of Hephaestus; foster son of Lernus, from Olenus

Paraebius: Phineus's closest friend; fated to toil without rest or reward as a punishment for his father's insolence; released after making expiatory sacrifice to a nymph killed by his father

Parrhasians: A people living in Arcadia; descended from Lycaon

Pasiphae: Daughter of Helios and Perse; wife of Minos; queen of Crete and mother of Ariadne; after Minos refused to kill his finest bull in a sacrifice to Poseidon, Poseidon cursed her with love for the bull; by the bull, mother of the Minotaur

Peirithous: King of the Lapiths of Larisa, in Thessaly; battle of the Lapiths and Centaurs occurred at his wedding to Hippodamia; journeyed to Hades with his friend Theseus in order to kidnap Persephone; trapped and serving eternal punishment in the underworld

Pelasgians: Broadly, peoples living in the region of the Aegean Sea; collectively used of Greeks or the Thessalians

Peleus: Argonaut; son of Aeacus and the mountain-nymph Endeis; king of Phthia and father of Achilles; exiled from his homeland Aegina after killing his brother Phocus before joining the Argonauts

Pelias: Son of Poseidon and Tyro; illegitimate king of Iolcus; sent his nephew Jason on the quest for the Golden Fleece; killed by his daughters through Medea's plotting

Pelopeia: Daughter of Pelias; sister of Acastus

Pelops: Son of Tantalus; grandson of Zeus, from Phryia; king of Pisa; Tantalus tested the gods by cutting up Pelops and serving him to the divinities at a feast; all deities recognized the deception and held back except for Demeter, who was grieving her daughter Persephone and ate Pelops's shoulder; was resurrected with an ivory shoulder made by Hephaestus; namesake for the Peloponnese; associated with the founding of the Olympic Games, which he established in honor of his chariot victory against King Oenomanus, father of Hippodameia; helped by Poseidon

Periclymenus: Argonaut; son of Neleus and Chloris, from Pylos; grandson of Poseidon, who gave him boundless strength and the ability to change shape

Pero: Daughter of Neleus and Chloris; wife of Bias; mother of the Argonauts Areius, Leodocus, and Talaus

Perse: Titan daughter of Oceanus and Tethys; wife of Helios; mother of Circe, Aeetes, Perses, and Pasiphae

Persephone: Divine daughter of Zeus and Demeter; snatched from the upper world and taken to the underworld by Hades; Demeter caused a famine while grieving and searching for her; unable to leave Hades permanently after being tricked into eating pomegranates there, allowed to spend part of the year with her husband Hades and part in the upper world with Demeter; once tended by the Sirens; associated with Eleusinian Mysteries, harvest, and vegetation

Perses: Titan son of Crius and Eurybia; by Asteria, father of Hecate

Perseus: Son of Zeus and Danae; founder of Mycenae and the Perseid dynasty; when King Polydectes of Seriphos demanded to marry Danae, was forced to retrieve the Gorgon Medusa's head as a wedding gift; with Athena's help, found the Gorgons' sisters the Graeae and then the Hesperides, from whom he received a special bag for the head; given Zeus's sword, Hermes's winged sandals, Hades's helmet, and Athena's shield; surprised the Medusa with her own reflection and beheaded her before she could turn him to stone; later rescued Andromeda from the monster Cetus and married her; used Medusa's head to kill Polydectes, then gave it Athena for Zeus's shield; also called Eurymedon

Phaeacians: Descendants of Ouranus; a people living on Drepane; led by Alcinous and Arete; in the *Odyssey*, a people descended from Poseidon and living on the island of Scheria

Phaethon: A name for Apsyrtus

Phaethon: Son of Helios and Clymene; traveled east to find his father and requested to drive Helios's chariot; lost control, causing chaos with the fiery heat; struck by Zeus's lightning bolt and fell dying into the Eridanus River; mourned by his sisters, Helios's daughters (the Heliades); Zeus pitied the women and turned them into poplars that shed tears of amber

Phaethousa: Youngest daughter of Helios and Neaera; shepherdess of her father's sheep on Thrinacia

Phalerus: Argonaut, from Athens; only son of Alcon

Glossary

Philyra: Daughter of Titans Oceanus and Tethys; by Cronus, mother of Cheiron

Phineus: Son of Agenor; husband of Cleopatra; king of Salmydessus, in Thrace; seer, given prophecy by Apollo and blinded by Zeus for sharing too much divine knowledge of the future; harassed by the Harpies

Phlegraean: Referring to Phlegra, a peninsula in Chalcidice; site of the Gigantomachy, the battle in which Zeus and the Olympians overthrew the Giants

Phlias: Argonaut, from Araethyrea in Argolis; son of Dionysus and Chthonophyle

Phlogius: A warrior of the Doliones; killed by Castor and Polydeuces

Phlogius: Son of Deimachus; brother of Deileon and Autolycus; joined Heracles on his quest to the Amazons but wandered astray; met the Argonauts, whom he and his brothers accompanied to Colchis

Phocus: Son of Aeacus in Aegina; brother of Telamon and Peleus; killed by his brothers

Phoebus: A name for Apollo

Phorcys: A son of Pontus and Gaia; sometimes conflated with Nereus and Proteus, also sea-gods; husband of Ceto; father of numerous monstrous offspring

Phrixus: Son of Athamas and the goddess Nephele; twin brother of Helle; the twins' hateful stepmother, Ino, arranged a false oracle demanding their deaths in sacrifice; they escaped on a golden ram sent by Nephele, but he alone survived to reach Colchis; presented Aeetes with the ram's Golden Fleece in exchange for the Colchians' hospitality; married Chalciope, and by her, fathered Argus, Cytissorus, Phrontis, and Melas

Phrontis: Son of Phrixus and Chalciope; grandson of Aeetes; brother of Argus, Cytissorus, and Melas; shipwrecked on a voyage to Orchomenus and later accompanied the Argonauts to Colchis

Phylace: Son of Deioneus and Diomede; husband of Clymene; founder of Phylace; father of Iphiclus and Alcimede

Phyxios: A name for Zeus, as god of escape and refuge

Pieria: A region in central Macedonia; site of Mount Olympus and the Pierian Spring, sacred to the Muses

Pierides: A name for the Muses

Pleiades: Seven daughters of Atlas and Pleione; born on Mount Cyllene and lived on Samothrace until transformed into a cluster of stars by Zeus; names are Maia, Electra, Taygete, Celaeno, Alcyone, Sterope, and Merope

Pleistus: River-god and father of the Corycian nymphs

Pollux: A name for Polydeuces

Polydeuces: Argonaut; son of Zeus and Leda; twin brother of Castor; along with Castor, one of the Dioscuri; associated with horsemanship, chariots, and sailors;

received permission from Zeus to share his immortality with his mortal brother; honored with Castor in the constellation Gemini; also called Pollux

Polyphemus: Argonaut; son of Eilatus and Hippea; founder and king of Cius, in Mysia; left in the land of the Bebrycians; wandered to the land of the Chalybes in search of the Argo

Polyxo: Elderly nurse of Hypsipyle

Poseidon: Divine son of Cronus and Rhea; brother of Zeus, Hera, Hades, and Demeter; ruler of the sea; father of the Argonauts Euphemus, Erginus, and Ancaeus, as well as Triton and others; associated with the sea, earthquakes, horses, and his trident; also called Earth-shaker

Priolas: Son of Dascylus and brother of Lycus of the Mariandyni; killed by the Mysians; commemorated by the Marindyni in a series of games

Prometheus: Titan son of Iapetus; father of Deucalion; known for stealing fire to give it and other secret knowledge to humans; punished by Zeus to be chained to a rock eternally; an eagle would eat his liver every day, only for the liver to grow back every night; in some stories, later rescued by Heracles

Promeus: A warrior of the Doliones; killed by Idas

Pytho: Site of Apollo's oracle at Delphi

Rhea: Titaness daughter of Ouranus and Gaia; sister of Cronus, Oceanus, and Tethys, and wife of Cronus; mother of the Olympian god; also called Cybele, Idaean, and the Great Mother

Scylla: Monstrous daughter of Phorcus and Hecate; transformed into a terrifying creature with multiple dog heads; living in a cave opposite Charybdis; known for snatching sailors from their ships

Scythians: Peoples living in central Eurasia

Selene: Divine daughter of Hyperion and Theia; sister of Helios; said to drive her chariot across the night sky; associated with the moon and her horns

Sicinus: A name for the island Oenoe

Sicinus: Son of Thoas and Oenoe; namesake for the island of Sicinus

Sinope: Daughter of Asopus and Metope, from Boeotia; taken away by Zeus, who promised to grant her desire; when she asked for her virginity, he was forced to keep his word and established a home for her in Assyria; later used the same request to trick Apollo and Halys to remain a virgin

Sintians: Early Thracian inhabitants of Lemnos; known for piracy

Sirens: Daughters of Achelous and Terpsichore; each part bird and part young woman; known for singing with sweet voices to lure passing sailors, whom they then killed; lived on Anthemoessa; once tended Persephone

Glossary

Sirius: The Dog Star, brightest star in the night sky, located in the constellation Canis Major

Sthenelus: Son of Actor; accompanied Heracles in the quest to take Hippolyte's belt and died in the ensuing battle with the Amazons

Stoechades: A name for the Ligystian Isles

Stymphalian: A lake in the northeastern Peloponnese; site of Heracles's sixth labor, in which he had to kill the man-eating Stymphalian birds

Styx: The main river in the underworld, separating the land of the living from the underworld; river upon which the gods swear

Syrtis: Region of the Mediterranean Sea where two channels meet off the northern coast of Libya; known for dangerous sandbars and shoals

Taenarus: Site in the southern Peloponnese; known as the entrance to Hades, the underworld

Talaus: Argonaut; son of Bias and Pero; brother of Areius and Leodocus; father of Adrastus, Eriphyle, and Pronax; king of Argos

Talos: Giant bronze man given by Zeus to Europa as a guardian around Crete; invincible except for his ankle; injured and killed due to Medea's sorcery

Telamon: Argonaut; son of Aeacus and the mountain-nymph Endeis; exiled from his homeland Aegina after killing his brother Peleus before joining the Argonauts; father of the Greater Ajax and Teucer

Teleboans: People of the island of Taphos; led by Pterelaus, attempted to claim land from King Electryon and the Mycenaeans; killed many of Electryon's sons and stole his cattle in a raid on Mycenae

Telecles: A warrior of the Doliones; killed by Heracles

Teleon: Father of the Argonaut Eribotes, from Locris

Teleon: Father of the Argonaut Butes, from Athens; husband of Zeuxippe

Terpsichore: Daughter of Zeus and Mnemosyne, the goddess of memory; one of the nine Muses; patroness of chorus and dancing; by Achelous, mother of the Sirens

Tethys: Titan daughter of Ouranus and Gaia; sister of Oceanus, Cronus, and Rhea; wife of Oceanus; mother of the Oceanids and river-gods

Theiodamas: King of the Dryopes; by the nymph Menodice, father of Hylas; killed by Heracles in a quarrel over an ox

Themis: Titan daughter of Ouranus and Gaia; second wife of Zeus; mother of the Fates; prophesied to Zeus that he would be overcome by a more powerful son; associated with justice, fairness, law, and scales of justice

Theras: Son of Autesion, from Sparta; colonized Calliste along with other Spartans

Glossary

Theseus: Son of Aegeus and Aethra; king of Athens; accomplished six labors on a trip from Troezen to Athens; labors included destroying the murderous robbers Periphetes and Sinis, monstrous Crommyonian Sow, deadly bandit Sciron, wrestler King Cercyon, and mutilator Procrustes; killed the Minotaur in Crete with Ariadne's help to survive the labyrinth; journeyed to Hades with his sworn friend Peirithous in order to kidnap Persephone, queen of the underworld; trapped in Hades until rescued by Heracles

Thetis: Daughter of Nereus and Doris; wife of Peleus; mother of Achilles

Thoas: Father of Hypsipyle; deposed king of the Lemnians; rescued by Hypsipyle when the Lemnian women killed their husbands; set adrift and later saved on the island of Oenoe, where he fathered Sicinus by the nymph Oenoe

Thrinacia: The island of Sicily; site where Helios grazed his sacred cattle, which were later eaten by Odysseus's reckless shipmates

Thunderers: The Ceraunian Mountains; literally, "Thunderbolt Mountains"

Tiphys: Argonaut and helmsman, from Thespis; son of Hagnias and Hyrmine

Titans: Gods who preceded the Olympian gods; children of Ouranus and Gaia; the Titan Cronus overthrew Ouranus before being overthrown by his own son, Zeus; replaced by the Olympian gods

Titias: Son of Anchiale; brother of Cyllenus; a metal-working Idaean Dactyl of Crete, associated with worship of Rhea

Titias: One of the strongest youths of the Mariandyni; defeated in a boxing match against Heracles

Tityos: Giant son of Zeus and Elare; father of Europa; grandfather of the Argonaut Euphemus; outgrew his mother's womb and was carried to term by Gaia; tried to rape Leto and was killed by either Apollo and Artemis or Zeus; sentenced to spend eternity chained in Tartarus with vultures feeding on his regenerating liver

Triton: A name for the Nile River

Triton: Divine son of Poseidon and Amphitrite; lived under the sea as a sea-god and herald of Poseidon; as Libyan king Eurypylus, gifted Euphemus with a dirt clod as a sign of hospitality; associated with his trumpet (a conch shell) and Lake Tritonis

Tritonian: A name for Athena; also used to refer to Lake Tritonis in Libya, associated with Triton

Tritonis: A lake in Libya where nymphs bathed the newborn Athena

Tyndareus: Father of the Argonaut Castor; stepfather of Polydeuces and Helen of Troy; king of Sparta and husband of Leda

Typhaon: Another name for Typhoeus

Glossary

Typhoeus: Serpentine monster, son of Gaia and Tartarus; by Echidna, father of many monsters; attempted to overthrow Zeus and was cast down either into Tartarus or below Mount Etna; also called Typhos, Typhon, and Typhaon

Wandering Rocks: Deadly rocks in the sea, close to Scylla and Charybdis

Zelus: A warrior of the Doliones; killed by Peleus

Zetes: Wing-footed Argonaut; son of Boreas and Oreithyia; grandson of Erechtheus; brother of Calais and Cleopatra

Zethus: Son of Zeus and Antiope; twin brother of Amphion; co-ruler of Thebes; associated with its founding myths; hunter and lover of agriculture

Zeus: Divine son of Cronus and Rhea; brother of Hera, Poseidon, Hades, and Demeter; husband of Hera; king of the Olympian gods; associated with the sky, thunder, lightning, and hospitality; also called Icmaeus, Genetaean, and Phyxios

APPENDIX

Excerpts from Euripides's *Medea*[1]

1–13, Medea's nurse speaks

I wish that the Argo[2] had never spread its sails
for Colchis,[3] winging past the blue Symplegades,[4]
and if only Mount Pelion's[5] pines had not been felled
to furnish oars for the hands of the heroes
who went in quest of the Golden Fleece
for Pelias's sake. For then my mistress,
Medea, would not have sailed to Iolcus's walls,
her heart shattered with love for Jason.
She would not have persuaded Pelias's daughters
to kill their father. Then she wouldn't be living here   10
in Corinth[6] with her husband and her sons, gladdening

---

1. From a forthcoming translation by Stanley Lombardo and Cynthia C. Polsley, by permission of Hackett Publishing Company.
2. The Argo was the ship that Jason sailed to retrieve the Golden Fleece. King Pelias sent Jason on this journey after he seized the throne of Iolcus from Jason's father.
3. The Golden Fleece was in Colchis, located on the eastern coast of the Black Sea near the Phasis River in present-day Georgia.
4. Jason had to sail through the Symplegades, or Clashing Rocks, near the Bosporus.
5. Pelion is a mountain in Thessaly near the kingdom of Iolcus to which Jason was the rightful heir. The wood for the Argo would have come from this region.
6. Although Jason returned to Iolcus with the Golden Fleece, Pelias did not give the throne to Jason. As a result, Medea, in guile, offered to teach the daughters of Pelias a spell to reinvigorate their aging father. She cooked a dead and dismembered ram and brought it back to life. Pelias's daughters performed the same act on their father, but he remained

Appendix

the citizens of the land to which she came.
She bore every burden for Jason's sake.

474–507, Medea to Jason

I will begin my speech from the beginning. First,
I saved your life, as is known by all the Greek crew
who boarded the Argo with you when you were sent
to tame and yoke the fire-breathing bulls
and sow the field whose only crop was death.
The dragon that kept watch over the Golden Fleece,
sleeplessly guarding it with its sinuous coils, 480
I killed, and so lit the way to your salvation.
Betraying my own father and leaving my home
I came with you to Iolcus under Pelion,
more enthusiastic than I was prudent.
I caused Pelias to die a most painful death
at his daughters' hands, destroying his entire house.
And after all I went through for you, you dog,
you betrayed me and contracted a new marriage,
although we had children. If you were still childless,
your desire to remarry would be pardonable. 490
Trust in your oaths is gone, and I cannot decide
whether you believe the old gods no longer rule
or that new ordinances are now in place for men,
since you must know you did not keep your oaths to me.
O right hand of mine, which you often took hold of
along with my knees, how empty the entreaty
of a worthless man who cheated us of our hopes.
But come, I will confide in you as in a friend.
(Why? How can I expect to benefit from you?
Your being questioned by me will make you look worse.) 500

---

dead. Because of this, Jason and Medea were forced to flee Iolcus and eventually arrived at Corinth, a city in the north of the Peloponnese.

Appendix

Where can I turn now? Perhaps to my father's house,
which, like my country, I abandoned for your sake?
Or to Pelias's poor daughters? They would give me
a lovely reception for killing their father.
This is how things are now: to my own family
I have become hateful, and I have made enemies,
again for your sake, of those I needn't have harmed.